A Tiny House on Wheels

ENNI AMANDA

To New Zealand, with love.

A Tiny House on Wheels

CHAPTER 1

Nina groaned. This was not what the first day of her new life was supposed to look like.

First, it wasn't supposed to rain. Second, the lot wasn't supposed to be empty. Her state-of-the-art tiny house, built on a trailer and packed with interior design goodness, should have arrived an hour ago, delivered by a towing company that wasn't answering the phone.

Nina tried to wipe the mud off her yellow gumboots by dragging them through the long, wet grass. There was nothing else to wipe them on as she stood on her empty lifestyle block on the outskirts of Raglan – a retirement village turned into touristy surfer town on New Zealand's West Coast.

Tired of inspecting the wet ground and planning her organic, perma-culture garden, Nina peeled off her rain jacket and slid back inside her car. She noticed the light grey interior getting muddy from her gumboots. Soon, she might have to upgrade to a pickup truck, but first things first. She had to call La La. Her best friend was a 70-minute drive away in Hamilton, missing the most momentous life change she'd ever attempted. Well, apart from moving to New Zealand. La La had offered a work-related excuse, but Nina suspected her absence had more to do with the forecasted rain. La La didn't mix well with mud and lack of fresh coffee.

Four months ago, Nina had dropped the news on her unsuspecting friend.

"You're moving into the bush just to avoid getting a mortgage?" she'd asked with an exaggerated eye roll. Nina could picture her friend's silky black hair waving as she shook her head. Her manicured nails curled around a coffee cup, seeking moral support from caffeine. There was nobody else in the office, after all.

They'd just finished the artwork for an urgent ad campaign and sent it away with minutes to spare. The creative director had left two hours prior, trusting them with the giant bus back their biggest client had poured thousands on. Back then, it felt like a compliment. Maybe they didn't earn that much, but they'd achieved some seniority within the agency.

Nina had held the lid on her big news all day and nearly burst from anticipation when they finally sat down for the well-earned hot drinks. La La spiked her coffee with cream liquor while Nina stuck to chamomile tea. She'd never enjoyed the office drinks. Being tipsy at work felt too out-of-control, even when you weren't working. She couldn't lose control; she'd built her life on it. By being in control, she'd saved the money for a lifestyle block, even if it was in the middle of nowhere. Saving and saving for years. She'd done the math. By not taking on a mortgage, she would save hundreds of thousands. She'd be free. It was worth every bit of self-control.

Staring into her best friend's eyes, Nina had painted a word picture of her future, growing her own food, living rent-free and having all the time in the world.

"To do what?"

La La's question had thrown her. Nina wasn't sure what she would fill her days with. But surely that wasn't the real problem. The late nights at work were the problem. Not having enough time to go shopping for essentials or return library books was the problem. Having a hopeless crush on a colleague who didn't return her feelings ... that was definitely a problem. She needed a new beginning.

"Well, if you must do this, I'll try to support you," La La had finally said.

She had sounded so abandoned Nina almost doubted her decision. Almost.

"Just don't be too proud to come back if it doesn't work."

Nina couldn't go back. She imagined the snarky remarks, the pity, the knowing looks. Her colleagues thought visiting the countryside was fine, but only retirees or aspiring cult leaders moved there permanently. They knew Nina had bought a piece of land but assumed she was just land banking – investing her money in something better than a low yield bond. She'd told no one about building a tiny, transportable dwelling, or the nights spent googling composting toilets, rainwater collection and gardening. For a while, she'd led an exciting double life – days in the office, nights planning her big break. Until the night she'd finally given her notice and come clean to La La.

"I should have told you earlier," Nina admitted. "I was just afraid you'd talk me out of it."

La La's blue eyes reflected hurt. "Maybe I would have! I could have asked, for example, why you would move there against winter. Isn't it going to be really hard to do any gardening or whatever you're planning?"

Nina had thought of this, but she didn't really have a choice. The building had taken longer than expected. Now that the builders had finished, she couldn't fit the 40-feet structure on her rental flat carpark. She also couldn't leave it in Raglan, sitting vacant. What if someone stole it? It was on wheels! She had to move in.

La La had cocked her head in understanding, eyes welling up. "I'll miss you. It won't be the same without you here. And I don't want you to be miserable."

"I won't be miserable."

And here she was, a few weeks later, cold and miserable. Nina took out her phone, but no longer felt like calling her friend. Not right now. La La would hear the desperation in her voice. Nina tried checking Instagram, but it wouldn't load. Of course! She had no data. At work, she'd been using the company wi-fi. In her apartment, she'd had a fibre connection – one of the hardest things to leave behind. From now on, she relied on mobile internet and hadn't even considered topping up her data before driving out to the sticks. Not smart. Just as she was about to text La La, she heard a distant rumble of an engine.

Nina scrambled out of the car, gazing down the dirt road she called a driveway. The engine sound grew louder, and a moment later a truck appeared from around the bend, towing her dear, sweet house. It looked just like she remembered from her visit to the builder's yard – a beautiful, stained cedar with arched custom windows and a roof covered with solar panels. Doll-sized, but perfect. The driver stopped at the edge of the boundary and wound down his window, motioning Nina to get closer. He had a perpetually sunburnt face and tired, droopy eyelids.

"Is this your trailer?"

Nina nodded, wondering if the guy had noticed the house on it.

"So where do you want it?"

The man was looking at the empty wet lot, covered in long grass, occasional bushes, and a few larger trees. Nina gestured towards the flat bit on the side of the hill she had planned. The driver killed the engine and clambered out of the vehicle. He took a few steps on the soggy ground, shook his head and retreated to his truck.

"Too soft. The wheels will sink in."

"Oh, it doesn't matter." Nina smiled. "I won't be moving it

any time soon. And the trailer tyres are extra wide."

The driver cast her a weary look. "I'm not talking about your trailer. I'm talking about the truck. If I go any further, I'm not coming back."

Nina felt the panic tighten her throat. "I have to get the house there. I paid for the delivery."

The house stood right at the end of her driveway, blocking the only entrance. She should have had the driveway extended all the way to the house location, but she had little money left. Every penny was earmarked for setting up the garden that would feed her in the future. She didn't want a mortgage – that was the whole point. Mortgages forced people into life situations they regretted. Like staying on a job that slowly sucked the life out of them. Nina had worked hard to avoid that, yet somehow ended up in more trouble than her half-million-in-debt friends.

As the tow truck driver detached the trailer and attempted a three-point turn on the swampy shoulder of her driveway, Nina woke from her despairing thoughts and ran to stop the truck.

"Okay, I get it. But what can I do? How can I get the house in the right spot? What do I need? A bigger truck?"

"We've nothing bigger than this. A tractor might do it."

"Where can I hire a tractor?"

The man looked even wearier than before. "Look. You're in the country now. Everybody has a tractor. Like that guy over there."

He pointed at the nearby hill. As Nina turned to look, the tow truck sped off, leaving her staring into the distance. Seeing it disappear round the bend, the tears came. This was a disaster. The house blocked her only entrance. She couldn't even get her little Toyota past it without falling into the shallow ditch the tow truck had revved its way out in and out of. She would have to carry bags of gravel on her back to build a driveway. How long would it take? Ten years?

After a moment of cathartic sobbing, a faint sound of an engine reached Nina's ears. She peeked through her tears and, to her surprise, saw a tractor far out on the hill, pulling an open trailer with something in it.

Nina wiped her face and hoped to God she wasn't looking too red and puffy-eyed. She would have to get to know her neighbours anyway, so why not now? Especially if they came with tractors. She drew a deep breath and set off up the hill.

It must have been some kind of countryside trick, the distance being longer than it seemed. It took Nina a good ten minutes and a lot of huffing and puffing (Pilates hadn't prepared her for this) to reach the top of the hill and another five to catch the driver's attention. He removed one earmuff and raised his eyebrows.

"I'm so sorry to bother you," Nina gasped, trying to catch her breath, "but I've just moved in next door... I mean the section down there, and I could really use some help."

As she explained her situation, the man turned to peer at her new home and let out a good-natured chuckle. Nina tensed at his reaction, but fought to keep her temper in control. She needed this guy on her side.

"I know it's a bit unorthodox, but it's a nice house, especially on the inside. And I plan to build a shed for storage."

The man nodded, still smiling. He had an infectious smile, the kind that immediately reached his eyes, paired with a ruffled dark hair. If he hadn't been wearing a paint-stained flannel shirt, he could have been in one of those beer ads, playing the guitar on the beach. Too bad he was such a jerk. Nina plastered on a friendly smile. "So, what I'm asking is… could you possibly tow the house to where it's supposed to be? They told me a tractor could do it."

The guy shrugged. "I'll give it a go."

He hopped out of the tractor and detached his trailer, then climbed back in, snapped his earmuffs back on and drove down the hill. Nina sprinted after him, her nerves on high alert. This was the most one-sided exchange she'd had with another human since visiting her demented grandmother. Had the guy understood her request, or would he mow over her precious home? Or maybe just drive past it to the local pub?

When Nina finally reached the house, she found the tow bar already attached to the tractor. Its engine revved and wheels dug into the muddy ground, but it was moving, inching her house away from the driveway. Nina ran before it, waving her arms to show where she wanted her house. She could hear the seams creaking as it drudged along the bumpy, soggy grass. Oh God, her expensive tinted windows!

Polished hardwood floors! The custom cabinetry in her kitchen... Would anything be left of it? The guy seemed to at least follow her hand signals and steered the tractor to the right, finally leaving the house under a large walnut tree.

Nina sighed like a deflated balloon. Her house stood in the perfect location. The tears tried to make a comeback, but she fought them off. She didn't want this smirky farmer to think she was a helpless, weepy female in need of rescuing. He'd just caught her on an emotional day, that's all.

Once the guy had freed her house from the tractor, he climbed back behind the wheel. Nina caught his attention as he was about to drive away.

"Thank you so much! You're a lifesaver. Sorry, I didn't introduce myself. I'm Nina, and this is Taina." Nina gestured at her house.

Her neighbour lifted his hand. "Jay."

"You live on the other side of the hill then?"

Jay nodded.

"You must have a lovely view?"

Another nod. God, this conversation was like pulling teeth. Nina was ready to give up as he spoke again, "Is it a play on the word 'tiny'?"

"What?"

"Taina, the tiny house."

"No, it was the name of my imaginary sister when I was little. It's a common female name in Finland."

"Finland, huh?"

"That's where I was born. But it's cool that it sounds like 'tiny'."

Nina smiled with delight, happy that she didn't have to carry the conversation. She waited for him to continue. Most Kiwis she talked to recounted their big O.E. – overseas experience – and how close they came to visiting Scandinavia. Nina didn't have the heart to tell them that technically, Finland wasn't even part of Scandinavia. In New Zealand, anything north of Germany counted as 'close to Finland'.

Jay stared in the middle distance, not bothered by the long silence.

"So how did you end up here?"

"It's a long story."

Nina smiled to encourage him to go on. He didn't. Instead, Jay nodded, put on his earmuffs and started the engine.

The tractor made its way back up the hill, with Jay's hand sticking up over his shoulder. It was either the world's most dismissive goodbye, or he was checking the air for signs of rain.

So, that weirdo was her neighbour. Nina should have been grateful for his help, but instead she felt offended and puzzled. Had living in the middle of nowhere affected his social skills, or was the guy a bit slow? Maybe the extended silences were just long processing times. Nina softened a little towards the odd farmer. He was cute; she had to give him that.

After unloading her car and organising her minimal kitchenware and bed sheets into her brand-new home, Nina gave herself a moment to sit down and take it all in. The bare plywood walls, the streamlined little kitchen, the endless greenery behind the windows. She felt like a little fish in an aquarium. She would have to get curtains. With no appliances running, she could hear her own heartbeat. It was too late in the day to charge the solar panels, so she couldn't even make a cup of tea before bed. Hopefully, the sun would shine tomorrow.

Nina had expected the tiny house to feel like a home. She'd chosen the floor plan, kitchen cabinets and floor coverings. It was all hers, nothing like those boring rentals she'd seen for the past years. But instead the space felt like a hotel room in a foreign country.

Meeting the new neighbour, as hot as he was, hadn't helped with the alien feeling. Nina wondered if everyone in the nearby village resembled Jay. Maybe she was the odd one out here. It all seemed backwards. As a Finn, she often came off reserved while the Kiwis made aggressively friendly small talk.

Nina dug up a chicken sandwich she'd packed earlier, hoping that food would ease her discomfort. But later at night, when she eventually climbed up on the sleeping loft and wrapped herself in two duvets, she still felt the penetrating chill. She had to order a load of firewood and christen her tiny fireplace. Could even a glowing fire dissolve the wobbly feeling in the pit of her stomach? Had she made a terrible mistake?

Chapter 2

Nina woke up to the sound of tuis in the walnut tree, her limbs stiff from the cold. She'd slept fitfully, but she felt better for seeing the sunlight pour in through the little loft window. What time was it? Her mobile phone had run out of battery and without power she couldn't charge anything. She reached for her laptop. It had two minutes of battery life left, just enough to tell the time. 7.34 a.m. Thank goodness. She had plenty of time to get up and drive to Hamilton to get the rest of her stuff. Cleaning up the rental would take the rest of her day.

Ninety-minutes later, Nina parked outside her old home, taking in the repeating pattern of townhouses, packed on a residential lot that left no room for outdoor life. After just one night away, her old flat in Hamilton East already looked all wrong. The neighbours were everywhere. Left, right, in front and behind. She'd lived in a modern 'gated community' which had nothing community-like about it. Everything was as easy care as could be, from the concrete driveway to the waxy decorative plants. Everyone had their own little backyard, the size of a postage stamp. The illusion of privacy created by the six-foot fence was constantly broken by the sound of the neighbours having conversations everyone could hear but pretended not to listen to.

After scrubbing the kitchen for two hours, Nina decided she needed food. She left the unit on foot and headed towards Two Birds where she knew she could get a healthy green smoothie, maybe even eggs. She deserved it.

The cafe buzzed with the lunch crowd and the queue moved as slowly as ever. Once Nina had placed her order, she noticed all the tables were full. She perched herself at the bar leaner with other people waiting for their takeaway coffees, wishing she'd also ordered takeaways.

As she reached for a magazine, she noticed the guy next to her tapping at his phone. Before her conscious mind kicked in, all the hairs on her body stood up. It was Tama. The indigenous specimen of male beauty she'd worked with for the past two years. Fun, flirty, and full of ideas. And the reason she had to get away. Both the boss and the clients loved Tama, who functioned as the agency's stamp of approval for all Māori elements they used in design. He often joked about being the token Māori in the all-white ad agency, serving all-white middle-aged clients.

Tama had once confessed to her that he often had little knowledge of the legitimacy of their Māori designs, but couldn't bother to run everything past the tribe elders. Even if he did, another tribe might have disagreed. So, he just made sure they didn't use carvings of his ancestors. Nina remembered her elation over his honest admission. He trusted her. Maybe he saw her differently to others in the office. For weeks, she waited for him to ask her out. There was more flirting, more compliments, more looks. Nina worked overtime to help Tama meet his deadlines. He returned the favour by bringing her takeaway coffees and praising her designs. On her new diet, Nina didn't drink coffee, but she took fake sips from the takeaway cups and drained them quietly at the end of the day.

Litres of coffee went down the drain, but the date invitation never came. La La, who had noticed the flirting, informed Nina that Tama was divorced and had a kid who lived with his ex-wife. For any sensible girl, that should have been enough of a reason to stay away. But having a crush was her way of coping with the stressful job. It made the days more fun, gave her something to focus on, other than her advancing age or her ex-boyfriend Matt whom she'd left behind in Auckland. And it gave her something to gush about with La La, who approved of the crush and thought Tama was delicious – although not her type. La La's type was older and wealthy. She wanted a man with an investment portfolio. Tama made good money but also spent lavishly and often had five dollars left come payday.

Scanning the cafe, Nina knew she could not slip away without Tama noticing. Even if she could, who would leave behind a nine-dollar smoothie? Steeling her nerves, Nina lifted her eyes at him, catching his attention at the same moment he turned. Tama dropped his phone on the table and broke into a gorgeous grin.

"Nina! What are you doing here?"

"Just cleaning the flat before I move to Raglan." He shook his head, eyes wide. "I can't believe you're not at the office. It's so weird."

"I know! I feel weird."

Nina wished she didn't smell like oven cleaner, or that she'd had the good sense to change out of her sweat-stained cleaning shirt.

"So, how's Raglan? Missing the city yet?" Tama winked.

"I'm only seventy minutes away."

It probably sounded like a flight to Australia to Tama, who lived right in the city centre, within a walking distance from work.

"Well, as long as you're happy. We'll just have to manage without you," he concluded, his face drawn in mock horror.

Nina wondered what he really felt under the silly act. Was he sad about her moving away, or just being polite? Maybe he'd just miss her help at the office.

"You're welcome to visit anytime, if you fancy a... trip to Raglan."

Nina cringed at her own words. It sounded like she was inviting him into her bed, especially as her house was so small that any visitor would end up checking out her bedroom.

"Absolutely. I do want to check out your wee house! Email

me some pics?"

So, he didn't want to visit. Nina's shoulders sagged. To her relief, the green smoothie arrived, giving her something else to focus on. Tama picked up his phone. Nina couldn't see what was on it, but she assumed it was Snapchat. His mates were pretty active on it, posting pictures of craft beers they were about to drink or had just consumed. She could hardly think of a more primitive level of communication.

Tama's fingers stopped typing, and he looked up. "We go to Raglan now and then for a surf. I'm sure Emma would love to check out your house, too."

Who the hell was *Emma*? Holding her breath, Nina waited for more; afraid to say anything that could sound catty. Tama seemed to read her mind.

"I haven't told you about Emma, have I? It's pretty new, she hasn't met my whānau, either." Tama pulled a face.

"How did you guys meet?"

"She … she's your replacement."

Holy shit! Nina fought to keep the smile on her face. She'd been out of the office for a week, sorting out her house move, and he was already going out with her *replacement*. How could anyone go from strangers to co-workers to boyfriend and girlfriend in that time? At least Tama had the decency to look embarrassed.

"Well, that was quick," Nina retorted.

"It's crazy, I know! They threw this big welcome party for her – any excuse for beers, right? She's new in town, so I volunteered to show her round. Anyway, she's really cool. You'd like her."

"I'm sure."

Nina stirred her drink, nausea welling in her stomach.

"I'm happy for you," she added, almost as an afterthought. She wanted to believe it.

Tama's takeaway coffee arrived. He made his excuses and rushed off, leaving Nina with a tornado of emotions. What the hell was wrong with her? She had thought Tama was just guarded and had come up with all kinds of theories on why. Maybe he'd been so burned by the divorce that he couldn't even contemplate another relationship. The unfairness of it made it hard to swallow the thick green drink, but she forced it down, gathered her handbag, and fled. On the way back to her flat, she texted La La:

Just ran into Mr Charming. Why didn't you tell me about Emma?

The reply came within minutes:

Sorry I didn't think you'd hear about it out there! Thought it might be easier to digest it later. We are all a bit??? abt this romance TBH. Martin's bending the rules to keep his golden boy :-O XX

So, the entire office already knew, and it was against the rules? In the two years Nina had spent fantasising about her colleague, she'd never considered the implications of an actual relationship. A wave of relief washed over her, followed by regret. What a waste of time! What she'd thought of as harmless fun had stolen two years of her life. She still want-ed a family, but her eggs were now two years older and she was restarting her life with no romantic prospects in a town with a tiny population.

Once back at her flat, Nina resumed cleaning. She relished the therapeutic aspect of scrubbing, rinsing and polishing, wiping off every trace of the past two years of her life. After two hours, her shoulders, arms and back ached. Perfect. The sensation both grounded and distracted her. But when she attempted to get up off the shower cubicle floor, a sharp pain shot through her lower back.

Oh God, not now, she thought. She still had to finish tidy-ing the backyard and drive back to Raglan.

Nina hobbled over to the deck and fetched the broom. She swept most of the little stones and debris into place. Done. Her back muscles seized again, forcing her to lean on the wall for support. If only she'd had someone in her life – someone who could take the car keys and let her lie down on the backseat. Did people who had that kind of support appreciate the luxury of it?

Nina double-checked all rooms and cupboards. Every-thing looked cleaner than before she'd moved in, but did it matter? For the first time in her life, she didn't have to worry about her landlord giving her a good reference. Even if she lost some of her bond, she would never have to declare that shameful fact in a rental application. The liberating thought buoyed her all the way out the door.

No matter how many times you moved house, there was always that unexpected surge of uncertainty and sadness when you locked the door for the last time. The moment of no return.

By the time Nina got back to her tiny house, the sun had fallen low on the horizon. Her arms felt heavy and her lower back was still sore, but the pain had reduced to a dull ache.

This time, stepping over the threshold of her tiny home, Nina felt more hopeful. Not quite at home, but there was a sense of relief. Her life was here now. There was no going back. The rest of her belongings burst out of her little Toyota, but she'd left nothing behind. The sunny day had done its job and charged the batteries. Nina plugged in her fridge and winced at its audible electric hum. The sound would reach her sleeping loft. She'd just have to adjust. Or get earplugs.

Observing the fridge, Nina also realised she'd brought no food with her. After dropping off her keys, she'd skipped shopping and bought a takeaway kebab, too tired to plan for the future. Her mind still reeled from the revelations of the day, playing out different scenarios. The drive had felt endless. Sitting on the built-in storage bench in her tiny, compact kitchen, Nina felt the exhaustion of the day catching up with her, the loft bed calling her name, enticing her to lie down. She had so much to figure out, but maybe she could do all that tomorrow.

CHAPTER 3

In Nina's old life, Sunday had been the day of sleeping in. But as the first light burst through the uncovered skylight window, gently stirring her from sleep, she remembered. This Sunday, she'd planned a trip to town to attend a crop swap – Raglan's version of a farmers' market – to stock up on fresh local produce. In the future, she hoped to swap her own organic produce. But since her garden was still nothing more than a pile of dirt and a dream, she'd prepared some handmade raw chocolate to use as collateral. Packing her chocolate treats, still in their heart-shaped silicone moulds, Nina thought of the money and effort that had gone into making them. Swapping one for a lemon seemed like a terrible trade, but she needed to get to know the other food growers in the area. She'd sacrifice her cocoa-based superfoods for the good cause. With an empty fridge, Nina had to skip breakfast. She took a couple of deep breaths at her doorstep to settle her queasy stomach, jumped into her wellies, and packed into her little Toyota. Driving away, she glanced at her tiny house in the rearview mirror. Dwarfed by the mature trees and hills around it, it looked even tinier. A miniature house. No wonder Jay had found it amusing.

Everyone on the narrow, windy roads seemed to drive faster than her. For a country that had a high road toll, New Zealand didn't believe in speed limits, more like speed targets Nina could never hit.

The drive to the village felt long, but the beautiful morning made up for it. The road twisted through the evergreen hills that dominated the landscape, giving frequent peeks of the ocean. After two years in the landlocked Hamilton, every glimpse of the turquoise waters lifted her spirits. Majestic and rugged with enormous waves, the Western coastline appealed to surfers. Nina already knew she wouldn't be making use of those waves. She didn't enjoy cold water and feared the powerful undercurrents. But she could do beach walks. Definitely. She'd take off her shoes and stroll along the shimmering black sand, even if the path from her new home to the water's edge currently seemed like an obstacle course of thick vegetation and a terrifyingly steep decline.

Twenty minutes later, Nina parked her car by the village hall and joined a trickle of people hauling large crates of fruit and vegetables. They seemed like proper farmers. In her flowery top and strappy sandals, she felt like a fraud. She missed the Hamilton farmers' market – the smell of freshly baked bread and ground coffee, crisp apples and vegan nut bars, and the fact that they accepted money.

The run-down village hall smelled vaguely of feet. Foldable picnic tables lined the room, displaying a variety of crops. With the cacophony of friendly chatter, Nina didn't notice the old man addressing her at the door. His gentle touch on her shoulder made her jump.

"Have you booked a table, dear?"

Nina stared at him with a flash of panic. Was she supposed to book something? She thought she would just walk in with her chocolates and see what happened. Now it seemed like a stupid plan.

"No, sorry, I didn't know. Is there not enough room?"

"What do you have in there?" He gestured towards Nina's cooler bag.

"Raw chocolates. Organic."

"How lovely. We wouldn't want to miss out on those."

The old man smiled reassuringly and led her to the side of the room. A woman of her age was setting up what looked like cheesecakes which – judging by her dreadlocks and hemp outfit – probably weren't the conventional kind.

"Earth here sells raw … um, things, as well. Maybe you two ladies can share. Two dollars each."

What kind of name was Earth? The kind that afforded its bearer with an air of superiority, it seemed. Earth folded her arms and dipped her chin, blatantly assessing Nina's outfit. Perhaps the viscose shirt and shiny hair didn't signal high enough commitment. Raglan was famous for its ferocious

Green Party supporters and alternative lifestyle.

"Sorry, I didn't know I had to book a table," Nina said with an apologetic smile.

Earth granted her a wary half-smile. "It's okay. I'll just stack my cakes. I have a three-tiered tray in my car."

Nina wondered what kind of car the woman drove. Probably electric. Or maybe something that ran on bio-diesel or rancid cooking oil. Nina tried to reel in her ugly thoughts. She loved electric cars and hated plastic bags as much as the next person. So what if her table mate seemed a little frosty? She was here to make friends. Evidently, she had to try harder.

"Thank you so much," she said.

The old man rubbed his hands together, pleased that everything seemed to work out. "Wonderful. I'll leave you ladies to it."

He left to attend to others at the door and Earth followed behind, presumably to fetch the tray from her car. Nina unwrapped her chocolates and placed them in little paper cups. By the time Earth returned, she'd organised her treats to take up only one third of the table. Earth rearranged her cakes, cutting uniform slices and placing them on the high tea tray made of vintage plates.

"That's beautiful." Nina traced the gold rim with her forefinger.

"Please don't touch."

Startled by Earth's clipped tone, Nina stumbled backwards. As she did, her sleeve brushed the berry sauce on one of the cake slices. "I'm so sorry! I'll pay for that, I promise. How much?"

Earth's eyes flashed with disdain. "This is not a bake sale. Normally, I would just swap with something of yours but I don't eat sweets."

"It's organic raw chocolate. No sugar of any kind."

Earth narrowed her eyes. "So, what do you use? Agave nectar?"

"Yes, with a bit of brown rice syrup. And organic cacao butter, raw cacao powder, lucuma powder and gelatinized maca. All organic."

Earth nodded, her expression softening a little. "Maybe I'll swap you for one, then. You can have the cake you touched. It's dairy-free, raw cheesecake with strawberry topping. All organic."

"Sounds great." Nina smiled and accepted the piece of cake. As she expected, it tasted of nuts – crushed nuts, mashed nuts and whipped nuts. Nothing like actual cheesecake.

"Cashews?" she asked.

"Activated."

Despite the nutty clump swirling in her mouth, Nina felt more at ease. She could speak the health nut language. She'd never used it in her previous life, but her recent diet overhaul had inadvertently prepared her for this moment. Maybe in time she'd embrace the shapeless layers of hemp and organic cotton. Wrapping her hair in a scarf instead of washing it would definitely save water if her rainwater tank ended up running low.

Earth selected one of Nina's heart-shaped, nut-covered chocolates and nibbled at it. The old man from the door announced that the swapping had started. The chatter notched up in volume and the locals began circulating the room with their canvas bags, crates and baskets in hand. Too nervous to jump in, Nina followed the action from behind the table – and that's when she spotted Jay. He crossed the floor in a few giant steps, carrying a vegetable tray across the hall to the last empty table.

Earth had perked up, watching him. "He's not organic, you know," she whispered.

"Who? What?" Nina blinked in confusion.

Earth nodded at Jay. "He douses his crops with Roundup."

"Really?"

"I grow all organic. Berries mostly. But now the season's over I bake from frozen."

Nina nodded appreciatively, trying not to ogle Jay. "Sounds great. I'm planning to set up an organic garden, but I've only just moved here, so I'm not very far with the plans..."

A flurry of elderly ladies interrupted them, wanting to hear how healthy and guilt-free their treats were. To Nina's surprise, people didn't swap individual items but wandered around the room, picking up what they needed. Following their example, Nina took her bag and browsed the other tables. Sensing Earth's eyes on her back, she skipped Jay's table, but collected hefty bunches of kale, spinach, apples, oranges and kiwi fruit from other growers. Slow down, she told herself. Everyone will think you're greedy. But there seemed to be plenty to go around, and after a round of polite refusals, she ended up accepting bags of lemon and grapefruit. She felt like she'd won the lottery.

When Nina looked up, she noticed Jay's table had emptied, apart from a couple of cakes he was just packing into his crate. Jay caught her eye, raised his hand and flashed her a smile. Nina waved back, wanting to say something but knowing her voice wouldn't carry across the room without drawing everyone's attention. Earth had packed up her plates and trays, having traded away all her cake slices.

Nina turned to her with a friendly smile. "Why does he come here? I mean Jay. If he has a big farm, shouldn't he be selling at a farmers' market or something, not swapping a couple of cucumbers for cake?"

Earth turned to look at Jay, her face hardening. "I suppose he just wants free cake."

"Well, it's not free, really."

"He grows large quantities. A box of veggies costs him nothing. It's cheaper than buying those cakes in the shops. And the old ladies love him. They don't care about Roundup when there's a young man..." Earth's voice trailed off as she looked over at Jay.

He was on his way over, carrying his cakes on the empty vegetable tray.

"Hi, Jay," Earth piped up.

"Hi."

"You're too late. I've no cake left."

Jay shrugged. "That's okay. I scored three cakes already."

Earth lifted her chin, peering at his treats as if from great heights. "As long as you don't mind getting cancer. You know cancer cells live on sugar, right?"

Jay drew an audible breath, a muscle on his jaw twitching. "There is no scientific evidence of that what-so-ever. But it's possible that the happiness I get from eating cake that tastes like cake will improve my mental wellbeing, which may even outweigh the negative effects of sugar." Nina couldn't tear her gaze off that stubbled jaw and fiery brown eyes. So much for the simple-minded theory. Jay could definitely string together a sentence.

"Did you read the article I sent you?" Earth demanded.

Jay scowled. "Which one?"

"The latest one! It is a scientific study. Your mum read it. She said she'd make sure you'd see it."

Jay sighed and switched his attention to Nina. "So, what are these?" He pointed at Nina's remaining two chocolates, already soft and sticky.

"It's organic raw chocolate," Earth replied for her. "Not your thing, I'm afraid."

Earth shifted closer and flashed Nina a conspiratorial smile, making her feel like they were allies in all matters of superior health and nutrition. Nina took an instinctive step away, her stomach clenching. She smiled at Jay. "They're not everyone's cup of tea, but if you like darker chocolate, you might like them."

To her surprise, Jay snatched one chocolate. They watched him swirl it in his mouth, waiting for a reaction. Jay swallowed, offering Nina a good-natured smile. "Not bad."

"Thanks."

"Is that an even trade?" Earth's voice climbed higher, along with her eyebrows. "I don't think she wants your pesticides. I saw her skip your table."

Her tone made Nina squirm. She didn't want pesticides, but she didn't want someone like Earth speaking on her behalf. When changing her diet, she'd sworn she wouldn't become one of those dietary nazis who sneered at other people's choices. Nina glanced at her full canvas bags. "I have more veggies I know what to do with. I don't need more."

Earth smiled conspiratorially. "See? She doesn't want your pesticide crops."

Jay shrugged. "That's okay. I'm sold out, anyway." Nina felt Jay's eyes on her as she packed her one remaining chocolate into the cooler bag.

"Money won't help if you lose your health," Earth continued. "Remember your dad with that Roundup container strapped to his back, walking around the farm..."

"Shut up!"

Nina risked a glance at them and froze. Jay stared at

Earth with an intensity that could have burned holes in more flammable fabric. The air sizzled with tension. What on earth - Earth, indeed - was going on between these two? Wishing to get out before the nuclear explosion, Nina thanked Earth, grabbed her bags and headed for the door. When she got to her car, she noticed Jay at her heels. "I wanted to say sorry."

Nina turned, bumping into the crate he was holding.

"Sorry for what?" she asked, stumbling backwards.

"That. There." Jay nodded at the community hall. "I didn't mean to make you uncomfortable."

His brown eyes bore into her, making her legs a little wobbly. She'd misjudged him. He wasn't slow, nor lacking in emotional intelligence. He also had the longest, thickest eyelashes she'd ever seen on a man. Nina dropped her gaze on her dirt-lined toenails, willing her heart rate to settle.

"Sounds like you guys have a history," she concluded.

"You could say that," Jay laughed. "Earth can be a bit ... she's passionate. But she means well, most of the time."

"She seems worried about your diet." Nina glanced at Jay's crate, bursting with homemade cakes and cookies. He huffed, a smirk playing on his lips. "Believe it or not, this isn't representative of my entire diet."

"It's not?" Nina matched his playful smile.

"Well, I grow vegetables. I eat vegetables."

"Conventional."

Nina wanted to kick herself. She sounded like Earth. "I

mean, she's really into organic," she added.

"I assume you are as well?"

"I try. I ... have my reasons." Nina bit her lip, heat rising on her cheeks. "But I don't judge other people for what they eat."

Jay stared at her, his gaze intense. "Good. Me neither."

Then he turned and walked away.

A man of abrupt exits, Nina mused as she packed her vegetables in the car. She still had to stop at the shops on her way home, to make sure she had other basics in her newly humming fridge. Driving down Raglan's palm-tree-lined main street, she wondered what kind of history Jay and Earth had. Jay hadn't referred to her by any title, but it didn't mean they didn't have a relationship. An ex-girlfriend maybe?

Chapter 4

Nina bristled with nervous tension. Three weeks into her new life, La La was coming for a visit. She would be the first visitor in her tiny home. Nina examined the small house, trying to see it through her friend's eyes. It was brand new and tidy, but still felt a little sterile. Hoping to add signs of life, Nina had hung a couple of art prints and set up a display of locally made ceramic coffee mugs. La La would appreciate a touch of class in the sticks. The Raglan La La was familiar with comprised the cute village with its hipster-surfer cafes and German tourists. La La only visited in the summer to ogle the tanned, shirtless guys and eat real fruit ice cream. What Nina had tried to explain to her (but failed to get across) was that her new neighbourhood wasn't anywhere near the village. She'd had to go rural with a capital R. Apart from her hot, Roundup-spraying neighbour, there was nothing but wild bush and cultivated grazing land around her house.

La La arrived about half an hour late. She got out of her

red Mini Cooper and, rather uncharacteristically, sprinted across the bumpy grass with no regard to her expensive black boots. Nina grinned, matching La La's 'woohoo' with a soft yelp as she enclosed her in a tight hug. Screaming with enthusiasm didn't come naturally to Nina, even with nobody else around.

"Nina! I can't believe you did it! You live here! How is it possible? There's nothing here. For miles and miles. Nothing!" La La whipped her head left and right, earrings whipping her cheeks, her blue eyes huge. She wore a black bomber jacket that matched her boots and her straight, black hair looked salon-fresh.

Nina chuckled. "I'm so glad you made it. I know this isn't really your thing, but I've missed you so much!"

"Me too! Now, come on, show me your crib."

Proud as a new mother, Nina introduced her house, its clever storage solutions, solar panels, rainwater collection system and the shower loop for filtering and cycling shower water. After a moment's hesitation, she even revealed her composting toilet, including the big outside barrels where she emptied the waste so it could compost further. La La followed her, 'oohing' with admiration, but gave the poop barrels a wide berth and announced she would not be using the toilet if she could help it. Nina doubted she could help it, considering her friend was here overnight.

After a cup of tea and a strong coffee for La La, Nina expected her friend to suggest a drive to Raglan for some shopping and dinner. To her surprise, La La didn't seem in a hurry to go anywhere.

"It's so peaceful here. I can't hear anything." She closed her eyes for a moment. "Well, I can hear your fridge, but nothing else."

Nina laughed. "Yeah, I'm considering earplugs."

"Do you have any neighbours?"

"I've only met one so far."

Nina recapped the story of Jay towing her house and how she'd bumped into him at the crop swap.

La La's eyes lit up. "Wait. He's young? Single?"

"I don't know."

"You don't know if he's young?"

"Ha ha. He's... maybe my age. Single? No idea."

"Sounds like a single guy. Why else would he show up to a meeting like that to score cakes?"

Nina shrugged. "Maybe his girlfriend doesn't bake? Besides, he hasn't been there for the last two weeks. I've been back twice to swap some water kefir I made. Last time, I got these amazing flower shaped zucchinis..."

La La raised a hand to shut her up. "Don't change the subject. You have a gorgeous and potentially single neighbour. This is interesting! Especially after..."

She didn't have to mention Tama's name. During the quiet nights in her new home, Nina had been thinking about her ex-colleague far too much, fighting the urge to text him. Maybe thinking about her new neighbour wasn't the worst idea. Anything to get Tama out of her head.

"I didn't say gorgeous," Nina corrected, suppressing her smile. "He's ... good-looking and also kind of weird."

"Well, I might have to decide that for myself. Come on, let's go for a walk." La La stood up.

Nina gripped the edge of her miniscule dining table. "Seriously? I don't even know where his house is. I think he has acres of land."

La La rolled her eyes. "Don't tell me you haven't even tried to find out! You're in the middle of nowhere with nothing else to do."

"I have heaps to do, thank you very much! I've been setting up my garden."

Nina knew she had to plant a few things before the summer was over to get at least one good crop by the end of season. After a day of shovelling, dislodging rocks and dragging bags of compost, she had no energy for pointless walks.

"Come on, let's go for a leisurely stroll in the countryside." La La pointed at her custom-made oak door. Nina pulled a face. "That sounds so weird coming from you."

"This is a once in a lifetime opportunity. My first and last country walk. You don't want to miss this one."

Nina laughed but lent La La her second pair of sneakers and followed her outside.

After twenty minutes of out-of-breath climbing, they reached the top of the hill. The landscape bathed in bright sunlight. Even though Nina had seen the view many times, it stole her breath away. Lush, green ferns framed the rolling hills, with the turquoise ocean shimmering in the distance.

La La raised her hand to shield her face from the million-megawatt sun. "I can sort of see why you like this place. This is a million-dollar view!"

"Literally! You can see why I could only afford to buy on the wrong side of the hill."

Despite her self-deprecating words, Nina felt proud. This was her home, her piece of the planet, and having someone else appreciate the scenery warmed her heart. As she was still soaking up the moment, Nina noticed La La moving ahead, towards the nearest house in the distance. Nina caught up with her friend. "Where are you going?"

"To see about those neighbours."

"Why? I mean, why now?"

"Because I know you. You'll put it off for months and then it's too awkward and you'll give up the idea altogether."

Nina ignored her friend's knowing look. "Hey! I've talked to one neighbour already. I'll get to the rest."

"No. You'll procrastinate and make it into a big deal in your busy head and end up backing out. I may prefer to live in the city, but I know the countryside. You need to know your neighbours. You rely on your neighbours. Sometimes, to survive. I know you're a capable person, but you're not an island."

Nina stared at her friend, her mouth hanging. "Do you not think I can survive here?"

La La gave her a compassionate look. "You're supercapable, but living on your own in the middle of nowhere is not about that. What if you were choking on a bone?"

"Why would I be choking on a bone?"

"Well, you make that ridiculous broth."

"Which I always strain."

"Not the point."

Nina knew what she meant. It had crossed her mind. She took extra care when getting out of the shower and wondered what she would do if her car didn't start, if she didn't have enough power to charge her phone or got violently ill. She hadn't considered choking, but now she couldn't shake the image of herself home alone, gasping for breath.

They strolled in silence to the neighbour's house. It turned out to be a beautiful, sprawling villa surrounded by a flowering meadow and a sea of vibrant blue hydrangea. A pickup truck stood in the carport and the front door was open.

"Looks like someone's home." La La nodded at the open door, but to Nina's relief, stopped to knock on it. Nina hesitated. She felt horrible not having a plate of biscuits or anything else to offer. But before she could duck away, a middle-aged lady in cut-off denims and a flowery T-shirt appeared at the door. She held a mixing bowl filled with dough, one hand kneading it as she raised a friendly eyebrow. La La stepped forward. "Hi! My name is Lauren. My friend Nina here has just moved here, over that hill, and since you guys are her closest neighbours, we wanted to say hi."

Nina smiled and raised her hand. “Hi!”

The lady’s eyes widened, and she broke into a smile, peering at Nina. “You live in the trailer house?”

“Yes. You know my house?”

The woman tried to pry the sticky dough off her fingers by swiping them against the bowl. “I heard about it and thought, how very brave! We’re so exposed to the elements around here I sometimes feel like the wind could just sweep me away. But on a good day it’s heaven.”

Nina’s stomach lurched as she imagined a tropical cyclone lifting her tiny house off the ground. “Well, I’m not sure if I’m brave or just stupid, to be honest. I haven’t seen a storm yet, so I don’t know what will happen. My house could just fly away and land in your backyard. And I guess that’s why we’re here. I was told it’s good to know your neighbours.”

Nina gestured to La La, who flashed an unapologetic smile. The lady nodded, wiped her free hand on a tea towel hanging on her arm, and held it out.

“That’s right. Neighbours are important out here. I’m Alice.”

Nina took her hand and repeated her own name. She had trouble memorising names. In Finland, people barely used first names in conversation. The concept of learning someone’s name during the first introduction and storing it for still felt foreign to her. But as Nina looked into Alice’s twinkling brown eyes, a small voice inside her whispered ⊠you should remember this’. When Alice asked the girls to step in,

Nina's brain recorded her name for all eternity, as she indeed lived in a wonderland.

Alice's cosy villa burst with plants and flowers, even more so than her garden. They came in all shapes and colours, in various pots and containers, including teapots and washbasins. Nina had spent the previous year studying perma-culture gardens and sprouting vegetables on her windowsill. She was no stranger to potting, but this was not your basic veggie patch or herb gardening. Apart from one fern and a range of orchids, Nina couldn't recognise any of the plants. With alien shapes and odd colours, they looked wildly exotic and purely decorative.

Alice noticed the girls transfixed by the wildlife and gently guided them to a small dining table.

"I run a wee side business. Houseplants are back in fashion. They want them in offices, living walls, features in receptions, things like that. And the rare species fetch a premium price." She joined the girls at the table, placing her mixing bowl on the table. "Although I don't always end up selling." Her face flushed and she smiled. "They're just so pretty and some are so hard to grow that I worry about them. It's safer to keep them here."

Nina smiled back, nodding in understanding. "They look so exotic."

"Many of them are from overseas. To be honest, I hate selling them. I just tell my son it's a business to get him off my back. I sell some now and then, but I don't advertise anywhere and only grow what I like."

She let out a hearty laugh. Nina couldn't stop staring into her eyes. There was something playful and twinkly about them. Something familiar. A loud oven timer woke her from her thoughts.

"Sorry, sorry." Alice jumped to fetch something from the oven. A heady smell of fresh bread mixed and mingled with the exotic flowers, making Nina a little light-headed.

"That smells amazing," La La remarked. "What is it?"

Her friend's frankness made Nina cringe. She might as well have queued up with a plate. Except that Alice was already coming back with plates, the steaming loaf of bread on a cutting board. Within ten seconds, a block of butter and cheddar cheese emerged and Alice cut the bread with a satisfying crunch.

Nina hadn't eaten bread in months, apart from some weird, gummy Paleo loaf she'd found in the supermarket. But if she was ever going to break her diet, this was certainly the time. Savouring the rich, yeasty scent, Nina buttered the offered slice. It smelled and tasted heavenly.

"It's kumara sourdough," Alice explained, which soothed Nina's conscience. Wasn't sourdough supposed to be more digestible? Something like that. Nina had dropped bread from her diet after researching how the conventional wheat growers used Roundup both during the growing season and pre-harvesting. The farmers had glyphosate, Roundup's active ingredient, in their urine and an increased risk of certain cancers. There was a Finnish saying 'knowledge increases pain', which applied well to her predicament.

This bread, however, was delicious. Their conversation flowed from the characteristics of Raglan and its surroundings to growing plants and beekeeping, which was another passion of Alice's. Nina found herself utterly captivated by the woman and her matter-of-fact attitude to country life. She seemed to just do what she liked and somehow make enough money to live on. Having spent years saving and surviving and now worrying about her survival in this new environment, Nina could hardly imagine such a carefree existence.

"So, what's your plan?" Alice asked her. "Are you just farming the land to feed yourself or going into business with something?"

"I ... I haven't figured that out. My first goal is to have a productive, organic garden, following the perma-culture principles, as much as I can."

"That's a great goal. You sound passionate about it."

"I am. Either that or just plain crazy. I don't know. I've read a lot and experimented with my little backyard plot in the city, but still feel like I know nothing about real farming."

Alice smiled and patted her arm. "You know what I do when I don't know something? I just google."

She winked and got up, indicating that the dough on the table needed her attention. It had doubled in size since they arrived.

"I'm sorry. We're keeping you from your baking. La, we should head back."

La La seemed to wake up and got on her feet.

"You don't have to leave," Alice called from the kitchen. "It's just that my son's coming for lunch. You're welcome to join us."

The front door creaked. Nina did a double take. *It was Jay.* So that's why Alice's eyes were familiar! La La, now wide-awake and alert, jumped in to introduce them.

"Hi! We're just visiting from the neighbouring tiny house. My name's Lauren and this is – "

"Nina?" Jay finished for her.

"You know each other?"

La La's voice dripped with meaning as she put two and two together. Nina's face flushed with warmth. Oh, God. This wasn't happening. She never blushed.

"Yeah," Jay confirmed.

"Jay helped me tow my tiny house in the right spot," Nina explained, partly to Alice. "The towing company just left it in the driveway. He totally saved the day."

"And Nina fed me some homemade health chocolate at the crop swap. But she refused to touch my non-organic veg-etables." The corner of Jay's mouth tugged.

Nina's face burned hot. "It's not that. I just didn't need..."

"Hey, be nice." Alice stuck a wooden spoon between her son's ribs.

Jay shrugged and moved on to the kumara sourdough,

cutting himself a hefty slice.

Nina turned to Alice. "It was so nice to meet you. Thank you for the bread and everything."

"Are you sure you don't want to stay? Pumpkin soup?" Alice asked, innocuously.

La La looked like she was ready to accept, but Nina shot her a stern look. She couldn't handle defending her organic choices to Jay in front of his mother. She liked Alice, but her son was another matter altogether. Having witnessed the sparring and familiarity between him and Earth, she felt like the third wheel in something she didn't quite understand. She also found it distracting to be around someone so attractive. Despite his decidedly understated wardrobe of jeans and a puffer vest, he had the hair and eyes of a Hollywood heartthrob, and he knew it. She wouldn't give him the satisfaction of more blushing and swooning.

Nina escorted La La out the door, but not before Alice gifted her a beautiful houseplant with heart-shaped leaves.

"A little housewarming gift," she said. "Hopefully it fits into your tiny house."

"It's gorgeous. Thank you!"

Nina ensured Alice she had a place for it and invited her to visit anytime. She might not have been elbow deep in baking, but she could always offer raw chocolate. Alice gave them both a quick hug, welcoming them to the area. Jay barely lifted his eyes from the newspaper he had spread across the table.

As soon as they were out of the earshot, La La turned to Nina.

"Good-looking? He's scrumptious. You totally played it down."

"He's also kind of ... prickly."

"Just like you. You're perfect for each other!"

"I'm not prickly! Am I?"

La La laughed and gave Nina a side hug.

"No, you're downright terrifying. You're the most head-strong, crazy girl I know! How you will ever find a man, I don't know."

Chapter 5

After a lovely night of talking and snacking on nuts and chips – another food item Nina hadn't touched in months – the girls ended up both sleeping on the loft, too tired to set up the guest bed, which had to be assembled out of several cubes and pieces of mattress. So much for the handy, space-saving solutions.

Nina's head reeled from the day's events. After two weeks of nothing happening (her major highlight had been building a compost bin), seeing both her best friend and neighbours felt like an overload of social interaction and new information. At least she'd have something to think about over the coming weeks as she turned soil and descended further into her hermit-like existence.

The next morning over breakfast smoothies – green for Nina, chocolate for her friend – La La presented her with a plan. "We should go hang out in Raglan. I need to get you out and about. Ideally, I would take you to Hamilton but that's more driving than I'm prepared to do right now, so Raglan it is."

Nina wrinkled her nose. "You make it sound like I never leave this house."

"I'm not talking about popping into the supermarket or hardware store. I mean, we should go out."

"You mean drinking? It's only 9 a.m."

"Well, not straight away. We could do a beach walk, get takeaways for lunch, hang out and get to know some locals, browse the shops. Then, we go for a drink. What do you think?"

Nina nodded. She didn't feel comfortable about the 'talking to locals' part, but everything else sounded laid back. She was relieved her friend hadn't suggested mid-winter surfing lessons or mind-altering drugs.

It took a good three hours for them to drink tea, enjoy the fire, and lie on the tiny couch before they finally started moving. They decided to take both cars. After the day trip to Raglan, La La would continue back home. The thought of her friend leaving already darkened Nina's mood, and she fought to focus on the present, as well as not losing sight of her friend's Mini Cooper. For a visitor who didn't know the roads, La La drove like a true local.

Turning from the main road, La La drove to the long peninsula that stretched in front of the town harbour, shielding it from the high ocean waves. The shape of it created a safe, calm bay perfect for swimming. The summer was long gone, but the sunny day had attracted a handful of beach combers and dog walkers.

Teenagers dove into the bay from the unnervingly high walking bridge that connected the peninsula to the pier. The water must have been freezing. Two elderly men sat on the opposite side, perched on the dock in their puffer jackets, holding fishing rods.

"So this is the part where we talk to the locals?" Nina asked, bristling against the cool breeze.

"Are you questioning my plan, young lady?"

"Of course not. But I didn't bring my togs. It would be much easier to strike up a conversation if I could join in." Nina rolled her eyes to emphasise the sarcasm. The sheer idea of removing even one layer of clothing was ludicrous.

"Great idea! Let's get you a bikini!"

"Ha-ha. A scarf would be more like it. Or mittens."

"Okay, let's get you a scarf. Whatever you need. I wanna go shopping, but not just for me. Let's find something for you, too!"

La La had expressed her concern after seeing Nina's new, simplified country wardrobe. Downsizing to move into a tiny house, she'd had to favour survival over beauty. And yellow gumboots went with everything, right?

"What about the beach walk?" Nina asked.

La La shrugged. "We can just walk across the bridge to the village. That counts, right?"

Nina laughed. She'd had her doubts about the walking part. La La wasn't the type to go barefoot on the sand, collecting seashells. She followed her friend across the walking bridge and towards the village. The only thing that worried her was money.

"The shops here are for tourists," she grumbled as they approached the palm-lined main road. "They're pretty expensive. There's no Kmart or anything."

La La rolled her eyes. "Who needs Kmart? Come on! But if you're worried about the cost, we can try the op shops. I bet you know them already. Lead the way."

They made it to the closest one, a little boutique close to the beach selling 'up-cycled' clothing.

"What is up-cycled?" asked La La.

"It's recycling, just more expensive. I think technically they should improve the clothes. Fix holes, change buttons, that kind of thing. But most of what I've seen here is just as is."

Nina knew her friend wouldn't be seen dead in anything recycled, updated or not, but she was trying to be a good sport.

"I knew you'd tell me the truth," La La laughed and forged ahead. "Look at these bins here! These must be cheaper."

Two containers outside the shop spilled with clothes the shop wanted to get rid of – for a reason. Nina lifted a pair of ripped, paint-splattered dungarees. La La snorted. She grabbed them off her and held them against her body as if measuring for size. "You know, I'm not a recycling expert, but surely there comes a point when it's actually okay to send something into landfill."

A shrill voice interrupted their giggling. "There is no need for anything to go into landfill. Fabric can be recycled into new fabric."

They turned to face Earth. She'd gathered her dreadlocks on top of her head, creating a bun the size of her face. In a pair of deep brown dungarees and an olive-green shirt, with a tanned skin, she radiated vitality and health. Her expression radiated contempt.

"You're right," Nina replied with haste. "I've read about recycled cotton but I'm not sure how it's made."

She hoped Earth would put her righteous anger aside and educate them on recycled fabric. She didn't take the bait.

"Your friend must be from out of town. Here in Raglan we don't mock other people's businesses," Earth hissed.

With that, she walked into the shop, straight behind the counter. Nina swallowed hard. Earth worked here. La La tugged on Nina's shirt. "Maybe you can show me one of the other op shops?"

La La took a step down the road, but Nina didn't follow. She stood in front of the shop, frozen. "I have to apologise," she whispered.

"Why? It's not your fault she has a stick up her arse. A very eco-friendly stick I'm sure, but still."

Nina's stomach tightened. "I live here now, and I kind of know her. I need her on my side. You said I need to be on good terms with my neighbours."

"Is she your neighbour?"

"In the wider sense, yeah."

Nina didn't want to admit that she was also curious. She wanted to know how Earth and Jay knew each other and what their relationship was. Chatting with Earth might shed some light on the mystery.

"Just wait here, please. I won't be long." She took a deep breath and entered the shop.

"Hi Earth," she said, waiting for her to look up.

Earth lifted her eyes from one of those non-glossy magazines. Nina loved those – anything printed on an uncoated stock with quirky photos of pot plants and people who could rock dungarees. She genuinely admired their dress sense, even if she'd never be able to pull it off in her previous life. But now that she lived in Raglan, maybe she could.

Nina took a step closer, fixing a pleading smile on her face. "I'm sorry for what my friend said. She's a real city girl. I don't think she's ever bought anything recycled. But she doesn't mean any harm. I love buying secondhand. Most of my clothes are recycled."

Earth's eyes signalled deep disappointment. "Uh-huh." She glanced at the door, maybe hoping that another customer would walk in and give her an excuse to dismiss Nina.

"I agree we shouldn't throw away anything still useful. I know people rip old jeans and T-shirts to make garden ties. Or use them as stuffing for pillows."

She watched Earth's mouth twitch. Was she fighting the

urge to educate her?

"Fibres like polyester and acrylic are toxic. You should never put them inside a pillow. If it's for a baby to play with or for sleeping, I wouldn't even use conventional cotton. The dyes keep emitting toxic gases."

Nina suppressed a victorious smile. "Oh, I hadn't thought of that. A good point."

Earth drew a breath, her voice rising higher. "Do you know the difference between organic fibre and organic fibre that's been processed organically? You should really watch what you put on your skin. Anything you eat goes through the digestive system, but when you absorb chemicals through your skin, they go straight into your bloodstream."

Nina touched the hem of her shirt. What material was it? Had she even checked before buying it? "That's good to know. I have to look into my wardrobe. I'd love to have all of my textiles fully organic, but it's so expensive."

Earth seemed to light up, her earlier apprehension gone. "Well, that's what we're doing here. We're recycling organic fibres to make them more affordable. And to reduce waste, of course."

Nina looked around the little shop with renewed interest. Two racks labeled ORGANIC had a few pieces hanging on each. Nothing immediately caught her eye, but the idea of her regular clothing slowly poisoning her was a great motivator.

Nina stepped closer to browse the racks. She hadn't lied

about her fondness for op shopping. Even when she'd been earning good money, she kept bargain hunting, largely because she was saving for her house and clothing seemed like the last thing she should have been spending on. Aware of La La waiting outside (she would soon grow bored with Instagram), Nina grabbed a pair of loose, light trousers. They felt a bit like linen but turned out to be a hemp blend. She could tell they would fit her in a way that any pyjama pants would, so she brought them to the counter.

Earth raised one eyebrow. "We have a fitting room."

"That's okay."

While paying for the pants, Nina wondered how she could bring up Jay. What could she possibly say that didn't sound like she had a crush on him? Nina couldn't think of anything. Well, at least she'd apologised and maybe got in Earth's good books. They didn't have to be best friends, but hopefully the dreadlock woman had no reason to sneer the next time they bumped into each other.

"One thing," Earth stage-whispered as she handed over her credit card and the pants. "Jay is taken. Just in case you were wondering."

Nina stared at her in disbelief. Was she trying to say she was Jay's girlfriend? Or that someone else was? Nina smiled. "Okay. I wasn't wondering. I mean, it doesn't really matter to me."

She felt like she was lying through her teeth. Anyone would have been wondering what was going on between

Earth and Jay.

Outside, Nina found La La sitting on a concrete block sipping a tall glass of beer.

"How did it go?" La La asked.

"I honestly don't know," Nina said. "But she said Jay is taken."

La La looked up in surprise, wiping froth from the side of her mouth. "Why? Is she his girlfriend?"

"That's what I was wondering. They didn't seem that friendly at the crop swap. But they clearly know each other really well."

"Weird," La La concluded and took another sip of her beer.

"Where did you get that?" Nina asked, tapping on the pint.

La La nodded at a bar down the road. She stood up and motioned Nina to follow. "Come on. I told them I'd come right back, I just needed to fetch you."

"And they were okay with that?"

Based on the bartender's expression, he hadn't been given a choice. He glared at them from across the bar as they stepped through the doors into the wooden interior dominated by a pool table. La La leant on the bar. "One more, please!" Nina shook her head to cancel the order, mouthing 'sorry'.

The bartender cocked his head. "You know we don't open until 4 p.m.? I'm just doing the accounts." He gestured at the selection of receipts on the counter.

He was a burly fellow with even features – handsomeness overridden by lifestyle choices. Despite the grumbling, he poured La La another beer. She pushed it over to Nina, who stared at the brown liquid in confusion.

"It's not even noon. Or is it?"

"1:35 p.m.," offered the bartender.

Nina bit her lip, searching for the right words. "The thing is, I don't really drink anymore."

Noticing La La's widened eyes, she continued, "No, I'm not pregnant. I just don't drink."

La La still stared at her in disbelief. "But ... why?"

Nina glanced at the bartender. La La grabbed both beers, and the girls shifted to a table in the far corner. Grateful for the privacy, Nina gathered her courage. "You're going to think I'm nuts."

La La smirked. "I already do. Go on."

"You know how Matt and I were planning to get married and have kids?"

La La stared at her, mouth ajar. "Yeah, like two years ago?" Nina grimaced. "Yes. We agreed it was time. I wasn't getting any younger – "

"Nobody is getting younger! I hate that saying," La La huffed, draining her beer.

"True. But anyway, you know how it all ended, right? We couldn't agree on how to live, or where."

"Because he thinks there's no life outside Auckland?" La La rolled her eyes. "Yeah, enjoy sitting in traffic fourteen hours a day, Matt!"

Nina chuckled, sadness filling her chest. "And I'm so happy I ended up moving to Hamilton and working with you. The best decision I ever made! But it didn't really change this problem I had to begin with... of getting older." She twisted her mouth, looking out the small window. "I still want a family."

"You'll find someone," La La said reassuringly, pushing the other beer at her. "Drink your beer. It might even help." She winked, glancing over her shoulder at the bartender.

"I can't," Nina whispered. "You know when Sarah from finance was going through IVF? She said I should get everything checked. I did, and turns out I have polycystic ovaries and may have trouble getting pregnant. So, I kind of went down this internet rabbit hole looking for information. And I found all these fertility diets. Apparently, there's a lot you can do to restore or improve your fertility, but it's a long game.

La La blinked at her, incredulous. "But you're only thirty-six. And single. Easiest way to get pregnant is to get drunk and sleep with someone. Seriously." She nudged the beer a little closer, her mouth tugging into a grin, eyes hazed over. She was definitely one beer ahead of Nina.

"I know it sounds crazy, but just one beer will affect your egg health. Or a bit too much sugar. And plastics can disrupt your endocrine system. There are so many things..." Nina hung her head. She needed to be locked up right about now, in a round room with padded walls.

La La leaned back on the vinyl seat, her eyes narrowing.

"So, that's why you went on that weird diet?"

"You think I'm a freak, don't you? I'm sorry, I didn't tell you. I was embarrassed. It's like my biological clock took over my brain and started calling the shots."

La La looked like she was watching a foreign film without subtitles. "Why would you do all that and simultaneously isolate yourself in the countryside? Where are you going to find a man in here?"

"I don't know. If it doesn't work out, maybe I need to think about other options. Like a sperm bank."

Nina surprised herself with her own words. Did she really think like that? When had she become so single-minded? Every male on the planet could probably smell her obsession, the same way dogs could smell fear. That must have been why Tama had never asked her out. Then she'd moved away and a normal girl – someone not secretly baby crazy – had stepped in like a breath of fresh air and captured his interest. So simple, so nauseating.

La La reached across the table and took Nina's hands. "You know I love you, Nina. You're like a sister to me. But you have to stop this and live your life. Even if it means your *egg health* will suffer."

Nina drew a breath, trying to steady her thumping heart. *"I know. But I keep thinking … it's healthy, you know? What's wrong with being healthy?"*

"Nothing. But it sounds like you're kind of slipping into the 'obsessed' category." La La gave her a long, hard look and took a long sip of the second beer. "You can't jump ahead to the next chapter. Don't worry about fertility before you've met the guy and tried to get pregnant. How do you know how hard it will be?" She drank more of the beer.

"But I do. If I keep using alcohol or caffeine, it'll get worse. I can't afford that. I don't have that much time left."

La La fanned herself, exasperation in her eyes. "You talk like you're dying."

La La peeled off her leather jacket, revealing a sleeveless, black top that highlighted her sleeve tattoo. It was warm, but Nina kept her denim jacket on. She liked the way it hid her. La La kept drinking the beer, as if getting drunk in the early afternoon would somehow validate her point of view. Nina wondered if her friend was planning on sleeping with the bartender. "Don't you ever think about it?" she asked. "That you have this finite number of months to have a baby and then it's game over? Doesn't it bother you? Even if you don't want a baby, it's a death of sorts, a door that will close for good. And we're all just meant to pretend we don't care, so we don't appear too desperate or something."

La La's lips curved into a sad smile. "It's because men don't care. They have plenty of time."

"It's so unfair!"

"True."

They sat in silence for a moment. When La La finally spoke, her voice held a tinge of uncertainty. "To be honest, I thought it would just happen. It seems to happen to most people, right?" The doubt that flashed in her eyes went straight to Nina's heart. She'd thought of La La as someone invincible. But she was also a woman – just not so hyper-aware of her own ageing as Nina.

La La lowered her voice. "Promise me one thing, though? All this stuff you just told me... never tell that to any guy, okay? I know you're all about honesty, but guys can't handle this stuff. So, if you really want to have a kid... just keep it to yourself. Trust me. Try to forget that stuff and just live your life, okay?"

Sod it, Nina thought.

She grabbed La La's beer and finished it for her in one arduous gulp. There were only a couple of mouthfuls left, most of it probably backwash, but it got her friend's attention.

"There," Nina said, "I need to live a little and you need to drink a little less. You might just have that one night of passion, and you might be ovulating ... and the egg that started taking shape three months earlier during this trip, might just be that much healthier and turn into a healthy baby, and you'll have me to thank for it."

"That's quite the picture you're painting there!" La La laughed, but her eyes glistened.

Nina smiled back through a film of tears. "I told you, I went deep into that rabbit hole." La La sucked in her bottom lip. "So... eggs take three months to cook, eh?"

"Yeah. They need to mature before they are released, and that cycle is three months long."

"Wow."

La La sat for a moment, digesting it. Finally, she grabbed her purse and got on her feet. "Right. Time to hit the proper shops!"

It was the last thing Nina felt like doing, but she dutifully followed her friend out the door.

They proceeded down the main street, popped into a little alleyway, and discovered a couple of new shops Nina hadn't noticed before, even one organic food store. La La rolled her eyes at the prices. She wasn't used to spending money on groceries – unless it was fine dining. Definitely not on anything fermented that came with *a mother*. Nina coveted a bottle of pomegranate flavoured decaf kombucha, but decided she needed organic pumpkin seeds instead. Something to offset the beer.

"See, we're not that different," La La remarked. "We're both freaking out about ageing and buy products that promise to turn back time. So far, I've gone for the eye cream more than drinking the green sludge, but..."

La La picked up a bag of maca powder, spinning on her heels so fast she almost lost her balance. "This one is anti-ageing, rejuvenating, enhances fertility. Hey, get this one!"

Nina laughed. She could tell La La had nearly two beers in her. "I have maca. I can't take too much. It messes up my cycle. But it's good for energy."

They spent the next two hours browsing the shops – La

La doing most of the buying – and chatting with the shop assistants. Nina loved being able to visit the shops with no one paying attention to her. With the shop assistants busy serving her friend, she could browse beautiful things without spending a dime.

The day turned out as lazy and hazy as Nina had dreamed of. After hours of walking around, sitting on the dock and talking, they went for an early dinner. Nina ordered a quinoa salad and La La went for a so-called 'healthy' burger with a black, activated charcoal bun. Nina doubted it had any real health benefit, unless you had just ingested poison. Still, La La's willingness to try health foods warmed her heart. In the office, they'd all known La La by the trail of candy wrappers and half-empty coke bottles she left behind. If Nina needed to relax her diet, La La needed to discover some nutrients.

When it was time for La La to drive home, Nina couldn't help tearing up again. They were only 70 minutes apart, so why did it feel like this? Again, the gnawing doubt over her life choice swirled in the pit of Nina's stomach. She hugged her friend a little too hard and let her go. As she watched her Mini climb up over the hill and out of sight, she promised herself a long, hot shower and three pieces of raw chocolate.

CHAPTER 6

Nina sunk into the reclined dental chair, willing her mind to focus on the silent episode of *Friends* playing on the ceiling-mounted TV. Better than focusing on her numb jaw and the sharp equipment going in and out of her mouth. It amazed her that somehow, even with the powerful local anaesthetic, the entire experience could be so uncomfortable. This was the worst dentist visit of her life. Not only because she had four cavities (four!), but because she had not budgeted for this to happen. She used no sugar or fizzy drinks. She had happily assumed that she would never need a dentist again, except for her annual (okay, triennial) check-up.

Manic googling in the last week had revealed that her new, healthy diet could actually be to blame. She'd eaten a lot of nuts, which apparently had high amounts of tooth decaying phytic acid. That she consistently forgot to floss probably didn't help.

The dentist finally removed the last metal vice out of her mouth and asked Nina to bite down on something. Her mouth was so numb she couldn't tell if it was closed or open.

I have to stop eating nuts, she thought.

Well, now she wouldn't have money to buy them anyway, so that must have been the silver lining.

Nina handed her debit card to the receptionist and watched in horror as the cheerful lady drained her account. She did the math. Her remaining funds were supposed to last until next summer, until she had an established, productive garden to feed her. She'd ordered a garden shed but had yet to build a greenhouse. And she needed that to produce anything over the winter. Now, if she built the greenhouse, she didn't have enough left over to buy food before the first crops were ready. So, no greenhouse. She would just try to survive.

Nina thanked the receptionist and sauntered to her car, saliva dripping from the corner of her dead-flesh-filled mouth.

Now that she had time, could she forage for food? She could collect mussels and ... surely there was something else she could find in the bush? Before the move, Nina had tried to fill the giant gaps in her knowledge by signing up for an organic gardening course. But she'd struggled to fit into her busy schedule and had missed most of the classes. Well, nothing beat learning survival skills in action, with a deadline. She had to educate herself on living off the land before she starved or developed scurvy. How was that for motivation?

When Nina arrived home, she checked her planter boxes. She'd only built three so far, and they were already looking wonky. It was probably too early for even the hardiest brassicas, but she'd planted a few anyway, hoping to get some early crops before Christmas. The little sprouts had grown, but something wasn't right. The baby broccoli and kale leaves sported a sprinkling of holes. A closer investigation revealed a handful of green caterpillars, happily munching on her food. They'd chewed the baby spinach so well only the stems remained.

Nina collapsed on the wet grass, tears bursting out with a growl of frustration. This was so unfair! She should have set up nets to protect the plants, but still. The plants had seemed fine a couple of days ago, and she had been busy putting together the tool shed, ordering a trailer load of soil and turning the ground with a shovel.

Allowing herself one more wail (she was in the sticks, nobody would hear her), Nina got up and fetched a container. At the last crop swap, she'd held a table next to a middle-aged lady, who had mentioned there were wild citrus trees growing close to her section. Nina wandered down her driveway and noticed a little path going into the bush. The path wound through densely growing ferns, first half-way up 'Jay's hill' (as she called it), then around it. Had she discovered a shortcut to the beach?

After ten minutes of walking, Nina felt better. Who could hold on to stress when surrounded by that much lush greenery and birdsong? Deep in thoughts, she nearly stumbled on the tree. It wasn't a citrus tree, but a kiwifruit one, full of ripe fruit. Her favourite! Nina picked the fruit into her container. She wanted desperately to eat some, but her tongue and lips were still numb and she couldn't risk biting into her cheeks. Last time, she'd ended up chewing up and swallowing a piece of her own flesh.

With her container nearly full, Nina followed the path further. A moment later, she arrived at a small opening. To her surprise, she found beautiful lemon and lime trees, all laden with fruit. Something about the view struck her as odd. Was this a planted garden? Nina examined the area and noticed a structure behind a large maple tree. Was it a house? A shed? The tree branches obscuring her view, Nina crept closer. She heard a rustling sound. Footsteps. A dark shape appeared around the building's corner, approaching her.

Nina froze. If she ran away, they would hear her. She was too close. Her heart pounding in her chest, she crouched down on the ground. She hid in the shade of a large bush, hugging her kiwifruit container. Maybe if she was perfectly still, they would just walk past. But no. She could hear someone ... something approaching. A dog. A friendly-looking Labrador, but its sudden appearance gave Nina a start. She tried to smile and dismiss the pooch by waving her hand. How were you supposed to tell a dog to ignore you? But the pup was too excited, bouncing around, barking and wagging its tail.

"Chloe! What is it?" A male voice called.

There was nowhere to hide. Time to get up and face the music. But before Nina got back on her feet, a pair of large, black gumboots appeared in her view. Growing from those like a dark, tall tree, was Jay.

"Oh. Hey, neighbour."

"Heyf." Oh, no! She couldn't speak. With the powerful local anaesthesia, her tongue still felt like a giant, swollen sponge. Why did this have to happen? Wasn't emptying one's savings account and being tortured for two hours enough for one day? Nina took a deep breath and scrambled to her feet.

"Thorry, I'f been to the dhentisth. I can'th speak."

She tried to smile and could feel it wasn't working. She must have looked creepy. Jay laughed.

Mortified, Nina covered her mouth. She watched Jay's eyes land on her fruit container. This was horrible!

"I didn't realithe thith wath your garden. I'm thorry. Here."

This was all too much. Tears burning behind her eyes, Nina pushed the container at Jay and ran down the path she'd come from. She heard the dog and Jay coming after her, but kept going, running until she heard nothing but her own heartbeat. Her mouth tasted of blood – from the running or biting her tongue, she wasn't sure. Finally, she reached her little home and clambered inside. She couldn't see anyone behind her. Jay must have turned back.

Nina filled her sitting tub – the highlight of her minis-cule bathroom – with hot water and soaked in it for half an hour. Then she made herself a cup of tea and a simple apple cinnamon smoothie from the last remaining ingredients in her kitchen. She'd been so upset over the dentist bill she'd skipped the grocery shopping.

As the anaesthesia gradually wore off, Nina found herself famished. After going through the cupboards and googling (slowly, but surely) for half an hour, she discovered a Paleo pancake recipe she had the ingredients for. Well, all except vanilla pods. With the delicious scent of baking filling her little house, Nina felt her equilibrium returning. It was getting darker outside, courtesy of the daylight savings, and she lit her one remaining soy candle.

It turned out the candle had all but lost its scent during the long storage, but it still created a lovely atmosphere. Nina changed into her softest slacks, a loose cotton tee and wool slippers. She put on her favourite song by a local indie band Paper Cranes and sat down to eat her pancake, whilst re-reading her favourite organic gardening magazine.

The doorbell rang.

Nina didn't even know what her doorbell sounded like – no one had ever used it. The 'ding dong' sound was so loud it made her jump up from her seat, bump into the table and spill some hot candle wax on her arm. Wincing with pain, she leapt to the door and peaked out of the little window. Jay and his dog. Nina's mind warred between wariness and nerves. She wanted him to see her house, but not right now. Not when she just wanted to sit down and eat her pancake.

But she also needed to stay friendly with her neighbours. She couldn't pretend not to be home – she lived in a tiny aquarium.

The evening's events flashed through her brain – getting out of the bath and changing her clothes. Walking around in her undies. She was so used to nobody being around that she hardly thought about it. Sighing at her own stupidity, Nina opened the door and smiled, now with a functioning mouth at least.

"Hi, Jay!"

Jay held out the container of kiwifruit. "You left these."

"Yes. I'm sorry. I didn't know I was picking your fruit. I'm … not having the best day."

"I gathered as much. But you left in such a hurry, I didn't get to tell you. It's not my garden."

"It's not?"

"No. It's a kind of community garden. It's on my land, but I didn't plant it and I don't really look after it. This Tongan family who live down the road started it. I said they could use the land since I wasn't growing anything out there. And they said I could pick anything I want."

"So it's their garden? And yours, obviously."

"No. I mean, it was years ago. Then the Tongans moved away and other neighbours and friends have been using it. We all know about it and I was going to tell you as well. In case you need some fruit or berries in the summer. There are quite a few trees. Lemon, lime, apple, orange, plum…"

Jay shifted, looking over his shoulder. Afraid that he would make one of his swift exits, Nina stepped aside and opened the door for him.

"Come in. You've come this far, you might as well have a tour."

Jay's hair brushed against the doorframe as he climbed the steep stairs. It felt strange to have a man standing in her tiny home. He looked out of place, like he'd just crawled inside a rabbit hole and ended up at a tiny tea party. Jay interlaced his fingers as if to avoid whipping his arms at furniture. He peeked inside the bathroom, checked out her reading nook, and glanced at the sleeping loft. Then he accepted the seat Nina offered him, patting Chloe, the dog who had followed him inside.

"Do you want some tea?" Nina asked.

"Nah, that's all right."

"I don't have any beer, sorry. Water kefir?"

"Water what?"

"Or... pancakes? I have pancakes, but they're Paleo."

"What?"

"They're made without grains, like wheat or oats. I used tapioca, green banana flour, and banana."

Jay stared at her in confusion. "You bake weird shit."

They sat in silence for a moment. Nina felt too exhausted to explain herself. She had done her duty by offering him whatever she had. If it was all too weird, he could just leave. Jay nodded. "Okay."

"Okay what?"

"Your chocolate wasn't too bad. I'm willing to try the pancakes."

Jay smiled and held her gaze, a little longer than required by polite society. Nina swallowed, suddenly nervous about her pancake. She always made pancake in the oven, Finnish style, so it was just one big pancake the size of her oven tray, about half an inch thick.

Nina set the table and dug up an old jar of jam she hadn't touched in months.

Jay looked at his plate. "It doesn't look like a pancake."

"It's an oven pancake."

They waited for a moment as the kettle boiled, filling the space with its loud rumble. Nina fetched her teapot and some tea leaves. She had nothing else than a raspberry leaf and nettle mix – perfect for regulating the monthly cycle. Nina wondered how these herbs affected the opposite gender, but kept her thoughts to herself.

"It's herbal," she warned as she placed the pot on the table.

"This is pretty good," Jay remarked, after shoving the second half of the pancake piece in his mouth. "Can I have another?"

Pleased with her baking success, Nina cut him a bigger piece. It felt weird to feed a man in her own house. She'd forgotten what it was like to have someone around.

A Spotify ad blasted from her laptop speakers, giving

them both a start. Why were the ads always so much louder than the music?

Jay swallowed the last piece of pancake and got on his feet. "Thanks. I should go."

"Okay."

Nina searched for words. She could sense the awkward mood between them, but didn't know how to change it. She'd been uncomfortable about letting him in. Now the thought of him leaving made her unsettled. Nina hadn't considered herself isolated or alone, but Jay's presence had burst her bubble. She was lonely.

There was also something about Jay's arms in that rolled-up shirt that made Nina's stomach tighten. She could see the veins and muscles twitching under the thick, tanned skin; arms so much stronger than hers. He has a girlfriend; she tried to remind herself, but the words did nothing to lower her heart rate.

Nina followed Jay to the door, thinking of what it would be like to kiss him. Oh, God. Jay stopped at the doorway, a couple of inches from her. He smiled his inscrutable half smile and studied her face, like looking for clues. She could sense the heat of his body and felt his breath on her face. It was time to say goodbye and break the spell, but every fibre of her being resisted. She wanted to lose herself in this moment, linger in his presence. She willed for him to read her mind, to touch her, kiss her, press her against the walls that were closing in. The silence stretched, growing a new meaning. Nobody stood this close to someone for this long, especially if they were just going out the door. But before she could think more of it, Jay turned, slapped his thigh and whistled. "Chloe! Oi!"

The dog, of course. Chloe appeared from Nina's reading nook, where she had been snoozing, and followed her master outside.

Nina sighed. Living on her own in the middle of nowhere was messing with her head. She'd become a cave woman who turned a neighbour's social call into a sexual fantasy. She had to get a hold of herself.

But she noted that once outside, Jay let out a breath. That night, she dreamed of his powerful arms grabbing her wrists as his rock-solid body trapped her against the wall, just like she'd imagined. Jay devoured her, stripping her naked with his gaze, touching her all over. By the magic of the dream, he was naked too, and they fit comfortably in her tiny foyer, using the wall for support, never bumping into anything, feeling nothing but his muscular body moulding into hers. She straddled the mysterious farmer, who turned into Tama and then back into Jay. She woke up to an orgasm and felt cheated, only experiencing the tail end of it while conscious.

CHAPTER 7

Nina stood inside her front door with a bucket in hand, trying to psych herself into action. It was time to empty her toilet bucket into the large compost drum perched outside. She did this every week. It should have been a quick routine task, but right now, it was pouring down outside.

She had to empty the bucket to use her bathroom, and she needed to go soon. This had to be done. Wrapping herself in a water-proof jacket, Nina stepped outside. The wind slammed the door in her face. She made it round the corner to the infamous 'shit tower' as La La had named her compost drum, climbed on the stepladder and lifted the lid off the drum. Holding her breath, she tried to tip the bucket's contents into the drum as quickly as possible. She had practiced this. Shit in, lid down, and a quick retreat. But this time, nothing worked as it should. Everything happened as if in slow motion; in a horrible, inevitable slow motion. Her foot slipped off the ladder and the contents of the bucket flew across the yard, partly landing on her new wheelbarrow.

Nina followed, landing on her bottom, her shirt and jeans covered in the splatter.

Ignoring the pain in her tailbone, Nina got up and picked up the bucket, staring at the disgusting mess. At least the rain was quickly washing away some of the poo on the ground.

What was she going to do? She was covered in faeces. This must have been the lowest of lows, stuff no one talked about on those tiny house forums and Facebook pages.

Nina glanced at her poor seedlings, soaking in puddles and flattened by the incessant rain. The rain had ruined everything. She wanted to give up, to throw herself on the ground and cry, but didn't want to plant her face in excrement. Eventually, the pungent smell rising from her clothes forced her to move. She undressed down to her undies and breathed a sigh of relief. There didn't seem to be any shit-to-skin contact. Thank God for small mercies. Nina stood in the rain, letting it rinse away any traces of dirt and sweat.

That's when she heard footsteps.

Jay appeared from behind the big poo drum and stopped in his tracks. Right behind her stood Alice. They stared at her, each holding a yellow umbrella, their mouths agape.

In a matter of seconds, a million thoughts rushed through Nina's head.

Why Jay? Why now? And why, oh why did she have to be topless, dressed in her tattiest undies?

Alice ordered her son to turn around and rushed towards her with a look of genuine concern.

"Stop! Stop there!" Nina yelled.

Alice halted and waited for Nina to approach her, negotiating the poo splatter like a revolting obstacle course.

"I'm sorry, it's just that there's ... shit everywhere. I slipped when I was emptying the bucket and it just sprayed..."

Alice's face lit up in understanding. "So that's why you undressed? Makes sense."

She was holding something wrapped in a plastic bag. Nina hoped it was one of her loaves of bread. She could really use a warm slice of kumara sourdough with butter right about now.

"I wanted to come and see your house, and I thought maybe you couldn't get to the shops in this horrid rain and needed sustenance. But I was afraid I'd slip and hit my head or get hit by lightning, so I asked Jay to come with me."

"That's so nice ... Welcome. But I really need to take a shower. Come in from the rain. Just walk around this way to avoid ... you know."

"Sorry, but I can't walk backwards." Jay turned around with a shit-eating grin, eyes lingering on Nina's body. Nina hugged her breast for a shred of decency, but her white undies had become somewhat see-through in the rain, which had now turned into a light drizzle, hardly obstructing his view.

Alice shot her son a warning look and ushered Nina towards her house. "Hurry before you catch pneumonia!"

Nina opened the door. Alice told Jay to leave his muddy

boots and umbrella outside. As they peeled off their rain gear at the crammed doorway, Nina squeezed past them to get inside, inadvertently brushing her chest against Jay. Dear God. The look in his eyes burned her freezing skin as she made her way inside. She grabbed dry clothes and a towel and rushed into the bathroom. As she closed the door behind her, she looked in the mirror. Her tangled hair dripped with rainwater, and her skin was turning blue. Great. A drowned sewer rat.

"I'll make us some tea," Alice shouted from her kitchen.

"Go ahead!" Nina called back, shivering from the cold, waiting for her shower to turn warm.

Alice's familiar manner felt odd, but Nina felt deeply grateful for her no-nonsense, practical approach. Maybe farmers were used to being around poo. Her own mother would have been talking about the dangers of slippery step-ladders and Nina's disgusting manual poo-composting solutions, dramatically thanking God for her daughter's survival and painting worst-case scenarios that rivalled any horror nightmares.

When Nina emerged from the shower, tea, fresh bread and pumpkin pie waited for her on the kitchen table. Jay sat in the same chair as last time, reading a copy of Organic Gardener. They looked so at home in her little space, Nina had to pause for a moment to take it all in. Despite the circumstances, it felt good to have company.

"I'm sorry about that. I must have given you such a fright."

Nina flashed her guests an apologetic smile.

Alice looked up, amused. "Oh no, I thought it might have been the other way around. I was just saying to Jay that our timing was unfortunate."

Jay smirked. "Yes, a minute later and we would have missed it."

Nina felt like kicking him back out in the rain, but she wanted the bread. As long as she could get a cup of tea and a slice of bread, she would tolerate his teasing. God, she really was a sellout.

After polishing a cup of tea and a buttered slice of the kumara sourdough, Nina took Alice for a tour around her house. She felt Jay's eyes on her back, but tried to ignore him.

Alice enthused over the details of Nina's kitchen and lounge, the clever storage solutions and multi-functional furniture.

"It's like a caravan, but so much prettier."

Alice climbed on the sleeping loft and stretched out on Nina's bed. "Oh, you have a skylight, how wonderful!"

Nina glanced at Jay, who gave her a knowing nod. "Yes, she's lying in your bed."

"I just wanted to test how it feels. I'm on the bedspread!" Alice sang out from the loft.

Jay's eyes widened in mock horror. "Once you let her in, she'll never leave. She's changing into your pyjamas as we speak."

"Come on Jay, not funny!" Alice climbed down from the loft and gave her son a friendly push. She turned to Nina with a coy smile. "Sometimes I forget the social protocol, especially here in the country."

Nina laughed. "I think we're way past protocols by now."

She thought of herself traipsing around naked in the rain. Yes, definitely not a show for the polite society.

It was easy to like Alice. She was matter-of-fact but also carefree – exactly what Nina hoped to be if she could stop stressing out about her life going nowhere and her money running out.

They sat for a good while, listening to the rain and drinking more tea.

"When we first moved out here with Jay's father, I hated this. Being trapped in a house in the middle of nowhere. When it rains, you can't do anything. Sometimes you can't even go anywhere when the road floods. Now it's the best part. Doing nothing, I mean. I guess I've just become that much lazier." Alice chuckled to herself. "Rain gives you an excuse to stop and think."

"Kind of like long-haul flights," Nina remarked.

"Exactly!"

Nina made a note of how she said 'Jay's father' in a way that sounded distant. She wondered where Jay's father was now. What usually happened? Divorce, death? Nina had little experience of either, so she steered clear. Alice took a sip of tea and continued. "I think it takes a while to get used to the rhythm. I remember feeling like I couldn't slow down or waste time. And when you're in that mindset, when you're young and restless, you can't see what's right in front of you, so you do waste time looking for things and…"

"Are you talking about me fixing the water heater?" Jay gave his mum a sideways look. "Because sometimes you don't find the tool you're looking for, because *someone* has reorganised the toolbox. Nothing to do with my mindset."

"Come on," Alice laughed. "See, this is what I mean!"

Nina smiled at their sparring. She could tell that they had a close and uncomplicated relationship. What must that be like? She hadn't called her own mother in two weeks, after informing her that the house move was now over and she was still very much alive, despite being alone in the countryside. Nina's mum meant no harm, but her anxiety was almost like a virus that spread through prolonged contact, even via Skype. After a longish phone call, she always felt the familiar dread in her chest.

The rain ceased, and Nina got up to clear the table. Alice joined her.

"I think we can make it safely back home now," she said, looking out the window. "You must have things to do."

"Not really," Nina confessed.

She felt the words slip out before she could catch them. Well, what was the point? They knew she lived alone in the middle of nowhere. She might as well be honest about the rest.

"I resigned from my job when I moved here and since then I've been spending my days just trying to set up the garden, but it's not going too well so... I really don't know what I will do over the winter. I think I have to find some work."

Alice's eyes lit up. "And what is it you used to do? Or, want to do?"

"Graphic design, mostly."

"Packages, labels?"

"Those, too."

Alice exchanged looks with Jay, whose face was unreadable. "Jay could use your help I think."

Jay looked away, uncomfortable. "Mum, no..."

Nina sensed the tension between them, but she couldn't pass up any work opportunity. "What is it?"

Jay rolled his eyes. "Mum wants me to go into the sauce business."

"Jay makes the most wonderful hot sauce," Alice confirmed, turning to Jay with a winning smile. "You would get a lot more for selling your own product than just the fresh produce."

Jay slowly shook his head. "The upfront costs and risks are much higher, too."

"What are you talking about? A few jars and labels. And now you've got a designer, too!" Alice clapped her hands like it was all sorted and the money was already rolling in.

"Breaking into the FMCG business can be tricky for small players," Nina admitted. Seeing their blank looks, she quickly added, "Fast-moving consumer goods."

"See? You already have someone who speaks the lingo!" Alice beamed.

"I don't know the industry that well, but I've worked with small businesses. Some have made it to the supermarkets, but most are still selling at the markets and gift shops. Those with good products and solid marketing strategy will make a living."

"I'm making a living growing vegetables," corrected Jay. "I don't need to sell sauce to survive."

He didn't sound convinced.

"Jay, bring her some sauce to try," Alice suggested. Turning to Nina, she said, "Jay makes this amazing chilli sauce that works on anything. I put it on pizza, pasta, in smoothies..."

"Smoothies?" Nina's eyebrows shot up.

"Chocolate smoothies," Jay corrected. "Probably wouldn't work with wheatgrass or whatever you drink."

Jay gestured towards Nina's kitchen, with a tray of micro greens growing on the windowsill.

"I make raw chocolate smoothies too," Nina said. "I wouldn't mind trying it with some chilli. It's good for digestion, muscle pains, nerve pain..."

Jay stared at her. "Do you ever just eat something because it tastes nice?"

Nina rolled her eyes. "Well, sometimes I accidentally end up enjoying something. I'm not proud of it but... it happens."

Jay laughed. "Well, if chilli is that good for you, I should make some more sauce. I'll bring you a bottle. I have to warn you though, it's quite hot."

"No problem. I love hot."

"Do you?" Jay held her gaze for a moment that seemed to stretch the fabric of time.

Nina's face flushed with heat. Her heart pounded against her breastbone and a delicious wave of desire made her body tingle. She felt sexy and fun.

Alice cleared her throat, bursting her bubble.

Nina took a quick breath. "Thank you for the bread."

"My pleasure." Alice smiled and winked. "It was great to see your little house. It's a treasure."

Alice peeked out the door to make sure the rain had indeed ceased. A patch of clear sky peeked between the rain clouds, already soft pastel from the approaching sunset. Watching her guests leave, Nina felt the pang of loss, just like the first time Jay had left her house. What was he really like? Did he really have a girlfriend? She found it hard to believe. Neither he nor his mother had mentioned Earth once. Surely a long-term significant other was worth mentioning. Nina sighed. She wanted so badly for him to be single that she was ready to grasp any flicker of doubt.

CHAPTER 8

Jay couldn't focus. He needed to check on his crops, add fertiliser, and pick out ripe tomatoes for a special delivery. At the end of the winter, tomatoes were not naturally in season and thus in high demand. He'd coaxed a hardy variety to produce a fairly decent crop in his greenhouse, which meant a great price from a local high-end restaurant.

He should have been paying attention, checking every piece of fruit for imperfections, but the image of the nearly naked woman, standing in the rain with her arms stretched out, kept entering his mind, playing in the background like a broken record. His brain had already deleted the rest of the unfortunate scene, zeroing in on one moment: Nina's shapely breasts, the arch of her back, the shivering legs, and the white underwear that was wet from the rain, revealing... The playback kept messing with his concentration, but he didn't want it to stop.

You better not get any ideas, Jay thought to himself.

As much as he'd liked to explore every inch of the gorgeous blonde in the tiny house, the prospect of actually asking Nina out made him break out in a cold sweat. He hadn't dated anyone in two years, not since his last girlfriend, Molly, had left him. He didn't even regularly talk to females, other than his mother.

Sparring with Earth was probably the closest thing to flirting he'd done in months, and it only annoyed him – and probably her. Jay knew Earth kept checking on him because of Mum. After his father's death, Mum had become obsessed with his social life, inviting people over and sending them to 'cheer up' Jay.

Jay argued that he wasn't depressed. Sure, some aspects of his life were depressing, but what people saw as manifestation of grief was partly just his character. He wasn't that cheerful to begin with. Molly had accused him of being closed off and glum, even before his dad's death. And afterwards, he'd been mourning, thus even less charming and sociable.

Would Nina judge him the same way? She'd chosen to move here, so obviously she didn't hate silence or solitude. Jay threw away a malformed tomato, his stomach clenching. Even if he found the right words to ask Nina out, he couldn't do it. Not yet. First, he had to sort himself out. A week ago, he'd found a lump in his left testicle. Every morning, he woke up to check it, hoping it had shrunk or disappeared. But it was still there, unchanged. Jay knew he should go to the doctor but was biding his time. He'd weed the capsicum beds, then go. He'd pick and deliver the tomatoes, then go. It was getting ridiculous.

Playing naked images in his mind was all good fun, but what if he was sick? He couldn't pursue a new relationship. He would have to tell her, and he didn't want her pity.

Yet, the strange Scandinavian woman drew him like a beacon. Maybe the hot sauce wasn't such a bad idea. Doing some work together would get him into her orbit. There was no harm in getting to know each other, was there? As friends.

Jay abandoned the tomatoes and traipsed over to the chilli peppers. If there was enough for a batch of sauce, maybe he could just go for it. The sauce would give him an excuse to visit. He could only hope she spent time naked around her house regularly.

To his disappointment, the chilli was ripening slowly. It would take another week or two before there was enough for a great batch of sauce. And it had to be a great batch.

Chapter 9

Nina sat at her little foldaway dining table, staring at a budget sheet on her laptop. This was not good. With the dentist bill, a new garden shed filled with dry firewood (so expensive in the early spring!) and a very unproductive garden, she'd blown through her savings too fast. Even relaxing her organic standards hadn't helped. The fresh produce was expensive in early spring.

Nina had been existing on brown rice, peanut butter, and hardy leaves of Swiss chard. It seemed to be the only thing she could grow that the caterpillars didn't like. She knew she had to get a net setup to protect her planter boxes, but with the slow growth and incessant rain, it didn't seem worth the cost or the effort. She would deal with the garden later in the spring. In the meantime, she had to deal with her non-existent income.

When walking out of the office, Nina had sworn she wouldn't go back for at least a year. She owed it to herself to give this organic 'living off the land' business a proper try.

Going back to design work had felt like a cop-out.

But staring at a spoonful of peanut butter and a cup of tea, she knew she'd been wrong. Finding work as a freelance designer in Raglan wasn't an easy option, either. A couple of local designers dominated the market. They seemed to have a loyal following and Nina knew she couldn't go after their clients. She'd done a little walk around the village business-es, had a few awkward chats, and left her business card with three people. Having spent most of her career behind the scenes of a reputable agency, she'd never had to approach businesses for work.

Aware of her options being slim, Nina picked up her port-folio and business cards and headed up the hill. Alice knew everyone in the village. Jay wasn't interested in her services – he still hadn't brought over the sauce or visited her in two weeks – but maybe Alice knew someone else.

The rain had stopped for a couple of days, but the grass seemed perpetually wet. Nina had opted for gumboots and a puffer jacket. This seemed to be the official business attire in Raglan.

Nina found Alice outside her house, turning over the flowerbeds.

She set down her shovel and waved. "Nina! Oh, perfect. I need a cuppa."

Nina smiled. It was getting easier and easier to hang out with Alice. She felt like a cross between a friend and a mum, someone who cared but didn't question her choices or worry about her every move.

Alice let them inside and put the kettle on. Nina peeled off her jacket and settled at the kitchen table. Alice's house had an amazing smell. It was like stepping into a rainforest where someone was baking. She had a loaf of zucchini bread on the table, still gently steaming in the morning light. On both sides, pink orchids bloomed in vintage glass jars. Nina sighed. She might have been financially ruined, but she had a lot of beauty around her, free of charge.

Alice placed a steaming cup of peppermint tea in front of her and glanced at the thick, black folder on the table. "So what's that? Have you come to audit me?"

Nina laughed. "That's my portfolio."

"Oh, thank heavens! My books are a disgrace."

Alice reached out for the folder and leafed through the first couple of pages, pausing on an upmarket honey brand. It was beautiful work. Nina had created the brand, down to directing the photography of the finished product, placed on a weathered wooden table with an eclectic outdoor picnic setting. Looking at it, you could almost taste the handmade spelt flour pancakes.

Alice pored over the images. "This is beautiful. Looks like a great product."

"It's just regular Manuka honey. But the packaging makes you think it's something special, right?"

"Absolutely."

"So... I need to find some work and I thought I'd start

with the only person I know around here. I was hoping you knew someone who needed some marketing help or maybe re-branding or starting a business ...” Nina felt hot. Did she sound like she was chasing after Jay? She hadn't seen a glimpse of him in the last two weeks, not even driving his tractor. But Alice was already looking through her address book. “There's this guy I know who runs a cafe in town. It's a bit run down and I remember him saying he was going to reno-vate and re-brand, to attract the right tourists.”

Alice held her finger on a name and handed over her book. It looked ancient.

“Why didn't you just save it on your phone?” Nina asked, pointing at the smartphone lying on the table.

Alice glanced at it, shaking her head. “Oh, I haven't got used to it, I guess. It seems so unreliable, runs out of battery every couple of days.”

Nina smiled. That sounded like a perfectly normal battery life, but she'd learned not to argue about technology with the older generation.

After writing down the phone number and business name, and enjoying a slice of zucchini bread, Nina made her way back home. She felt disappointed that Alice had said nothing about Jay's whereabouts. She could have asked, but had felt too awkward. Alice would have thought she was after the hot sauce branding job, or worse, her son.

Chapter 10

Jay was about to take a shower when the doorbell rang. He assumed it was probably Mum. He didn't get that many visitors, being so out of the way. Wrapping a towel around his waist, he answered the door.

Earth stood on his doorstep in her usual hippie gear, carrying a big shoulder bag that looked like a rug.

"I'm sorry about last time," she said. "I shouldn't have mentioned your dad."

"Yeah, okay." Jay nodded.

He didn't want to hold a grudge, but also didn't feel like inviting Earth in. Ever since her lifestyle transformation, she'd become fairly unbearable to be around.

Jay motioned to his towel attire. "I'm about to take a shower, so..."

Earth didn't budge. "That's okay. I won't take long."

She stared him down, immovable, until Jay relented and invited her in. JWs were easier to deal with. And more tactful.

Earth proceeded to Jay's kitchen counter, pulled a thick

binder out of her satchel bag and opened it, motioning Jay to get closer.

"I heard about the lump," she said.

Jay closed his eyes. Mum. It had to be. Two days ago, Jay had told his mum. Why would Mum talk about his groin to this nut bag?

He'd only talked to Mum because he needed to know how quickly the lump in dad's armpit had grown. Jay was fairly sure his was still the same size. Mum had recounted the early stages, with the lump doubling in size over a month, coupled with growing exhaustion and other symptoms.

To Jay's relief, it sounded different.

He'd relaxed a little, but Mum had wanted him to see the doctor immediately. They'd argued for a while. Jay had left, announcing that he would deal with this on his own terms. He doubted Mum really understood what she'd done. She'd told about his testicle lump to the woman who already believed everything in his life, from his farming practices to his diet, was carcinogenic. Jay knew Mum had a soft spot for Earth and perceived her preachy style 'informative'. Mum kept inviting her around and claimed she learned something every time they talked. Jay found he could easily disprove a lot of what Earth said by simply typing her latest claim, plus "debunked" or "myth busted" on Google.

"Look," Jay said, keeping his voice as measured as he could. "I'd rather deal with this without your involvement. You're not a medical professional, are you?"

"That's the thing, though," Earth jumped in, as if triggered. "The traditional medicine does not want to cure cancer. The treatment of cancer hasn't improved at all in twenty years. You really don't want to go down that road! They will pump you full of poison and you'll never get well again."

Her every word was baiting Jay to engage, but he didn't want to get sucked into this argument. Not now. Not ever.

Jay secured the towel around his waist. "I don't even know if it's cancer. Could be something else. Could be nothing."

"Obviously, you have to get it checked out."

"By a doctor who practices traditional medicine? I thought you were against that?" Jay scoffed.

"No, I'm against the traditional treatment of cancer. You should get checked out, get a biopsy. Find out what it is. Sooner rather than later."

"Why is this so important to you?"

It was a good question. Earth had made it clear she despised Jay's farming practices, and they disagreed on several topics, but she kept coming around and engaging with him. Jay wondered if she saw him as a project, someone she needed to convert. Or was she still, deep down, harbouring feelings for him?

A long time ago, before the dreadlocks, hemp, and alternative medicine, they'd gone out for drinks. Jay had thought of it as friends catching up. He'd never found Earth that attractive, and she'd just broken up with his brother. Sure, his brother was an asshole, and Jay was happy to commiserate over this with an old friend. But Earth had taken his emotional support as a sign of something more, and Jay had ended up gravely disappointing her at the end of the night.

They'd never talked about it again. Instead, they argued about farming, medicine, diet and politics. It was mostly good fun, like sparring with a sister. But Jay was not ready for Earth to involve herself in his private health issues. That signalled ownership.

"Did my mum put you up to this?" Jay asked as Earth seemed to have momentarily lost her sharp tongue.

"Not really," she finally said, her eyes defiant, "but I know she would approve. She really wants you to get checked out. She's worried."

Jay's cheeks flamed as he imagined his mum talking about his balls with this woman. He needed everyone to back off right now. The towel flapping against his thighs, Jay marched to the front door and held it open for Earth, silently staring her down, until she stepped outside.

"Fine," she muttered. "Just don't come complaining to me if…"

"If I die of cancer? Don't worry, the dead don't complain."

Jay closed the door, sighing with relief as he heard the lock click.

CHAPTER 11

Nina had a skip in her step. She'd just invoiced her first client and got paid within forty-eight hours. The modest sum of money was doing wonders to her mood as she browsed the farmers' market in Hamilton.

Turned out Alice's friend hadn't been in the process of re-branding his cafe. Instead, he'd sold the cafe and was starting a business manufacturing handmade leather bags. Beautiful and pricey, they made perfect executive gifts. Nina had never spent that much on a bag, or even rent, but she'd nodded along and made all the right noises to show her appreciation.

The client, Trevor, was in his fifties, a charming man with sinewy hands and that hard-hitting, stressed-out vibe common with cafe owners. Nina found it interesting that cafes – where customers enjoyed relaxation and refreshments – were often run by people deprived of both. Maybe tinkering with leather was exactly what Trevor needed. Thankfully, he had a budget. The cafe had been profitable, even if it attracted more weed-smoking surfers than city professionals on mini breaks.

Nina had shown him her portfolio and listened to Trevor explain his marketing strategy. She'd left the meeting with her head full of brand ideas and, two days later, had sent through her first draft. Trevor had been happy with her work and wonderfully decisive. After a couple of weeks, her client had a beautiful business card and a Facebook page, and Nina had an invoice to send.

Seeing the money appear on her account had prompted Nina to drive out of town to stock up on necessities at more reasonable rates.

The farmers' market was in the winter hibernation mode. There were no avocados, persimmons, or even tomatoes. But someone strummed a guitar in fingerless gloves, and the smell of coffee and pancakes drifted in the air. Nina ambled through the aisles, enjoying the familiar buzz she hadn't experienced in weeks. For the next morning, she had a meeting lined up with another prospective client – a friend of Trevor's. Things were looking up.

Her bags heavy with pumpkins, apples, and egg cartons, Nina wobbled back to her car. Driving through the neighbouring suburb, she called La La. She wouldn't have dreamed of phoning before 9 a.m. on a Sunday morning. At 10 a.m., La La still yawned her way through the hellos.

"Are you still in bed?" Nina asked.

"Of course. It's morning."

"Okay. Get up and put your slippers on. I'll bring you a coffee."

"Are you in town? Fantastic!"

"I'm approaching the cafe down your street." Nina yelled into the speaker in her lap. "Flat white?"

"Decaf, please."

Nina nearly crashed the car. "Ha-ha. Sorry, I thought you said decaf."

"I know! Crazy, right? I'll explain later."

***

The Sunday morning brunch was in full swing. A string of tightly parked cars surrounded the cafe like an impenetrable, metallic wall. Nina drove around the corner and squeezed into the last parking spot. Ever since Jay had towed her tiny house in place, she hadn't thought about parking at all. After weeks of roaming free with hardly anyone around, standing in line for coffee felt odd. By the time she placed her order, Nina had already forgotten about La La's request and ended up getting her a regular flat white.

Ten minutes later, Nina stepped into La La's small but tastefully decorated unit. Her friend had dressed up and brushed her hair, the traces of makeup under her eyes the only reminders of whatever had happened last night. Nina wondered if she should ask.

She handed over the takeaway cup. "I'm sorry I forgot

about the decaf! My brain's scattered."

La La laughed and shook her head but accepted the coffee and took a swig without hesitation.

"So, why decaf?"

"Well, to protect my eggs, of course. You of all people should know."

"So you're planning… to have a baby?"

"Of sorts," La La shrugged.

Seeing Nina's astonished face, La La led her in, and they sat down on her emerald velvet couch. Nina doubted anyone under the age of eighteen had ever sat down on it. Everything in La La's space was beautifully impractical. Hearing her talk about her eggs sounded out of place. Had she swapped bodies with someone else? La La put down her coffee and lowered her voice. "I went to the baby clinic, you know."

"Fertility Associates?"

"That one. And they did these tests and told me I qualify for IVF, but that I'd have to quit alcohol and coffee, basically."

"IVF? Really? I thought you wanted to meet the right person and…?"

"I know. But you got me thinking. And it turns out I don't want to adopt a kid. The only thing I could ever handle is having my own. I'm not Angelina Jolie. But I don't want to be Jennifer Aniston either. What if I never meet anyone? Time is running out, you said so yourself!"

Nina stared at her friend in utter disbelief. Was her baby panic contagious? Had she broken her happy-go-lucky friend and turned her into a high-strung ball of nerves like herself?

La La leaned back on the couch. "Anyway, turns out IVF is expensive, so I'm not sure. I thought about hooking up with someone, saying I'm on the pill..."

"You can't do that. That's horrible!" Nina shuddered, remembering her own thoughts from months ago. She'd been contemplating the same thing. She needed to get off her high horse. "Sorry, didn't mean to sound so judgy. I've thought about it, too, I just... couldn't pull it off."

"I know it's dodgy, but IVF is so expensive and all you really need is one swimmer."

Nina chuckled. "No, you need like a hundred million. Even under 20 million is considered a low sperm count."

La La closed her eyes, sighing dramatically. "Please, Wikipedia. Anyway, the guy wouldn't have to know anything. How would that hurt him? Besides, I'd make it worth his while."

Nina cringed. "But... do you expect him to just disappear? What if he liked you and kept coming back? Hamilton's not that big. People are going to see you with a baby. They'll talk."

"I know. It's not a brilliant plan. And I won't do it. Unless it's like a perfect opportunity."

"Like a well-hung businessman who's visiting from overseas?"

La La laughed. "See? You get me!"

"So, have you met any lately?"

La La slid lower on the couch. "Zero."

"Same."

Grunting, La La peeled herself up and rummaged through her fridge. Nina glimpsed an old takeout container, a dried-up block of cheese and a random assortment of salad dressings. What the hell was her friend eating?

La La slammed the fridge door like Smeg was responsible. "Sorry, I thought I had… something."

"That's okay."

"You should have given me a proper warning. I'd have stocked the cupboards. I feel like I never see you anymore."

"Sorry," Nina wailed.

La La leaned over her kitchen island, sticking out her lower lip like a toddler. "I'm waiting for you to just … come to your senses and move back, I guess."

Nina tried to laugh, but felt a sting of guilt. "Me too. It just hasn't happened yet. I don't think I have any sense left."

After some creative thinking, La La put together a morning tea of nuts and corn chips. She recounted all the office gossip she could think of, including how Tama had been acting oddly lately, being frequently late and distracted. To Nina's surprise, the mention of his name didn't elicit the familiar buzz. Maybe she was finally getting over him. She even hoped that he was okay. It was a new feeling. All she'd ever wanted before was for him to love her and need her – or suffer without.

After a couple of hours, Nina got up from the couch and stretched out her stiff body. She needed some proper food. She hugged her friend goodbye and headed out to Subway. To avoid eating alone in what felt more like a poorly lit hallway than a restaurant, she bagged the wrap and ate it in the car on her way for some much-needed second-hand shopping. Two hours later, she had a bag full of cheap thermals and even one nicer looking top that she definitely had no use for in the bush – except for that client meeting in the morning.

On the drive back, Nina kept replaying the conversation in her mind. Something about La La's baby plan, laid out like that, had made her sober up. She wanted a baby, but maybe she didn't want a baby in that 'damn the consequences' kind of way. It sounded too premeditated, at least for her. She was a planner. La La had a lot of crazy ideas, but she wasn't one to carry out long-term plans. Her friend had never stuck to any diet for more than a week. Her life was much more about instant gratification. She bought what she fancied, ate what she craved, and pursued anyone she found attractive.

Nina felt jealous of La La. With her inherent impulsiveness, she would likely fall pregnant with no scheming or other sociopathic behaviour. Nina couldn't do that. Even when drunk, she sensed the consequences somewhere behind the haze of intoxication. Vividly imagining the next day's hangover really took the fun out of drinking. And since changing her diet, she hadn't touched alcohol in months.

Nina sped up her Toyota, weaving through the green hills faster than she felt comfortable with. What the hell was wrong with her? Why couldn't she just live in the moment? Maybe it was her upbringing, and how much her family had appreciated rational thinking. She'd rationalised her way through her thirties, doing the smart thing, gaining skills and work experience, and now she was conquering yet another challenge she had set for herself – to live self-sufficiently. It was the hardest one yet.

Could she stop trying?

The thought had come out of nowhere and it gave her such a jolt she nearly drove off the road. Her heart pounding, Nina squeezed the steering wheel, bringing her focus back to driving. She didn't even know what it meant ... how did one go from planning and steering their life to just letting go?

CHAPTER 12

When she arrived in Raglan, Nina slowed down. She had no errands to run, no reason to linger in town. Stopping for the sake of stopping felt like the first tentative step towards veering from the plan. Maybe she could still surprise herself.

It was turning into late afternoon when Nina parked at a little pub on the main road. She'd driven past many times, often wondering about people who had the time to sit around and drink beer every night.

Before getting out of her car, Nina glanced in the mirror. Thankfully, there was an emergency mascara and powder stashed away in her glove compartment. And that nice new top from the second-hand shop. She was an expert at changing in the car, quickly removing the shirt from underneath her cardigan, and replacing it with the silky top.

Smoothing her defiantly wavy hair out of her face, Nina stepped into the pub. A handful of old guys had gathered around a TV screen to watch a rugby game. One booth had a young family tackling a plate of hot chips and a middle-aged lady with a glass of wine fiddled with her phone at the bar. Flames flickered in an open fireplace, casting a warm glow on a pair of vacant couches.

Perpetually cold, Nina gravitating to the warm seats. After sitting down, she realised she should have ordered a drink first. No servers hovered about, but before she could get up, someone appeared. Not a staff member, Nina gathered. A gorgeous man, the type she had always considered suspicious. Or predatory. He'd rolled the sleeves of his dark collar shirt and had such perfect nails Nina immediately hid hers. She felt grateful for the silk top and the minimal effort she'd put in with the mascara. Things could have been worse.

"Can I buy you a drink?" the stranger asked.

Nina stared at him, words eluding her. Even back in the agency days, she never went out alone. The gang from the office created a buffer against strangers approaching. If she felt particularly introverted, she let La La tell her where to sit, what to order, and who to talk to. Nice and easy. What was she doing here, all by herself, without backup? Her muscles tensed, ready to bolt her out the door.

"Let me guess. You like... Sol?" the stranger smiled.

"No. I prefer local beer. But I'll get it myself." Nina rushed to the bar. She picked a light sounding beer out of the Good George lineup. The young bartender took her card, looking over her shoulder, eyes flashing flirtatiously. Nina guessed the stranger stood right behind her. She took a deep breath and turned around. He grinned, scanning her body.

"Are you here with someone? Don't tell me you're taken." He flashed a wicked, pleading smile.

"No, but I prefer to buy my own drinks." The bartender handed back Nina's credit card. She struggled to jam it back into her wallet, fingers cold and stiff, hands shaking.

"Do I make you nervous?" he asked, amusement dancing on his lips.

Nina filled her lungs with the scent of his cologne. She couldn't flirt, but she could scare him off with brutal honesty. "Yes, you do. It's because I overthink. You might think we're just chatting. But my mind's already a million miles away. I'm thinking... what if we hit it off? What if you suggest we leave together, go somewhere... and what if I don't want to sleep with you? Or what if I do, but then change my mind? You might be one of those idiots who think that buying someone a drink means they owe you something, so you throw a hissy fit, call me names ... Or you're one of those psychos who thinks no means yes..."

Nina drew a breath, seeing that her opponent was no longer smiling.

"Has that happened to you?" he asked, genuinely concerned.

Nina bit her lip, ashamed. "No. I don't accept drinks from strangers."

"I suppose you're safe then," the stranger remarked. "So, what are you doing in a bar on a Sunday afternoon? I gather you're not into sports."

"Why?"

"Well, you sat down on a seat where you can't see the screens."

So that's why the couches were vacant.

"I sat by the fire because I was cold. But you're right, I don't really care about sports. I just came to… well, I kind of challenged myself to do something different. I might as well have gone to church. Or a bingo night."

The stranger's mouth pulled into a lopsided smile. "I know a great bingo night around here if you want to try that next."

Nina pulled a face. "Great."

"Don't know many churches, sorry. But I can be the stranger you meet in a bar if that's on your list. I'm not a rapist, though. And believe no means no."

"Good." Nina gave him a rueful smile and took a sip of her drink. It was nice. She drank a bit more, wondering if she should move back to the fire. Would he follow her? She wanted him to, but had probably blown it already. Why did she have to talk like a mental patient? It would have actually been nice to just chat, flirt, laugh, and enjoy the sexual tension like normal people did.

"I'm a bit cold." Nina glanced at the fireplace.

The stranger took this as an invitation and followed her to the leather couches. They sat down facing each other. The flickering flames reflected in his eyes, making them even more enigmatic. Nina noticed the faint lines around his mouth and across his forehead. His hairline was receding ever so slightly and he had two broken capillaries on the side of his perfectly shaped nose. Nina relaxed a bit, relieved to find signs of age and imperfection. He leaned back in his chair, holding her gaze. "Do you give that little speech to everyone?"

Nina twisted a strand of hair around her finger, her stomach doing flips under the intense gaze. "Not really, since I don't go out much. But I know I have a tendency to scare people off, even when I don't mean to. I find that in bars, people speak in a kind of code. Certain phrases mean certain things. And I'm terrible at that. English is my second language. So I say what I mean. And that kind of ruins the ambience. It doesn't sound sexy, or mysterious, or suave, or whatever people go for."

"Like, if I said that I wanted to kiss you, because I find you sexy?"

Nina blushed. It sounded like a cheesy line. Why was it having such an effect on her? This wasn't fair. Part of her wanted to say something to break the spell, but her brain offered more blanks than useful words. The other part of her, the more primal part, volunteered to overlook the cheesiness, sending a gush of heat to the pit of her belly. The stranger leaned in and gently brushed the side of Nina's mouth with his finger.

"You had a bit of beer froth there. It didn't bother me at all and I could have just told you, but I wanted an excuse to touch you, so I used it..."

His hand lingered. Nina had to admit he was doing a great job, being both blunt and seductive. Her entire face tingled at his touch.

He leaned back on the couch and sighed with mock disappointment. "I see what you mean by the ambience. Can we go back to speaking in code? I can teach you some, show you the Kiwi way of talking without really saying anything."

With a start, Nina realised that the man hadn't asked her where her accent was from. Was this the first conversation with a Kiwi that sidestepped the question? Not having to always start by explaining her origins felt refreshing.

"Okay. How does it work?" she asked. "When you're speaking in code?"

"What do you mean?"

"I mean, when you pick up a woman who's actually playing her part?" Nina smiled, hiding behind her beer glass.

"It's pretty straightforward. I buy you a few drinks. You laugh at my bad jokes. I ask you questions, and you tell me about your life, your cat, your ex-boyfriend, whatever you want to talk about. I nod and look like I'm listening, but I'm really just thinking about what you look like naked. Then I suggest a coffee at my place and you say sure, let's go. And we have sex. Unless you change your mind, in which case I call you a cab and say good night like a gentleman. And jerk off in the shower."

Something about that story depressed Nina to her core. Put like that, one-night stands sounded formulaic, not nearly as spontaneous and magical as she'd thought. At least this guy's evening line-up didn't include coercion or rape. He was funny and gorgeous. He probably didn't have any issues with the 'enthusiastic consent' or whatever was the definition of not raping someone.

"That's... nice of you," she replied, rolling her eyes. "You should teach a sex ed class."

The guy looked mildly amused. He shrugged. "Most women just go along. I haven't met that many sexy strangers who put me on trial but still don't..."

"What?" Nina's mouth dried as he narrowed his eyes, holding her gaze.

"Well, you're not exactly pushing me away. Your words say one thing, but your eyes say something else. That's code too."

Nina felt hot. She should have protested. She should have told him he was reading into things. But why bother? She took another sip of her beer and smiled. Despite the embarrassment, she felt laughter bubbling under the surface. This moment thrilled her. The warmth of the fire, the fizzing drink at the back of her mouth, and those brown eyes locked with hers.

"What are my eyes saying?" she asked.

The stranger leaned in, as if to study her eyes. "I see... a fountain erupting, a train entering a tunnel... wait, is that a rocket?"

Nina laughed. She could feel the pit of her stomach radiating. It was sweet, intoxicating. She giggled behind her glass. "So… you're watching a sex scene from a fifties film playing in my head? Well, that's embarrassing."

"Not as embarrassing as what's playing in my head right now." His voice turned thick, and he took a drink.

Nina shifted in her seat and looked away. "That's probably why we speak in code, so that we don't have to be that embarrassed."

If she'd known the code, she would have sent him a signal to shut up and kiss her. The stranger cocked his head, his eyes still firmly on her. "What's your name?"

"Nina. What's yours?"

"Tyron."

Nina couldn't believe it had taken this long for them to introduce themselves. Tyron told Nina he was in town visiting his mum, killing time until she got home. He fetched Nina another drink. "Are you sure about breaking your rule?" he asked. "You're not a stranger anymore, right?" Nina said. She took a sip, enjoying the warm glow in her belly. She didn't want to break the spell.

Tyron's phone beeped. He looked at it and frowned. "My mum's still an hour away, driving from Tauranga."

Nina looked at her own phone. 6.37 p.m. Suddenly she remembered the groceries in the boot of her car, wilting away.

She stood up. "I… just remembered I have groceries in the car. There's chicken and… frozen peas. Thawed peas. You wanna come see my tiny house?" she blurted.

Tyron got up and smiled. "I'd love to."

Tyron grabbed his coat and followed Nina outside. She headed towards her tiny Toyota, but stopped. She had downed two beers and could definitely feel the effect.

"I don't know if I should drive," she said. "I might be over the limit."

Tyron smiled and gestured to a new Audi with darkened windows. "Get your groceries, I'll take you home."

"Are you sure? You've been drinking, too."

"I can handle one beer," Tyron stated matter-of-factly.

Nina fetched her shopping, embarrassed about her second-hand clothing bag, and loaded them into his Audi. The leather seats inside felt luxurious for Raglan. Around here, cars were more likely to run on cooking oil and smelled like rancid french fries. She would have been more comfortable with a bearded man who ate beans out of a can and had a mattress at the back of a van than with this polished guy with the faint scent of expensive aftershave that mingled with the leathery new car smell.

La La would have loved this car, Nina thought.

Being driven by someone else made her blush with desire. Or maybe it was the beer. Wasn't alcohol supposed to lower inhibitions? She was definitely thinking inappropriate things. Her gaze lingered on the rippling muscles in Tyron's forearms as he turned the wheel and sped away from the town centre. He held the wheel in a tight grip. Oh, that grip. Nina drew a breath, her head spinning. She needed to be more spontaneous, right?

The hills and valleys flicked past behind the dark window. She could only make out blurry shapes. All that mattered existed inside this car. Simple. Primal. Why couldn't life be like this sometimes? They needed no words, explanations, or hard truths. She didn't even need coherent thoughts; she was so tired of those crowding her mind. Nina gave herself over to the pulse, the thirst, the hunger.

With a few 'lefts', 'rights', Nina directed them to her house. Tyron lifted her bags out of the car and carried them inside. The house was still warm, but Nina turned on the heater and low lighting. This wasn't a real estate tour.

"Tea?" she asked, hoping he would say no. She wanted him to just touch her, kiss her, carry her away... They'd done enough talking already. Anything more he said could reveal something that made her wake up. Her drunken haze was fading away. She needed to make this stupid mistake and enjoy it to the full before reason kicked in.

Tyron stopped at the doorway, looking around the small space, fascinated. "It's so small."

"It's a tiny house," Nina smiled.

"It suits you," he concluded.

"Because I'm small?"

"Because you're cute."

Cute, not beautiful. He had probably dated a lot of beautiful girls who lived in stately, impressive houses. But she was happy with hers and, right now, she was happy to be cute. Nina smiled and searched for words. How did people get from "want to come over for a coffee?" to ripping each other's clothes off?

"I don't have a lot of visitors," she said.

"I can see why." Tyron chuckled, gesturing at the size of the space.

"Oh no, I can easily fit eight people in here, but nobody wants to drive out here, especially in winter."

"I might. Now that I know what's out here."

Nina could see the desire in his eyes, a little invitation she had been waiting for. "So you'd come if I threw a party?"

"I wouldn't call eight people a party. But I would definitely come, just to see the miracle of you fitting them all in here." He grinned.

"Come on. Some people have smaller egos; they take up less space."

"Touché."

Nina kept her eyes on Tyron's and waited. After all that talk about rapists, he must have felt cautious. Maybe she needed to sit down and sign a consent form?

Tyron took a step closer, and Nina caught his scent. The expensive cologne held notes of something spicy. She inhaled and placed her hands on his chest. Hunger flashed in his eyes as he accepted her invitation. He cupped her face into his hands and crashed his mouth on hers. Nina felt like she was plummeting, floating underwater, suspended somewhere outside time and space. Every nerve ending in her body fired up simultaneously, like woken up from a deep sleep, sending fiery signals through her core. She could almost see her reasoning brain scurrying away in panic, releasing the last half-baked thoughts on its way out: He could be married. He could be a serial killer. Then a door slammed, leaving her head swimming in a sea of hormones.

They tumbled up the steps leading to the loft, undressing with acrobatic skill on the way. She wanted to feel his bare chest, and the rest of him. Everything else was in the way. Tyron kicked off his pants on the last step and landed on top of her, his arms catching the weight of his upper body just in time. He lowered his mouth onto hers, savouring, taking his time. She could feel he was hard, pushing against her bare leg. Her centre pulsed with need.

Tyron lifted his head, panting. "Do you have protection?"

Oh, no. Nina seized, her thinking brain whirring to life like a rebooted computer. This couldn't be happening. Of course, she didn't have protection. She lived alone and ultimately wanted to get pregnant. But she couldn't tell him that. How had she not considered this? She couldn't say she was on the pill. She just couldn't.

"No. Do you?" she whispered.

Tyron patted the pockets of his discarded jeans and shook his head. "Sorry. I've run out. Just remembered."

They looked at each other, both confused. How had they ended up like this? Wasn't it clear from the start where the evening was going? The whole charade of saying what they meant, not speaking in code... why hadn't she followed through? They could have swung by a petrol station to get condoms on the way.

Sobering up, Nina pulled the bedsheet over her breasts. "I am an idiot."

Tyron rolled off her, sitting on the bed. "No, I'm an idiot. I should have thought about it. 'Would you like to see my tiny house' is basically a euphemism. It's probably considered vulgar slang somewhere in the world."

Nina laughed, almost hysterically. She now had the hiccups and her nose was running. "I'm sorry."

She dropped the sheet and scrambled down the stairs to her bathroom. She splashed water on her face, dried herself, and changed into comfy slacks. An oversized sweater completed the look. Tonight was so weird. Was this what happened when you tried to loosen up a little? Maybe she wasn't cut out for this.

"Nina?" Tyron called through the bathroom door.

Nina smoothed her hair and stepped out.

Tyron stood in his boxers, a questioning look on his face. "Are you okay? Do you want me to... go for a condom run? Or just go?" He smiled, gesturing at Nina's new outfit.

"Yeah, I was getting cold. Sorry."

"Stop saying sorry. Do you want me to go?"

Nina allowed herself to study his face. He was gorgeous, but the moment was over. She glanced at the clock on the wall. "Your mum will be home soon."

Nina noticed her groceries, still sitting on the kitchen counter. She loaded them into her fridge and freezer. She heard Tyron dressing up behind her and felt bad for treating him this way.

The sound of an engine gave her a start. It couldn't be Tyron, who was still buttoning up his shirt. Nina looked out the window and saw the dark shape of a tractor on a hill behind her house. Its headlights swept over the long tufts of grass as it slowly drove towards her house, veering past it to the driveway and out of sight. Who was driving around this late at night? Jay?

Thinking of Jay made Nina suddenly uncomfortable about Tyron. She didn't know the guy and now his presence felt too prominent, filling every nook and cranny of her tiny space, making her muscles tense. Underneath all that, hunger pangs twisted her stomach, and she realised she didn't want to cook for this man. She wanted to make an egg sandwich and eat it by herself.

Tyron appeared next to her, now fully clothed. Nina listened to the engine sound gradually fade out as the tractor drove away. She exhaled.

"Who was that?" Tyron asked.

"Not sure."

Tyron peered out the window. "Do you often have tractors driving around here?"

"Um ... not really. The neighbour has one, but he doesn't really drive at night."

Tyron looked unconvinced, fidgety. "You mean Jay?"

Nina nodded.

A strange look flashed across Tyron's face. "You guys know each other?"

"Well, yeah. We're neighbours. Why? Do you know him?" Nina asked.

Tyron dug up his phone and flicked through it. "Sorry, I have to go."

Before Nina could respond, he stepped outside. It was only when she heard him start his car that she remembered her own. She needed that car. She had a meeting first thing in the morning! Nina ran outside in her socks, but only caught the taillights of the Audi as it disappeared down the dark driveway. Oh God. What was she going to do?

Chapter 13

Nina knocked on Jay's door, freezing from head to toe. She'd already tried Alice, hoping to catch her before she turned in and beg for a ride back to town. She felt terrible asking, but even worse when she discovered Alice wasn't home.

The only other house within walking distance was Jay's. So here she was. She had only ever seen the house from a distance. Up close, it looked cosier – a solid Lockwood construction with a wraparound deck and probably a nice ocean view, currently swallowed by darkness. The porch had no flowers or embellishments, apart from three pots of woody herbs Nina recognised as Alice's handiwork.

Nina drew a breath and knocked again, then banged on the door for good measure. She was too cold and miserable to care anymore. She needed her car. No taxi companies serviced the area. The idea of hitchhiking terrified her, especially with very little traffic on the road.

Thankfully, a light turned on and the door opened. Jay stared at her with a raised eyebrow. He seemed irritated.

Nina swallowed hard. "I'm so sorry to bother you, but I really need some help."

"What happened?"

"I... I've left my car in town and I really need to pick it up before tomorrow morning. I have a meeting. A work thing."

"What do you mean, you left your car? Did you walk home? It's thirty-five kilometres."

"No. I got a ride with a friend and they ... left."

Nina's own words rang in her ears. Why couldn't she say it was a man? Why did her little hookup, which wasn't even technically a hookup, sound so seedy when she tried to describe it to this curmudgeon? Nina didn't want Jay to think she regularly entertained male guests, but surely, she was entitled to one slip-up?

Jay cocked his head and looked at her, unnervingly deadpan. Chloe the dog appeared on his side, panting excitedly at the sight of Nina. At least she wasn't angry with her.

"Some friend, to drive off like that."

Nina held his gaze, looking for that familiar hint of jest in his eyes. Why was he being such an arse?

"Maybe I asked him to leave," she shot back.

"So your date went so badly you couldn't even sit in the same car to get back to yours?" A hint of a smile flickered on Jay's lips.

"No! I just didn't remember that my car was in town. Or I remembered, but too late."

"Must have been one hell of a date."

A flush of embarrassment washed over Nina, and she tried to look away. She could feel Jay's gaze on her, searching for answers.

Why was he like this?

After what felt like an eternity of awkwardness, Jay pulled on a bulky hoodie, grabbed his keys, and walked out to his car. He didn't even glance at Nina on his way out, but she followed him, along with the dog. Maybe she had already come to expect this kind of behaviour from him. Jay started his old station wagon and Nina hopped in. Chloe settled on the back seat, her warm breath on Nina's neck. The dog's uncomplicated happiness eased her discomfort.

"Thanks. I appreciate this. Really."

Jay responded with a nearly undetectable nod and drove on. Nina couldn't help but compare her earlier journey with Tyron to this bumpy ride with the moody, unpredictable farmer. The air between her and Tyron had prickled with sexual tension, with Jay it sat heavy with tension. Along with the discomfort, Nina detected an unmistakable dose of guilt. She didn't know why, but travelling with Jay felt like sitting in detention.

Jay kept his eyes firmly on the road, hands squeezing the steering wheel. The way his knuckles whitened as he tightened his grip made Nina think of what Tyron had felt like, lying on top of her. It felt like a lifetime ago. So much had happened in a few hours. Until today, her life had been so uneventful, she'd considered finding two avocados for five dollars the highlight of her week.

The lights of Raglan appeared from behind a hill. Nina glanced at Jay. He hadn't spoken a word for the last fifteen minutes. At least she didn't have to answer any more questions about her 'date'. Silence suited her perfectly. But as he turned on the main road, she had to tell him where to drive – to the parking lot behind a bar. She knew it would complete the terrible picture Jay had about her evening.

Nina gathered her courage and directed Jay to the right place. He parked next to her Toyota and – to her surprise – turned off the engine and released his seatbelt.

"There's a game on," he said and hopped out.

Nina got out of the car. "Thanks for the ride. That was a huge help."

Jay looked restless, pacing by the car. Suddenly, Nina realised what she'd done. "I made you miss the game, didn't I?"

"It's still on. I might catch the last ten minutes." Jay nodded towards the bar.

"Yes, great. Go!"

Jay jogged towards the bar entrance with the dog at his heels. Nina felt terrible. She had to smooth things over with him. They were neighbours.

This was probably not the last favour she would need, she thought as she ran after him.

The bar had filled with people. A rugby game blasted on three giant screens, each with its own crowd of spectators. Nina spotted Jay at the nearest one, wedged between two older guys, all quietly engrossed in the game. Nina headed to the bar, bought a craft beer, and tapped on Jay's shoulder. As he turned, she tossed him the beer and fixed her attention on the screen. She wasn't here to yap into his ear. Jay raised the bottle. "Thanks."

Nina could barely hear him over the noise. She understood little about rugby, but could read the timer in the screen corner, announcing the game had ten minutes of playtime left. Part of her wanted to sneak out, but she couldn't leave without apologising. She was also starving. Nina made her way back to the bar and ordered a plate of nachos without cheese and some onion rings. Not healthy, but she'd already abandoned her sound judgment so many times. What was one more?

Nina found a little table and bar stools behind Jay. The food arrived when the game ended. The somber mood told her New Zealand had lost. As Jay turned away from the screen, she waved at him, pointing at the table.

"I didn't know you ate this kind of stuff." he remarked, grabbing an onion ring.

"I don't, really. But I haven't eaten since lunch and I'm starving."

Jay seemed to digest this for a moment. Or maybe he was digesting the third onion ring he'd now consumed. "So, the date didn't involve a candlelit dinner?"

"No. You know what my baking's like. It's not really candlelit dinner material." Nina pulled a face, but Jay didn't seem amused.

What was his problem? He was still acting like a hurt baby. Maybe she needed to change the subject.

"You know I went to your mum's tonight but she wasn't home."

"Yeah… she's out."

The way he said it didn't welcome further questions. They ate in silence. Jay picked up the last corn chip and let Chloe snatch the last onion ring.

"Thanks for this." Jay nodded at the finished meal, then turned and headed out the door, followed by his faithful furry companion. Nina stared at his fleece-covered back, her mind reeling. Was he angry with her, angry about losing the game, or just being a dick?

CHAPTER 14

Nina got up early, took a shower and made herself presentable. Her head felt funny. Could drinking two beers really cause this? It felt good to focus on something else. If the dating scene wasn't her playground, she still had her career. Well, the beginnings of one, if she could bag this next client.

Precisely two minutes to nine, Nina entered the cafe. The Monday morning was busy, with most tables occupied. Nina knew little about her prospective client. Trevor had mentioned she was switching careers after thirty years, which made her at least fifty years old. She was going into fashion retail, which made her either passionate about clothes or gravely misinformed about the financial opportunities within the industry. Nina looked around for any outrageously dressed middle-aged ladies but saw no singles what-so-ever.

Eager to grab the last vacant table, Nina propped her laptop on it and ordered a decaf, almond milk flat white. After a couple of minutes of searching for a free wi-fi, she concluded there was nothing she could do with the computer and grabbed herself a dog-eared architecture magazine featuring houses roughly a hundred times larger than hers.

Over her magazine, Nina kept her eye on the door. A cackling burst of laughter at a nearby table caught her attention. She turned and immediately recognised Earth. She wasn't the one laughing though, merely smiling graciously and nodding at her middle-aged table companion, who had a flapping cotton dress and a messy chignon rivaling the size of Earth's hair. What if it was her?

Nina's stomach seized. Why hadn't she googled the woman? She grabbed her phone. As she waited for the network connection, her coffee arrived. Swiss water decaf, almond milk. The server made a point of repeating her order with poorly concealed contempt. She could feel the shift of energy at the neighbouring table as they turned to peer at her. Nina drew a breath and smiled at Earth. "Hi."

Earth responded with a half-smile. On the table in front of her, an open folder burst with fabric samples. Dress fabrics.

Nina's throat tightened. "Are you by any chance starting a fashion business? Meeting with a designer?"

Earth's eyes widened in disbelief. "How did you know?"

Nina reached into her bag and pulled out a business card. She was proud of her cards, having finally organised nice ones with gold foil that cost an absolute fortune. Earth turned over the card and showed it to the older lady. "It's her. She's your designer."

The older lady, who Nina now knew was her new client

Marlena Watts, turned to her with a friendly smile. "Oh, hey there!"

Nina smiled back. "Hi! Nice to meet you. So sorry, I didn't know it was you."

"Not a problem. I wondered how we'd find each other. Maybe we should have agreed to bring red roses or wear yellow scarves," Marlena laughed. She had a nice, bubbly laugh.

"We've met," clarified Earth, "but I didn't know her name or that she was a designer."

Earth's matter-of-fact tone had a chilling edge to it. Nina tried to ignore it. What was she doing here, anyway?

Marlena offered Nina a chair, and she joined their table. "My daughter Esther here is helping me out with the business."

Nina was about to clarify she'd heard the name correctly when she caught Earth's expression. She sensed a conflict she wanted no part of. Esther had probably been reborn as Earth, but that was none of her business.

"Can you tell me more about the business?" she asked Marlena.

Marlena's eyes lit up and she launched into a speech about how there was nothing unique for women her age to wear and how her little shop would make Raglan, if not the entire world, a better place. At one point, Earth jumped in and talked about ethical fashion. Her mother seemed less enthusiastic but nodded along. She seemed more excited about finding something to wear that flattered her shape.

Nina wondered how often people went into business just to get items they coveted for wholesale price. She tried to steer the conversation to their customers. Who would pay the retail price and why? The answer was tourists. To Nina, this sounded a little naïve. Most of the tourists seemed to be in their twenties, surfers buying surfing gear, camping gear, and overpriced burgers. Nina swallowed her doubts. She wasn't here to poke holes in Marlena's business plan. Hopefully, they wouldn't blame her for lack of foot traffic or sales later on.

Within half an hour, Nina had a good idea of Marlena's taste in clothes, which she could translate into a brand she would probably like. She considered asking for a 50% advance payment, as she often did with new clients. But these people weren't complete strangers. Surely she could trust them. Plus, she really wanted to get back home, away from Earth's opinionated tone.

She closed her laptop and stood up. "Thank you so much. I'll be in touch with the first drafts by Friday."

Nina rushed out the door, relieved to reach her car.

She'd just open the door when Earth reached her. "Can I have a quick word?"

Nina's stomach dropped. "Sure."

"I just need to warn you about Tyron. A friend of mine saw you with him the other night."

Nina ground her teeth, her temper sizzling under the surface. Who had been spying on her? She steeled her nerves, arched an eyebrow. "Is that right?"

Earth cleared her throat. "I just thought you should know he sleeps around. A lot."

"Really?" Nina tried to sound surprised. Tyron seemed exactly like the type that slept around. She'd fancied him after a couple of beers, and he'd jumped on the opportunity. Earth gave her a slow, meaningful nod. "Really. I mean, he's charming. Fun to be around. But I wouldn't trust everything he says, that's all."

"Did you?" Nina asked. She wanted to hit back. Earth's preachy tone was getting under her skin.

Earth blinked. "Did I what?"

"I mean, how did you find out? Did you trust him? Did he cheat on you?"

Earth's eyes flashed defiantly. "If you must know, I went out with him. A long time ago. I didn't know he was like that, but I found out."

Her facade cracked for a second and Nina glimpsed genuine pain behind her eyes. She softened her tone. "Well, it's a good thing I didn't sleep with him then."

Earth's mouth dropped for a second, but she quickly gained her composure. "Good for you."

For a moment, they stood in awkward silence.

"Jay's not like that though," Earth said.

Nina tried to process the words. Why was she comparing Tyron to Jay?

"Well, that's good," she replied, hoping for Earth to

elaborate.

"I just thought you should know, since you guys are neighbours. Jay's not a bad guy, apart from spraying his crops. It's Tyron who took his inheritance and ran away, left Jay to look after the farm and their mum."

They were brothers! Nina thought of Tyron's smile, his eyes, how he'd reacted to Jay's name. Of course. It was obvious. How had she not seen it?

"Inheritance?" Nina repeated, her curiosity trumping politeness.

Earth tilted her head, sending the dreadlock bun lolling on one side. "I mean, it's not like there was a lot of money, I don't think. They're not dairy farmers. But Tyron put his land up for sale before they even buried his father!"

"Wow. Sounds like you ended up with the right brother, then?" Nina stared at Earth, waiting for her to deny or confirm their relationship status. She had to know. Earth's inscrutable smile was getting more annoying by the second. "Jay and I have a long history. We have our disagreements, but there's this special bond, you know? That little something that tells you it's going to last a lifetime."

She spoke with warmth and conviction, but the words sounded like a parable. But whatever their exact relationship, she had feelings for Jay and transmitted serious 'back off' vibes. Nina sighed, thinking of the moments she'd swooned over Jay. She had to stop wasting her time on unavailable men.

On the drive home, Nina recounted her recent life choices. So far, she had managed a move to the country, a pointless crush on a neighbour, and an almost-one-night-stand with his philandering brother. She needed to change tack.

CHAPTER 15

Jay chopped up chilli peppers with careless abandon. He'd already touched his face twice, causing both his left nostril and left eye to burn. The previous night's events had kept him up for much of the night.

It had all started with his mum calling him about Tyron's visit, begging for Jay to welcome his brother, as she was on her way back from some market in Tauranga, two hours away. (She'd sold five plants. Great use of petrol there.) Jay had told her he was busy, which was partly true, and that Tyron could entertain himself in town (also true). Jay was still reeling from Earth's visit and his willingness to please his mum had plummeted to an all-time low.

Mum had given up, and Jay had gotten back to his hot sauce. It had just the right consistency, and the taste was even better than last time. He'd been ready to take a bottle to Nina. It had been late, but not too late. The perfect time for a cuppa, or maybe a beer – although he doubted Nina had anything that mundane in her fridge and bringing alcohol with him would have looked too presumptuous. So hot sauce it was.

Being after dark, Jay had taken his tractor. This way, he wouldn't accidentally sneak up on her. She still hadn't set up proper curtains, and as much as he wanted another glimpse of her naked body, he preferred not to build a reputation as a voyeur. Maybe one day she would willingly undress for him. Feeling both nervous and hopeful, Jay had driven down the hill towards the tiny house. But as he'd gotten closer, he'd seen Nina wasn't alone. She had a male visitor, the shape of his shoulders unmistakable behind the window.

Jay had swerved into Nina's driveway, and that's when he'd seen the car. He would have recognised Tyron's pompous Audi anywhere. Soon after the funeral, his brother had sold their father's perfectly useful pickup truck and bought the pretentious, leathery penis-replacement which was so low-riding he could barely visit the farm. Not that Jay wanted him to, anyway.

Jay threw the chillies into the pot and started peeling onions. Thinking of Tyron and Nina together, the unfairness of it all hit him again like a ton of bricks. Why Nina? Why last night? Hadn't his big brother done enough already? Since their father's death, the best thing about him had been his willingness to stay away from Raglan. Jay couldn't even decide which one was worse – that his brother had snaked his way into Nina's bed for a one-night stand, or the slight possibility that he was genuinely interested in her. Both options made him physically ill.

When Nina had turned up at his door later that night, asking for a ride, Jay's spirits had lifted. Tyron hadn't spent the night, and Nina didn't seem that besotted with the date. Why hadn't she gotten a ride back to town with Tyron? That part made no sense, but Jay hoped it was because the date had been cut short. He had tried to pry a little more out of Nina, but didn't want to come off too curious. She'd apologised for making him miss the game. Jay couldn't have cared less about the game, but it had been a handy distraction. The only reason he'd watched it at home that night was to distract his brain from the image of Nina and Tyron together. And the only reason he'd headed for the pub was to avoid returning to his empty house with all those thoughts swirling in his mind.

Jay wasn't sure why he was making another batch of hot sauce. Maybe because he still had ingredients left. Or maybe he needed something to occupy his hands, to avoid picking up an axe and turning that Audi into scrap metal. Jay knew Tyron was spending the night in their mother's guest room. The most amicable thing he could do was to stay home and wait for him to leave.

Jay looked at the bottle of sauce on the kitchen counter – the one he'd earmarked for Nina. Could he take it to her now? He needed to see her, regardless of what had happened with Tyron. He'd spent his whole life losing to Tyron, always waiting for his brother to leave so he could have his share of the attention and resources Tyron seemed to hog anywhere he went. This time, he wouldn't bend over. He would fight back. Jay fully appreciated the irony of his thoughts. He lived next door to Nina and hadn't even asked her out. He had no right to be upset. And he still had no idea of the state of his health. He should have been focusing on self-care instead of directing his energy on Nina and Tyron.

But Tyron didn't spend the night, the ugly, jealous part of him insisted. *It's not over yet.*

Jay grabbed the bottle and looked at the clock on the wall. Was Nina back from that meeting? Could he just rock up at her door?

Chloe pushed her head against Jay's legs. He reached down to pat her, but she backed away, let out a soft whimper, and threw up on the floor. Jay could see the worms in the vomit. *Oh shit.* This was not the time to make sauce deliveries. It was time to look after his best friend. The sauce would have to wait until tomorrow.

Reluctantly, Jay set the bottle back on the table, cleaned up the floor and guided Chloe to the car, hoping her stomach was now empty.

CHAPTER 16

After spending a good day and a half working on logo concepts for both of her new clients, Nina decided she needed a break. She wanted to talk to Alice about Trevor and maybe ask what she knew about Marlena and Earth, but didn't want to go in empty-handed. She wanted to bring a cake. Wasn't that what neighbours did around here?

Nina was just taking a carrot cake out of her oven when she heard a knock on the door. It was Jay, holding a bottle of something red. The chilli sauce, Nina remembered. She flashed him a smile. "Hi!"

"Nice puppets."

Nina looked down at her oven mitts, which had faces on them – a silly gift from her dad. Oh well. She was home, and allowed to wear whatever she wanted. Jay handed over the sauce bottle and took a step back, as if he was making a delivery. "Let me know how you like it."

"Thank you, I will."

Jay looked over his shoulder. Was he about to bolt? Nina

gestured at her kitchen. "I'm baking. Do you wanna have a taste? I'll make you a cup of coffee."

He has a girlfriend, the sensible part of Nina's brain reminded her. She ignored it.

Jay looked at her quizzically. Why was he so hard to read? After a much-too-long break, he just nodded and stepped inside. Nina noted that Chloe wasn't with him.

"Where's Chloe?" she asked, hoping to buy some time. She had a vegan chocolate cake and a carrot cake. The first one was for her, the second one meant for Alice. Which one should she offer? The carrot cake was probably what Jay preferred, but it still needed icing.

"I left her with my mum. She had to be wormed and now she's sleeping it off."

Nina nodded, clueless about dogs and their worms. "Does your mum like carrot cake?"

"Um... I think so, sure. Why?"

"Sorry, I was just planning on taking this cake to her, but I think you'd like this better than the vegan chocolate cake, so – "

"Try me." Jay smiled.

"You mean the vegan...?"

"Now, when you say vegan, you mean you *didn't* use any meat in it?"

Nina laughed. "No meat, no eggs, no dairy."

"So, what's left?"

"Ha-ha. Cocoa powder, flour, oil, sugar..."

"No wheatgrass?"

"Why do you think I use wheatgrass in everything?"

Jay pointed at the micro greens on her windowsill. They looked a little wilted. Nina was trying to keep them alive for a few more days to boost her morning smoothies.

"Those are mustard greens and barley grass. I thought you were the one in the veggie business," Nina quipped.

"Well, barley grass looks a lot like wheat grass. And I don't grow micro greens."

Jay accepted a piece of the vegan chocolate cake and bit into it without hesitation. After a moment of chewing, he nodded. To not seem like she was waiting around for a compliment, Nina focused on making coffee and a cup of tea for herself.

"What's your biggest... um... item? I mean crop," Nina asked, wishing she hadn't tried to tease him. She read a lot about nutrition but was weak on the farming lingo.

After rummaging through her pantry, she found the coffee she'd bought for La La's visit. Thank goodness there was still some left. Right behind her back, she heard Jay chew and swallow a mouthful of cake and clear his throat.

"I grow potato and kumara, cauliflower, kale, beetroot, tomato, capsicum... and some chilli and other herbs. And of course we have some citrus and other trees but not heaps for resale."

That sounded like a lot of variety to Nina. "So you'd be self-sufficient if society collapses?"

Jay shrugged. "If you don't need a lot of protein. Why – is it going to collapse?"

"I don't know. My dad's always talking about that. He's a bit of a survivalist."

"Really? Living in an underground bunker with canned goods and a shotgun?"

Nina laughed. Maybe 'survivalist' was too extreme. She sat down across the tiny table, placing two cups on it.

"No. He has a rifle for hunting and a cabin by the lake, but he spends most of his time running a small business in town. I haven't seen him in ages, though. He says he can't leave the business long enough to come and visit. But I'm hoping he eventually retires."

Nina couldn't believe she was sharing this much with a guy who had shared nothing of himself. She made a mental note to stop blabbing.

"Business owners never retire. What's his business?"

"Um... it's a printing press."

"Back in... Finland?"

Nina nodded and got up to make the coffee and tea. She poured Jay a cup and offered him some almond milk, since that's all she had. He declined it but took the coffee, pulling a face as he sipped.

"So, what does your father do?" Nina asked, then immediately remembered he was dead. Oh crap. Was she meant to know that? Jay looked out the window, his face unreadable.

"He was a farmer, like me. He died two years ago."

"I'm so sorry."

"He was much better at it than me, though. He knew how to sell." Jay looked at her square in the eye, and Nina felt her stomach tighten. For a moment, he wasn't aloof or unreadable. He was just sad.

"What do you mean?" Nina asked, "I've seen you at the crop swap, with all the ladies flocking around your table."

Jay smiled and shook his head. "Well, that's crop swap. You only need to be a male who still has his own hair."

Now that Nina thought about it, Jay had been the only male in the room with a full head of hair.

"My dad knew how to sell to businesses, how to talk up the product and push for a good deal. I hate going out there. I'm not much of a sweet talker. You might have noticed."

Suddenly, he looked like a little boy, and a picture emerged – a picture of an enigmatic dad and two brothers, one of them a real sweet talker and the other one … Jay. Nina had an overwhelming urge to hug him. "I find it quite… refreshing. I don't really care for the sweet talk."

"You don't?" Jay's eyes flashed.

Was he talking about Tyron? Did he know? Did he assume something? Nina wanted to scream that she hadn't slept with his brother, but how could she say that without sounding like a complete ass? Besides, she probably would have, if he'd had a condom. She'd been attracted to Tyron. She wouldn't plead innocence or apologise for anything. Jay had a girlfriend.

Nina got up and cleared the empty plates.

Jay took the hint and stood. "Thanks for the cake."

"Thanks for the hot sauce. I'll let you know how... I react to it."

"Are you expecting a rash, or a fever or something?" Jay deadpanned.

Nina suppressed a giggle. "Well, at least some hot flushes. Maybe euphoria? We have to figure out what warnings to put on the label."

Nina cringed at her own words. She hadn't meant to push her professional services to him. Working with friends got complicated. She always ended up charging less, or nothing at all, and then feeling stupid about it. And she couldn't ask Jay to pay. What would Alice think of her?

Jay looked at the unlabelled bottle of chilli sauce with his eyes narrowed. "It needs a label, doesn't it?"

"Well, if you want to sell it."

"And you could do that?"

Nina drew a breath. She had walked straight into this one. "I could do it. Or someone else could do it."

Jay looked puzzled. "Who?"

"I mean, there are other designers. Lots of them. Even in Raglan. Well, maybe not lots, but there are ... others."

Nina listened to her own ramble, wishing she knew where she was going. She wasn't much of a sweet talker either. Or any kind of talker.

"So... you don't want to do it?" Jay asked.

"No, I just mean you don't have to go with me because I'm your neighbour. That would be silly."

Jay looked at her, now even more puzzled. "It's Raglan. We always go with the neighbour."

He wasn't being clever. He was just stating a fact. La La's words about the neighbours replayed in Nina's mind. Was Jay offended that she hadn't bought her veggies from him? She couldn't even afford the organic vegetables anymore. She was buying more and more conventional produce from other shops. Why wasn't she buying off Jay?

"I'm sorry. I should have bought from you," she said.

"What?"

"I mean your veggies. I should have bought directly from you, right? Because we're neighbours."

"I thought you wanted all certified organic," Jay replied. He didn't sound offended.

"Yeah, that would be great. But right now, I can't afford to go hundred percent organic, anyway."

Jay looked at Nina for a while, making her feel heady all over again. "You know I had zero residue?"

"Residue?"

"I had most of my produce measured for pesticide residue this year. They didn't find any."

"Really? How is that possible?"

"Well, I spray sparingly, only when necessary. It's expensive anyway, so you want to avoid it as much as possible."

Nina had never really considered the cost of pesticides.

She felt like an idiot. "So, your veggies are technically organic?"

"I'm not certified. But yes, in many cases it's technically the same thing."

"Wow. I had no idea."

"Many people don't." Jay shrugged and opened the door to let himself out. Nina followed him outside.

"We should do a barter deal," she said.

She didn't want Jay to leave. This seemed to happen every time he visited. She remembered the relief after Tyron had left. With Jay, she felt the opposite. When he left, she felt an acute sense of loss.

Jay turned to study her face. "What kind?"

"I design your sauce label and help you launch the product. And you give me veggies."

"Is that a fair deal?"

"I don't mean like half of your crop. Just the amount I would normally buy elsewhere. And not for life either, just for as long as we're working together."

"Well, that's why I'm asking... is it a fair deal for you?"

"It's brilliant. The house and land are paid for, so most of my money goes into food. And petrol, when I have to go shopping... for food."

Jay seemed to consider this for a moment.

"Okay," he said, extending his hand for a handshake.

Nina smiled and offered her hand. The strength of his grip took her by surprise, warm and reassuring like a hug. She could feel her heart rate rise and her nerve endings tingled. The handshake seemed to go on for a long time, neither of them wanting to let go. This was ridiculous. A little giggle escaped Nina's mouth, and she dropped her hand. Jay cleared his throat.

"That's how we seal a deal here in Raglan," he said, his voice gruff.

He's someone else's boyfriend, Nina reminded herself.

"I hope Chloe feels better soon," she called after him as he turned to leave. In his signature style, Jay waved his hand over his shoulder, but this time, turned his head enough for Nina to see he was smiling.

Why, oh why, couldn't he be single?

CHAPTER 17

Nina found Alice in her garden, hunched over her sprouts, talking to them. Nina couldn't make out the words, but it sounded like baby talk.

Holding out her iced and decorated carrot cake, Nina took a couple of steps closer. "Sorry to interrupt."

Alice turned and smiled at her. "No problem, I'm done here anyway and hey... what did you bring? I could definitely take a coffee break!"

Alice got to her feet and led them into the kitchen. "That is such a lovely-looking cake! Is it very healthy?"

"Umm...it's a carrot cake, and I replaced some of the sugar with brown rice syrup, which is pure glucose, so it doesn't raise your blood sugar as much as fructose. But no, it's not really that healthy."

"Sounds healthy to me," Alice decided, and put the kettle on.

"I wanted to come and thank you for the lead. Trevor's great to work with, and it's already led to another job."

"Wow, you've been a busy girl!" Alice set the table with two plates and cut the cake.

"I feel so much better having some money in the bank," Nina admitted.

"This is divine." Alice sighed, sneaking a piece of cake into her mouth. "Just what I needed to get me through the afternoon lull!"

Nina smiled and tried to tackle the much-too-thick slice Alice had plopped on her plate. It tasted delicious – way too easy to overdose on.

"I heard you're helping Jay as well." Alice's eyes twinkled.

Word travelled fast around here. Jay had only left her house an hour earlier. Then she noticed Chloe peacefully asleep on a small rug in the corner. Jay must have come by on his way back. Alice followed her gaze. "Poor Chloe is still tired and Jay had to go pack up. He's got a pickup truck coming."

"Does he do that by himself?"

"He has a couple of farm hands who come to help on the day. They're probably there already. It has to be done quickly, so it's all freshly picked when they take it away."

"Who is he selling to?"

"Mainly restaurants, and one of those food boxes I think."

Nina had assumed Jay's produce just ended up in the supermarkets, not in the hands of chefs. "Sounds great."

"Well, it's better than the supermarkets," Alice confirmed. "But I really hope the sauce business takes off. It would change his life."

"How?"

"Jay works long hours on the farm. It's backbreaking work. I just want him to have an easier life than his father."

"Absolutely. I don't know how he's making the sauce right now, but small businesses often struggle to scale up when the demand grows."

Alice's eyes lit up. "That's the best part. My husband – before he died – bought all this equipment from a liquidated jam and chutney factory. It's there in the shed, just gathering dust. I think Jay took out a couple of pots to test the recipe, but he can easily set up a production line."

"That's great!"

It sounded like Jay was following in his dad's footsteps in more ways than one. Nina wondered how Jay's dad had died.

Alice clapped his hands together. "Having a real designer working with him is going to make such a difference. He was so excited about your deal!"

Nina had a hard time imagining Jay showing excitement, but smiled. If she could make a difference to Jay's budding business, she would. She wanted to keep that smile on Alice's face. Maybe one day, she'd see that excitement in Jay, too.

Chapter 18

Jay stood in his shed, staring at the enormous pots and pans, strainers and other chutney making equipment piled up on a long shelf. He'd started out by making one batch in his own kitchen, working off a recipe his dad had left behind. He wanted to reduce the eye-watering hotness and add more flavour. Experimenting with one pot of sauce had been fun, but the idea of producing large quantities with an unfaltering taste and consistency and bottling it without making a mess… he could smell a challenge. But if he was ever to give this a go, it would have to be now. He had a designer – a gorgeous blonde designer.

Nina was such a mystery to him. She invited him into her house, fed him strange baking and now had suggested this deal that made no sense – her professional services for his vegetables. Surely, she could buy a box of veggies for far less than her going hourly rate. Maybe she was after something else? Wishful thinking, but he couldn't help it.

Jay's growing feelings for Nina had finally prompted him

to schedule a visit with his doctor. He had to find out if there was anything to worry about. The sense of impending doom alternated with glimpses of hope. If he could get a clean bill of health, he could actually see about this girl. He had to give it a shot.

Jay grabbed two big pots and carried them inside his house. Everything in the shed needed a good wash, and he had to start somewhere.

Scrubbing the stainless steel, Jay thought of the next time he could see Nina. It would be when he made the food delivery. He'd have to wait for the capsicums to ripen. Nina would love them. Jay wondered why it was so hard to go over for a visit. She was new in the area and lived in a ridiculously small house. There was good reason to worry about her, in the neighbourly sense. But Jay hadn't taken those opportunities. If he'd got to know her straight away, he could have warned her about Tyron. He'd done nothing and hated himself for it.

Now they had a deal, a reason to stay in touch. He'd have to make the most of this.

CHAPTER 19

Nina felt jittery. She had a date at the Cherry Tree Festival outside Hamilton, and the sun had turned up for the occasion. Every cherry tree in Waikato bloomed like a cloud of candy floss, and it felt like at least fifty percent of them graced the grounds of the manor hosting the annual event. Nina had never seen so much pink.

La La had helped her set up an online dating profile. When Nina lost her nerve, she'd even published it for her. But when the messages began popping up, Nina found herself entertained by the little conversations. She enjoyed the attention, the little buzz her phone emitted when a new message arrived. It made the long, lonely nights at the tiny house more bearable. Especially when the internet was acting up and she couldn't watch anything on Netflix. But it had been just that – harmless chatting – until today.

It felt like a blind date. However honest and 'herself' Nina tried to be online, it was a different version of her. She suspected this guy also had an online personality he curated separately from his real-life persona. Meeting in the flesh was almost like deleting those carefully curated identities and entering the messy, three-dimensional world. He could judge her on the way she played with her hair or the way she walked. Everything about her was on display.

Nina straightened the hem of her mustard yellow dress and looked around. She couldn't see anyone matching the photo she'd stared at for so long she practically had it memorised. In fact, she could only see black hair. The Cherry Tree Festival was almost exclusively attended by Asians.

To be fair, Nina hadn't been that drawn to the photo of Adam, but he seemed sane and had expressed his desire to have two kids. A girl and a boy, although Nina couldn't imagine how this level of planning was possible. So, as Nina had promised herself, this warranted at least one face-to-face meeting. She'd also promised herself she wouldn't be too picky or fixate on little details, like flimsy arms, a feminine bum shape, or a body odour. No, she couldn't help herself. Those were deal breakers, but she would definitely tolerate a shorter stature or hairy knuckles. She would at least try.

A fresh group of Asians wandered through the gates, flocking in every direction, their cameras pointed up at the canopy of pink blossoms. As they dispersed, Nina saw a man in a baby blue collar shirt waving at her. He looked as described, about six feet tall and slender. His hair was an unremarkable shade of dirty blond and his face somehow blank – like it was currently unused by its owner. He flashed her a perfunctory smile, which disappeared quickly, never reaching his eyes.

"You must be Nina," he said in an even tone.

"I must be." Nina smiled.

She had to stop judging this guy before he'd even warmed up. Everyone seemed unnatural when nervous.

They toured the grounds and took pictures of the cherry trees. It was the most romantic setting you could have asked for, like floating around inside a pink, fragrant cloud. Nina felt awkward. The setting didn't match their relationship. They'd only just met. It was too early to even casually brush against the other person, let alone hold hands or take couple selfies. Not that Nina had a lot of experience with those. Matt had been so averse to being photographed, it was hard to find any visual evidence of them ever being together.

After the long silences she'd experienced with Jay, Adam felt like an unstoppable chatterbox. He talked about his family, his work at the council (yawn), and then described his love of chess, long distance running, and making fresh pasta. These were respectable hobbies, in which he clearly excelled, yet Nina kept tuning out. Adam was not a storyteller. He had a sharp memory and could rattle off countless details of flours he'd successfully used in a pasta maker or marathons he was training for. Nina dutifully expressed her admiration, and Adam seemed pleased.

When it was Nina's turn, she tried to spin a good tale of her move to New Zealand and her life in Hamilton, working at the ad agency. And then, moving into her tiny house in the middle of nowhere. It didn't really have a dramatic arc or a proper ending, but she was desperate to entertain herself with something other than marathon results and the secrets of perfect tagliatelle. She described the regrets, the loneliness, the hard physical labour she hadn't expected, but also the joys of connecting with her neighbours, eating fresh produce straight off the ground and having the freedom to start her day with a swim (well, in theory) or foraging for oranges.

Adam listened carefully and inserted questions. He seemed very impressed that Nina had no debt, and that she was adding to the value of her property by building a shed and gardening. Nina had never thought of her gardening in terms of property value, but the appreciation made her feel nice. Maybe she was doing something right.

After a full tour of the cherry trees and the surrounding gardens, they stopped at the food truck and ordered nachos. Nina asked to leave out cheese and sour cream, and she was grateful Adam didn't comment on this. She wasn't yet ready to have the conversation about her weird diet. Adam paid for the food and they sat down.

A gentle breeze shook the cherry trees, making a handful of light pink petals fall on them like snow. Nina looked up and sighed. "This must be the most beautiful moment of spring. Everything will be downhill from here."

Adam looked at her questioningly. "Why is it going downhill?"

"No, I'm just saying... when you see something this beautiful, it's almost sad, because nothing can surpass it. You know what I mean?"

It was clear from Adam's expression he did not know what she meant. Although he was definitely trying. "Is it like when people cry at weddings?"

Nina smiled and nodded. It wasn't really that at all. She was pretty sure wedding guests didn't cry about the beautiful decorations. Or maybe they did. She'd never fully understand other people.

At the end of the date, Adam walked Nina to her car and gently mentioned that she should get it washed to avoid corroding the metal. Nina nodded in agreement. She drove her poor car in a lot of mud and dust. She didn't have an outdoor hose, only a bucket and rainwater. It was unlikely she could ever keep her car spick and span, but she appreciated his concern.

Based on the lukewarm date, Nina was expecting maybe a peck on the cheek and half-hearted promise to keep in touch. But Adam had other ideas. As Nina was about to say goodbye, he cupped her face in his hands and planted a kiss right on her lips. It wasn't a long, wet one, but it took her by surprise.

"I like you. I'd like to see you again. When would suit you?" Adam asked.

It was so efficient, so straightforward. For a moment, Nina felt awestruck by his laser-focused intention. There was no time for that awkward dance at the doorstep, sexual tension building up, both looking for the right words... Adam had the words, as rehearsed as they sounded.

"Oh, really?" Nina stammered.

She tried to gather her thoughts and hide her surprise. On the surface, the date had gone well. They'd had pleasant conversation, nice food and the most beautiful surroundings. Maybe Adam found their level of connection perfectly acceptable.

Nina didn't know what to say, but Adam jumped in. "I know there's a distance between us, but if all goes well, I'm willing to move. Currently, I'm renting, saving up for a house. I wouldn't have any work in Raglan, but I would consider Whatawhata or somewhere else on that side of town."

Nina swallowed hard. The practicalities of living in different towns didn't really concern her. She would have dated someone from a different country if they were in love. She wanted to be in love – properly, irreversibly in love. Surely that's how it was all supposed to start. But it hadn't happened, not like she was hoping, so maybe it was time for a different approach. Maybe, by just dating someone, you eventually fell in love. She'd heard of arranged marriages that, over time, developed into genuine love and affection. Could it work for her?

***

On the way home, Nina tried to make sense of the decision she'd just made. She had agreed to a second date the following week, this time in Raglan. She wasn't ready to invite Adam into her home, and he hadn't pushed for that. Instead, they'd agreed to meet at the local pub and go for a walk around the village. Nina was already nervous about it. It was easier to date outside her home turf. She already knew a few people in Raglan. Someone could see them together and report to others that knew her. Earth's mum, Marlena, was a real busybody. She'd introduced Nina – referring to her as 'my designer' – to many other locals. What if she saw them together? What if Alice did? Or Jay? Was she ready for that? Nina couldn't give herself an answer, but she had to admit she had mixed feelings about all this.

CHAPTER 20

Nina sat at the cafe, the same one where she'd met with Marlena the first time. This time, she was meeting with Earth. She'd called out of the blue and demanded a meeting as soon as possible. Nina didn't have a good feeling about this. She'd already emailed the first drafts and Marlena had sent an enthusiastic response, saying she loved all options and would talk to a few people to help her choose.

Nina's coffee arrived at the same time as Earth, who burst through the door, followed by a thick cloud of sickly incense scent. Despite the scent, she looked somewhat tidier, like a business version of her usual self. She wore a tight little blazer on top of a floral outfit that may have been a jumpsuit or just harem pants with a top.

"Okay, I'm just going to be straight with you," she said as she grabbed a seat opposite Nina "It's not working. It's not you, you've been great, but we have to take a different direction."

Was Earth talking about her mum's business or breaking

up with her?

Earth blew out a dramatic breath. "Mum's too embarrassed. She wants to just keep going so as not to offend you, but... you and me both know that's not right. We have to do what's best for the business."

Nina took a deep breath and tried to put the pieces together. What could have possibly happened since the last email she'd received? "Has... something happened?"

Clients sometimes backed out right in the beginning, usually for a good reason. Nina didn't have that much experience with small businesses, but her friend who did more freelance work had told her she lost work mostly for financial reasons – to artistically inclined cousins, Fiverr or other websites where you could buy cheap design work mainly from the developing countries. Some of those clients came back, having wasted time and money. Others were just happy to cut down the cost, regardless of the outcome. Nina didn't really want to work with the latter kind, anyway. People who couldn't tell the difference between her work and something their nephew had made in Microsoft Paint were impossible to please.

Earth had the decency to look uncomfortable. "We've received another offer, and it's too good to pass. At this stage of starting a business, we need to be very careful with our budget."

"Of course," nodded Nina.

She'd made them a very reasonable offer, a fixed price for

a logo, business cards and branding of social media channels. Nina dug up her phone and logged into her time tracking app. "I've spent eight hours so far, so I can just invoice you for that."

Earth squirmed. She obviously hadn't considered Nina would charge for the time already spent. Nina's chest filled with white, hot anger. Nobody did this to their mechanic or their hairdresser. If you agreed on the price and started the job, the client couldn't back out without paying. That her work took place on a computer somehow made it so immaterial that some people considered it not worth anything. They probably imagined her sitting there, pushing one button while the laptop did the rest.

Earth's eyes narrowed. "Yeah, I understand you've probably done some work already, but... you see, we can't use anything you've done, so for us, it's not really worth anything at the moment. I hope you don't take this the wrong way."

That 'probably' irked Nina more than Earth's unwillingness to pay. That she had the nerve to doubt if Nina had done anything, after she'd sent Marlena a PDF of four different logo options, each spelling out their ridiculous but also unique business name, Raglan Fair Thread.

"I do not base my pricing on whether or how you use my designs. It's based on the hours I work. So, if you make a million dollars with something I create, I won't come to demand my share." Nina tried to keep her tone light.

Earth looked away, her jaw tensing. "Look, I didn't want

to say this, but I've checked your quote and your website. You don't have terms and conditions. If you stated that in the event of a cancellation, the client must pay the accrued hours, that would be a different deal. But right now, you have nothing. A friend of mine is a lawyer, so he looked into it for me."

As Earth talked, she kept looking slightly past her, only allowing the briefest eye contact at the end, making sure Nina was listening. This must have been very hard for her. She was right. Nina didn't have a 'terms and conditions' page. Most small businesses and freelancers didn't. She relied on the goodwill of her clients. A big mistake.

"I have an email thread between myself and Marlena, proving that I've delivered part of the work. But I also think it's not worth the trouble for me to go to court over five hundred dollars."

Nina wasn't sure what her options were in a situation like this. Was there any office apart from the actual court that could sort out disagreements between small businesses? There must have been something, but she already knew she would never go down that road. She would have to leave this behind and move on.

Earth gave her a tense smile. "I'm glad you can be sensible about this," she said magnanimously, which infuriated Nina even more.

She couldn't lose her cool now. Nina gathered her things and got up. "All the best with your business."

Earth looked like she had something to add, but then thought better of it. Nina didn't want to hang around for whatever stupid might come out of her mouth next. She was out the door and on her way home within a minute. After two minutes of driving, she pulled over and dialled La La. All those things she'd wanted to say burned in her throat. She had to rant at someone.

"Calm down, girl," La La soothed her. She sounded distracted. "You're going to have these bad eggs now and then. That's what it's like with freelancing. Or you can always come back to town and work for a reputable agency and respectable clients?"

Nina could hear the smile in her voice. "This is not funny. She is like the only female of my age I even know around here. And I really thought, over time, we'd become friends. At least I tried. I don't care about the five hundred bucks. It just sucks to be treated this way!"

"I get that. But I would care about the five hundred bucks. She's stealing from you. Not worth befriending, in my opinion."

"Yeah, I know."

"Now, take a breath, go home and make yourself a drink."

Nina sighed and finished the call. She wasn't sure La La really understood. If she didn't, then who would? Raglan was feeling more and more like a stupid idea.

CHAPTER 21

Nina sat in the orange tree in the middle of the community garden, plucking ripe fruit and dropping them on the ground. Some went straight into her basket, others rolled around. The meeting with Earth had put her off doing any more design work, so she was foraging. After all, Jay had told her it was okay. Somehow, knowing that she had all this food available without making a dime made it easier to accept that she wasn't making a dime. God was still looking after her – growing all this fruit.

Still, sitting in the tree, far away from anyone's sight and hidden within the leaves, the tears came. Would she ever feel like she belonged here? Would other clients do the same, just because they could? Even if she slammed a chunk of small print on her website and in her quotes, it didn't really stop people from doing whatever they wanted. If she had to chase them and take them to court to get her money, she would never make a profit.

A familiar bark drew her attention. Was that dog tracking

her down? Nina didn't want to see anyone, especially Jay, but she had no way out. Chloe had picked up her scent and arrived under the tree, barking excitedly. At least she was over the worming episode and back on her feet. Nina had to admit she rather liked Chloe. She'd been the most supportive and accepting individual in Raglan, apart from Alice, maybe. The thought made her well up, and she tried to blink the tears away.

After a few moments, Jay joined Chloe and peered up between the branches. "Hi there."

"Hi." Nina climbed down from the tree, dabbed her eyes and gave Jay a sad smile.

"Are you okay?" Jay asked. He seemed genuine.

"I'm... not having the best day. But I'm fine," Nina assured. "I came to pick up some fruit since you said..."

"Yes, absolutely. Take anything you want. I'm after some limes myself."

He swung an empty plastic bucket on his arm.

"I saw some here," Nina offered, leading him towards a smaller tree on the side of the garden.

Jay picked three ripe ones carefully in his bucket. "Thanks, these are great. I needed some more for the hot sauce. I'm cooking another batch."

"That's exciting. I should take a photo of you doing this. We could use it for the website one day. It'd make a great product back story," Nina said.

She couldn't help her mind running down this track. She

wasn't a gardener. Design and marketing were her game. Even if nobody ever paid her.

"So, what happened?" Jay asked.

Nina thought of a way to sidestep the question. Earth was possibly his girlfriend. She was the town newbie. A foreigner. She didn't belong. Could she actually trust Jay with this story, or would it make everything worse?

"Come on," Jay said. "You look like you need to offload. My mum has the same look. She needs less prompting, though."

Jay smiled disarmingly, and Nina talked. Having someone's full attention was irresistible. As the story flowed out, she reminded herself to stick to the facts and keep her emotions in check. She tried to spin the story, so that Earth didn't appear as the bad guy, that she'd been merely doing her mum's bidding.

"I'm not angry with her," she said. "Just disappointed with the whole thing. And I feel stupid for not having Ts and Cs on my website. It's so basic."

"You should be angry with her," Jay retorted. "That's a really shitty move."

Jay's tone caught Nina off guard. Why was he taking her side?

"I give my clients credit if they have trouble paying. I'm pretty flexible," Nina added.

"I wouldn't give too much credit. The good ones pay up. The shitty ones will come up with all kinds of excuses. No amount of credit is enough for them."

Nina realised Jay must have had his share of local clients, good and bad. As a farmer, he was running a business.

"To be honest, I feel like I'm not cut out to be a freelancer. That I should just go back to working in Hamilton."

Jay pulled a face. "It's a bitch of a commute."

"Yeah. Not ideal."

"Do you want me to talk to her?" Jay asked.

"God, no! I don't want this to become an issue between you two."

"Why?" Jay gave her a strange look.

Nina frowned. Wasn't it obvious that these kinds of issues were potentially flammable between couples? She was trying to save them from the unpleasant argument. This was between her and Earth – and Marlena.

"Look," Jay continued, "if you're thinking this thing with Earth is a common occurrence around here... it's not. She's a piece of work. If I'd known she was your client, I would have warned you."

"Really?"

"Yeah."

Nina couldn't believe how harshly Jay talked about Earth. If they were indeed a couple, Jay could have at least attempted to take her side, whether or not she was in the wrong. Nina almost felt bad for her.

"Apart from the payment thing, Earth hasn't been horrible to me or anything. She warned me about your brother."

"Did she?"

A strange look settled on Jay's face.

Nina gave her a rueful smile. "Maybe a little late, but still. She only had nice things to say about you, though. She really loves you."

Jay looked confused. "Loves me?"

"Yes, obviously."

Jay looked like he'd lost the plot. "Why would you say that?"

Why had she said it? Was she trying to mend their relationship – or just meddling?

"I don't know," Nina admitted. "To state the obvious, I guess. Sorry."

"Don't be sorry. I just don't understand. I mean, she's a family friend, but we're not involved."

Not involved? Nina felt a surge of elation. "Sorry, I must have misunderstood her. She talked about your history, and your special bond ... something about lasting a lifetime."

Jay shook his head in disbelief. "She's delusional. We went out once after she broke up with Tyron, but it didn't end well."

Nina felt stupid, but deeply relieved. She wondered what was going on with Earth. Was she trying to keep her away from Jay? Was she in love with him?

Jay kneeled down to her level and tentatively touched Nina's shoulder. His hand was warm, perfect. She didn't want to move.

"Don't write us off just yet, okay?"

"I won't," Nina promised.

Jay got up and Nina followed, sad to lose the physical connection but suddenly tingling all over with the new possibilities. Jay was single! Or, at least, he wasn't Earth's boyfriend. She tried to remind herself it didn't mean he was into her, but it did nothing to settle her heart rate.

Nina searched Jay's face for clues. He was a good friend, but she didn't want to misinterpret that as anything more like Earth had done.

Just as she was about to form a more personal question, Nina's phone beeped. It was Adam, sending her a link to a real estate listing in Raglan. Her neck flooded with heat. She'd completely forgotten about Adam. Why was he sending her a house listing with nothing but a smiley face as the message? Nina quickly closed her phone and slipped it in her pocket.

"Everything okay?" Jay asked.

"Fine."

"So, I'm putting together your first veggie box," Jay said.

Oh, yes. The barter deal!

Nina thought about their agreement. She would make those sauce labels for Jay, and they would look amazing. She'd already started, but wasn't a hundred percent happy with them yet.

"I am working on your labels," she said to Jay. "I'll send you the first drafts by the end of the week."

"No rush. You gotta give me some time to bring you veggies so that you at least get something out of this deal."

Jay was being so nice. Nina had to swallow down her tears one more time. She reached to pet Chloe. The dog was a willing recipient of her affections, placing her head on Nina's shoulder like she'd done this a million times. Maybe she was a trained 'hug dog'.

Once she composed herself, Nina released Chloe and got up. "Thanks for being so nice."

To Chloe, she whispered, "And thanks for the hugs." She waved them both goodbye.

"No worries," Jay called after her as she wandered off with her basket of oranges.

CHAPTER 22

Jay stared at a piece of lasagne on his plate. He had finished work late and accepted his mum's invitation to reheated leftovers. As they sat down to eat, Jay could tell Mum had a speech prepared.

"I wanted to apologise," she started. "It was wrong of me to discuss your health with Earth. She's just so knowledge-able, I thought maybe she could have some insight..."

Jay scoffed. "She reads crap online and believes every-thing she hears. Most of it has no scientific basis."

"Well, you can't trust everything online," Alice replied diplomatically. "But Earth means well, in her own way. Ty-ron really did a number on the poor girl."

Jay sighed. He knew Mum still felt responsible for Tyron's actions, but that didn't mean Earth had a free pass to mess with everyone. Jay swallowed his mouthful and recounted Nina's experience with Earth and Marlena, hoping he wasn't breaking her trust by doing so. He left out the part about Earth implying she was his girlfriend. That part annoyed him more than all the rest combined – she'd done that just to keep Nina away from him.

"That's terrible. But I'm sure Nina knows we're not all like that," Alice said. "She won't think less of you because of Earth."

Jay could sense his mum had guessed his interest in Nina, and he wasn't ready to talk about it. "I don't want us, as a community, to treat anyone that way. It's not right."

On the way home, Jay thought about what to do. It probably wasn't wise to get involved in whatever was going on with Earth. First, he wanted nothing to do with her. Second, he would probably make things worse. But he could be a better client himself. He would make Nina's veggie box the most varied, freshest food delivery she'd ever received. He'd make Nina understand that someone here wanted to treat her right. The idea of her taking a job in Hamilton made Jay uneasy. He wanted her around. The least he could do was to keep her fed.

The next day was sunny and crisp – a winter's day with a hint of spring. Jay stepped into his greenhouse and checked the watering system was working as it should. Sometimes, the hydroponic pipes got blocked. This was the time of year when nothing really grew outside, apart from citrus fruit. He could grow some brassicas in the polytunnel, but the winter tomatoes always fetched the premium price, even with his limited sales skills.

Jay walked around and, as he checked the crop, picked a

few of the very best tomatoes and herbs and packed them into a small cardboard box for Nina. Thinking of Nina filled him with an equal measure of excitement and frustration. She was beautiful, clever, and seemed so determined it almost scared him. But she was also vulnerable, all alone. He felt responsible for her.

Nina didn't know the land she was living on used to be their paddock. Tyron had sold it to a developer as soon as he could, accepting such a low-ball offer it had made Jay's blood boil. For a moment, it had looked like the developer might build something on it, but then probably figured the service connections would cost too much. So, as Jay had suspected, they flipped. He hoped Nina hadn't overpaid.

After his dad's death, Jay's mum had been trying to make him leave the farm and study something in town. He knew it wasn't just about finding an alternative career path or even for a change of scenery. She worried he would never find a wife, doing what he did, living where he lived. She wasn't mistaken about the lack of opportunity, but what she didn't understand was that Jay wasn't really that good at grasping those opportunities. At least here with his vegetables, he couldn't constantly fail at talking to women. Well, until Nina. Amazingly, her appearance had brought an end to Mum's talk about the University.

Jay didn't know what his mum imagined was going on with him and Nina, but he was grateful for the breather. He didn't want another career. There was nothing wrong with farming. Mum insisted it was his father's lifestyle of hard physical labour that had brought on his cancer, but Jay could easily list a few other factors, such as heavy smoking and a diet shockingly low in the vegetables he grew. Jay had never taken up smoking and quite enjoyed the plant-based foods. To his dad, farming had been a way of showing off. He had wanted to boast with the largest pumpkins and heaviest, juiciest tomatoes on the West Coast.

For Jay, it was an opportunity to make a living without having to deal with too many people. He was happiest with the plants and machinery, breathing fresh air, and spending time with his own thoughts, with no one breathing down his neck. Getting a degree in engineering to spend the rest of his life comfortably sitting in front of a screen in an air-conditioned office sounded about as appealing as lying in a hospital bed, being fed through a tube. Which is what might happen to him anyway, Jay thought with heaviness.

But it was times like these, when he was preparing to visit Nina, that he really wished he had the verbal skills of his late dad and his asshole brother. They always knew what to say – a gene he had missed out on. There was so much he wanted to say, but it all sounded stupid when put into words, even inside his head. He couldn't just say he liked her – that sounded pathetic and school-boyish. He definitely couldn't say he wanted to touch her, kiss her, and ... That sounded like sexual harassment. To further complicate things, they were now business partners. They had a deal. All he could do was to keep his end of it and hope she would give him a hint, help him out. He had an inkling she liked him, at least a little.

I haven't been with anyone since dad died, thought Jay with a start.

Maybe it wasn't such a surprise. Molly had found him too serious and sarcastic at the best of times, and during his father's illness, he'd had a permanent dark cloud hanging over his head. Jay didn't blame Molly for leaving his side, but he wondered if someone like Nina would have stayed. She seemed so headstrong and principled. Almost as if she didn't expect life to be easy or fun. Not that Jay wanted to make anyone's life less enjoyable. But life kept hitting his backside with a big cricket bat, which meant that anyone who got close to him ended up getting their share.

The latest setback was Tyron. His brother was back from Auckland, asking for the rest of his inheritance – the money he'd agreed to invest in the farm only three months ago. Jay didn't know how to pay him, other than by selling the farm. So far, he hadn't demanded that. And Mum, being a soft-hearted idiot, had agreed to invest her savings into his latest business venture. All this did nothing to help Jay's mood. If stress really caused cancer, he was a prime candidate.

Jay gathered the rest of the vegetables, arranging them beautifully on a bed of shredded brown paper. He turned over two potatoes to hide minor bumps and imperfections. The quality was on a par with the supermarket, maybe even better. For a moment, Jay allowed himself to feel pride. Maybe he wasn't that skilled in other areas of life, but he grew beautiful food.

At Nina's door, Jay stopped to listen. It was too quiet. Was she even home? Jay walked around and saw two cars parked behind. Did she have a visitor? What if it was a date? Jay knew he could have just left the box on the stairs. It was a beautiful day, unlikely to rain. But he had to see her, even if it was only for two minutes at the door. If nothing else, he had to find out who she was with.

Jay knocked on the door and waited. There was no answer. Just when he was about to set the box down, he heard sounds behind him. A burst of laughter. It was Nina, and she was with someone he recognised. It was the girl he'd met at his mum's house. What was her name? He remembered her looking at him with interest, winking.

She reminded him of the drunk tourist girls that sometimes ended up at Raglan bars, looking for a fling with a local – an authentic Kiwi holiday experience. The way they looked at him, openly measuring, assessing... Like he was just one more thing to tick on their holiday checklist, right after white water rafting, glowworms and bungee jumping. He never wanted to be that guy and stepped aside with relief when his friends jumped at the chance to chat up the German blonde. They could offer the easy flattery and laughs; recycle the same old jokes, anecdotes on cultural stereotypes. If he was honest, it didn't seem that difficult. The drunk girls laughed at anything and found flimsy excuses to touch you. Picking up tourists had been a popular pastime in the sleepy little Raglan village for a long time. And his two remaining local friends – Bill, the surf instructor and Gary the musician – had continued this hobby well into their thirties, even though Bill was now divorced and had a kid.

Awaking from his thoughts, Jay could tell the girls had noticed him. Nina smiled and gave him a little wave, making Jay feel better about intruding.

"Jay! You remember my friend La La?"

La La flashed him a pearly smile and nodded at the vegetable box. "What have you got there? A home delivery?"

"Just my end of the deal."

Seeing La La's eyes light up, he regretted his choice of words. "A deal you say? Dare I ask...?" La La wiggled her eyebrows.

Nina pulled a face. "It's highly confidential. And unsavoury, of course."

La La snorted, and Nina shot Jay an apologetic look. Jay tried to think of a quick comeback. If there ever was a time to be more fun, this was it.

"We simple folks in the country rely on exchanging goods and services." Jay did his best South Island accent, his face deadpan. "Miss Nina here keeps my loins warm and I help her fight off scurvy."

La La laughed so hard she started hiccupping. Jay nodded towards the door and Nina opened it to let him set the veggie box on the kitchen table.

"These are beautiful!" Nina exclaimed, examining the vegetables. "Thank you so much! I needed to go shopping, but this will tie me over. La La just came for a surprise visit and I have nothing in the cupboards."

"Great." Jay smiled and shifted towards the door, eager to get out of the way of the girls' night or whatever would happen next.

The scary-looking friend with a black fashion haircut blocked his way, still smirking. "So, you get your payment every time you do a delivery, or is it every Saturday after bingo?"

Jay had no choice but to play along. "No miss, I come after my weekly wash in the river."

"Well, the least she could do is offer you a hot beverage before sending you on your way." La La winked knowingly at Nina, who looked like she was over the joke.

"That's okay, I need to get back to work." Jay squeezed past La La. He needed to get out of here when he was still winning, before he put his foot in his mouth.

Nina followed him outside. La La stayed inside, spying on them through the window. Nina looked over her shoulder. "I told her to stay back," she confessed. "I love her to bits, but she can be a real busybody. Sorry about that."

"No worries."

"But you really held your own with her. I think she's pretty excited. She thinks you're hot." Nina's cheeks turned pink.

"And what do *you* think?" Jay asked. He couldn't help himself. It was such a perfect opportunity. He smiled and tried to look relaxed, like he couldn't care less, trying to read the answer hiding somewhere behind those blue eyes. No. Green-blue eyes. She had orangey rings around her pupils, like little splashes of mustard on a smokey blue tablecloth.

Nina laughed. "I think ... she's a terrible tease. I wouldn't believe a word she says."

Jay exhaled in mock disappointment. "Just when I thought I had a shot," he sighed.

Nina's eyes rounded. "Would you like me to set you guys up?"

Jay's stomach dropped two inches. How could he backpedal his way out of this one without insulting either woman?

"Um ... that's okay. I didn't mean..." Jay smiled in a way that he hoped conveyed no offence.

"I'm sure she'd go out with you. I'm not kidding. She really thinks you're cute." She glanced over her shoulder and dropped her voice, eyes turning serious. "But you should know that she's recently expressed a desire to have a baby. She's pretty determined."

Jay looked at Nina for a moment, unblinking. Was she really trying to set him up with her friend? The idea of fatherhood immediately made Jay think about the lump in his testicle and words came out of his mouth before his brain caught them. "I'm probably not the best choice, then."

"How so?"

Jay wanted to go back and edit his wording. The last thing he wanted to discuss with Nina was the state of his testicles.

"I'm just ... not quite there yet." He shrugged, hoping he came across endearingly nonplussed, not immature and commitment-phobic.

Jay had given little thought to having babies. When you didn't have a girlfriend, questions like that didn't feel very topical. And now that issue was hanging somewhere between them, as if suspended in mid-air, refusing to float down with the pollen and dust particles.

Nina stood there looking at him, so still and serious. "So... you wouldn't go out with someone who wants to have a baby?"

Why was she being so dire about this? They were talking about her friend, who Jay barely knew. He didn't want to go out with the tattooed woman, much less have a baby with her. Surely Nina could understand that.

"Can I just pass... this one time, without being judged as a heartless bastard?" Jay stretched his mouth into an apologetic smile.

Nina seemed to relax a little. "I understand," she said, switching gears. "Now, I think I can get the first draft of the label for you by the end of the week. Can I email it to you? What's your address?"

Jay dug into his pockets, but couldn't find paper or a pen. Nina disappeared into the house and came back a moment later with a beautiful business card.

"Here's my email. Can you just send me a quick message before Friday?"

Jay took the card and nodded. "Where did you get these from?"

The card had a glossy pattern on top of a geometric, colourful one, making it glint in the sunlight.

"I ordered them from the UK. They're not very expensive, if you want something special for yours?"

"Mine? I thought we were doing... stickers?"

"Labels," Nina corrected. "Yes, but you'll need business cards when you meet with retailers or go around promoting your products."

Jay nodded, feeling stupid. "Sorry. I must be the most clueless client you've ever had. Can you make a list of things you think I will need? So I can be prepared?"

"Sure, no problem."

Talking about work, Jay relaxed. He knew where he stood and what was going on. But he also wanted to rewind back to that previous bit. He should have been able to steer that conversation on the right track to say what he wanted to say. That he didn't fancy Nina's friend. He wanted to go out with her.

Jay looked up at the door, to a pair of eyes behind the small window. La La had tiptoed from the window to the doorway to a better eavesdropping position.

Jay flipped the business card and nodded. "I'll email you."

He strolled away, forcing himself to not look back like a

lovelorn idiot. On the way back, Jay remembered the hot sauce. He hadn't even asked for Nina's opinion on it – the one question he had prepared as an icebreaker before leaving home.

Chapter 23

Nina admired the fresh vegetables filling up her tiny dining table. She could smell the fresh soil. She could almost smell the nutrients. When you knew more about them, you knew they packed so much more than you'd ever guess by just looking at them. There was something similar about Jay, but she couldn't put her finger on it. He seemed to say more than he actually did, but she couldn't be sure she was reading it right. However, she's just learned something new. He didn't want a baby.

La La reached over the vegetables and touched her arm. "You asked him if he wants a baby?"

"Well, sort of. You should have seen his face when he heard the word 'baby'. It was just this ... blank stare. Like he couldn't understand why anyone would want a baby."

"But... how did you even bring that up? It's not exactly a casual topic."

Nina shook her head. "It doesn't matter. What matters is that I have to get over him and focus on relationships that have a future. Like Adam."

She let the realisation sink in, an overwhelming sadness washing over her. Even if Jay was single, he didn't fit in with her plan. Maybe she needed to just get over it and do what La La had done. She'd gone to a sperm bank and chosen a baby daddy. This was the big news she'd wanted to surprise her with. As excited as Nina was for her friend, she felt even more lost. What if she never found the right one? She was still undecided about Adam. He kept texting her, complimenting anything she said or did, but seeing his name pop up on screen didn't elicit the excitement Nina had felt with Tama, or Jay.

"Are you sure?" La La smiled knowingly. They had discussed Nina's lack of enthusiasm for Adam. Her friend couldn't understand why she'd agreed to a second date with someone like that. Or as La La had put it, someone 'so dull he makes your vagina dry up'.

"What did they say about your eggs?" Nina asked, hoping to change the subject.

La La had explained something about her latest test results – something scary that Nina had missed with the thoughts of Jay crowding her mind.

"That my AMH is low for my age and I may have trouble conceiving. Which means it may take a few tries to get pregnant."

Nina admired her friend's carefree tone. She knew enough about AMH – the ovarian reserve – and how concerning a low count was in terms of fertility. 'A few tries to get pregnant' sounded very optimistic, but Nina didn't have the heart to correct her. Maybe believing in her fertility would help her conceive.

"What's the sperm donor like? Tell me about him!"

La La smiled and looked away. "He's very successful. Tall. Very smart. And he has the most beautiful blue eyes."

She had a giddiness about her, almost like she was in love.

"That's great. So why is he doing this?"

"Well, he's married and already has two kids, so he doesn't want to start another family. He said his sister suffered from infertility and he felt if he could help someone else, he should."

"He's married?" Nina knew little about sperm donors, but she'd imagined them to be single guys, eager to sow their wild oats or something stupid like that. A sperm donor being married didn't seem right, somehow.

La La nodded. "Of course. Most of them are. You wouldn't want a single guy. It'd be some pathetic nerd who couldn't find anyone to have a baby with. Imagine that poor loser."

Nina had never considered the possibility that there could be men out there who wanted to be fathers but couldn't. The whole concept sounded made up. Surely, for every man who wanted to procreate, there were at least 15 women with the same desire, all within a walking distance. That these baby-crazy men would join a sperm bank sounded even more far-fetched. But La La was prone to wild theories. Nina chuckled a little. "But if they're married, it means there's not even a small possibility that … you know."

La La scoffed. "That we find each other through a sperm bank and fall madly in love? Oh, come on!"

"But it's like a modern fairy tale!"

"No! It's like an icky story that ends up in *That's life!* magazine."

Nina shrugged. "Yeah, you're probably right." She must have read too much into that dreamy look. Maybe La La didn't really have feelings towards her sperm donor.

Light outside the window had dimmed. Nina got up to make tea, planning a meal with the new ingredients now piled up on her table. Maybe a vegetable roast? Or just a veggie omelette? She could serve it with Jay's hot sauce, which had turned out to be amazing and not actually as hot as she'd feared. It had a lot of flavour and was great just sprinkled on top of anything.

Nina started chopping capsicum. "So, you don't mind not doing the whole falling in love, getting married thing?"

La La looked out the window. She twined her dragon tattooed arms around each other – one dragon disappearing under another in a tight embrace. "I just know it won't happen. Not like that. The men I fall for, they don't want babies. So, I have to do the baby thing myself. Then one day, when the child is older, I'll fall in love again. And it won't bother me he doesn't want babies because I'll already have one. And they'll be able to see that I'm not a desperate 40-year-old woman trying to get pregnant in my last hour of fertility."

This all made sense in the warped way that La La always

did. Nina thought about the men La La had dated. The description fit. She couldn't imagine any of them wanting a family. Some already had families, all had high-flying careers. As crazy as La La's plan sounded, maybe it was the best of many poor options.

"But will the child have a relationship with their father? Will they know who he is?"

"You can choose either way. This guy is happy to be part of our life and I think it's easier. I don't want to make up some stupid story for the kid. Or like… wait until they're 10 and flip their world upside down. It's a lot easier if they know from the beginning. Lots of kids don't live with their dad."

Nina made a note of how La La talked about 'our life' like she was already pregnant. It must have been nice to have that level of confidence. She couldn't even muster enough confidence in her ability to find someone – anyone – to have a baby with. Let alone trust that she could fall pregnant.

"It's cool he wants to be part of the kid's life. I thought sperm donors were anonymous."

"Yeah, some are. But I chose this guy because he wasn't. And because of all the other stuff."

There was that dreamy look again. Nina had to admit, her friend had the magical air of someone taking charge of their own life. Why couldn't she do that – find someone who offered the future she wanted. Someone like Adam. All she had to do was to shake off this silly crush on Jay and forge ahead with the plan.

CHAPTER 24

Nina approached Jay's door, buzzing with excitement. The glass bottle samples she had ordered from China had finally arrived, and she had printed out mock-up labels to test out how they looked. She had her favourite – a gorgeous, streamlined bottle that showcased both the sauce and the labels beautifully. But this was Jay's decision.

Over the last two weeks, she and Jay had fallen into a comfortable routine of emails and meetings, planning upcoming markets and other sales opportunities, setting up a website, ordering business cards and other bits and bobs. It was easy to work with Jay. He trusted her expertise, made swift decisions, and was willing to spend money on what mattered. Nina tried her best to save his money – organising the best deals with the printers and googling for the right bottle supplier in China. Ordering straight from the manufacturer was riskier, but the savings were huge.

Every time they met, Nina felt the rush of adrenaline. Being around Jay was like a drug she craved, even though their relationship remained platonic. They slotted perfectly in their roles as designer and client. There were no more long silences and Nina had discovered Jay was actually a lot of fun to talk to. Just like Nina, he enjoyed digging deeper and exploring any topic from different viewpoints. With the work on the table, Nina found it easy to discuss anything and everything, related or not. Jay might not have wanted children, or a more intimate relationship, but he was a good friend.

Nina knocked on the door. She could tell Jay was home as his muddy gumboots stood by the door. Chloe barked, and Jay's footsteps approached the door. He let her in and they sat at the kitchen table. It had become their office.

Jay's house had a hunting cabin feel to it. It felt sturdy and bare, like one of those remote Airbnb houses Nina had stayed at when she first toured New Zealand. Except this one didn't have a random selection of expired canned goods left behind by other travellers. Jay had a proper kitchen and comfortable chairs. Otherwise, the decor looked tired and mismatched, as if he couldn't care less.

Nina pulled the bottle samples from her bag and lined them up on the dining table. Jay looked at them in awe, turning each one around, bringing it close to his face, then further away. This was the first time they saw the finished product – the bottle, sauce and the label all working together. Nina had filled the bottles with Jay's hot sauce to create realistic mockups.

"They look so real," Jay remarked.

Nina smiled. "So, which one do you think...?"

Nina held her breath, willing him to pick the right one. She wasn't sure why it mattered so much. She could always try to talk him into picking her favourite. So far, Jay had showed a keen eye for design. He couldn't draw or create anything, but he could tell the difference between something that worked and something that didn't – a quality only the best clients possessed. Nina waited, tapping her fingers on the table.

Jay eyed her with amusement. "I sense there is only one right answer."

Nina broke into laughter. She had to relax. "You're right. I have my favourite, I just wanted to see if you'd agree."

Holding her gaze, Jay slowly circled his hand above the bottles. Without even looking at them, he picked one, the right one, and displayed it to Nina with barely controlled glee.

"This one!"

Had he done a blind draw? He seemed so sure of himself. Nina nodded. "Yes, but why?"

Jay assumed a look of sharp concentration, with a hint of a smile. It was so cute Nina wanted to kiss him. "Because … it makes it look like there's more sauce. Or… because it shows off the label better?"

Nina wouldn't have worded it exactly like that, but she was impressed. "Wow. I have nothing left to teach you!"

"Don't say that, Mr. Miyagi, I can't do this without you!"

It was so much fun to work with Jay that Nina was almost scared of finishing the project. What would happen when the sauce was in the shops and he didn't need her anymore?

It still felt like a long way away, considering how hard it was to get into either of the two supermarket chains that seemed to operate like a cartel. But they'd nearly finished the design, and that meant fewer meetings, fewer emails, less contact. She would have to shift her focus back to her garden and finally learn to grow her own food. With a start, Nina realised she didn't really care about gardening. She enjoyed this. Design, ideas, collaboration... it had turned out the dream of living off the land wasn't really her dream at all. She liked it on paper. It sounded good to be self-sufficient and work outside in the sun. But it wasn't what she truly enjoyed.

Once they'd decided on the bottle, Nina went over the finances with Jay. They were spending more on the labels but a lot less on the bottles and were overall well within the original budget. They talked about the next steps, the Christmas markets and producing content for the website. Nina wanted to get high-quality photos of Jay's chilli peppers, and Jay himself. He seemed uncomfortable with the latter but agreed that it might be a good idea.

After they'd gone through the agenda, Nina packed up her things. Jay rarely walked her out, but this time, he followed. His eyes had the familiar hint of a smile, but also softness Nina hadn't seen before. It wasn't much, but to Nina, it felt significant. She kept her eyes firmly locked with his, lapping up the strange intimacy she wanted so badly, even if she knew it wouldn't work. Something about Jay just seized her, making it hard to think straight.

Jay shifted, looking like he had something to say, but the words refused to materialise. Then he suddenly raised his hand and ran it through Nina's hair, sending shivers through her whole body. She fought the urge to close her eyes. His hand moved slowly and gently and finally pulled away, holding a piece of something wilted and green. Nina recognised it as spinach – something she had put in her morning smoothie. Had that thing been hanging in her hair all day? A flush of embarrassment made Nina erupt in giggles. Jay smiled and flicked away the leaf. It landed on his doormat.

"Wait! I was saving that for dinner!" Nina laughed.

"Sorry." Jay smirked. "I can give you something fresher if you'd like?"

Nina sighed. She wanted to just step in and kiss him, but it felt like she'd have to climb over a wall to get there. He was so close, yet so far away. Besides, he wasn't ready to start a family; she reminded herself. She couldn't build her future on a pleasant working relationship. Even the physical attraction could easily be one-sided. She'd already made this mistake with Tama; she knew how it would end. It was time to rein in her silly, fluttering heart.

Nina took a breath and ran her hands through her hair to check for other smoothie ingredients. All good.

"I better get going," she said.

Jay nodded. Nina waved her hand and walked away, down the hill to her tiny house. It felt like the longest walk in the world.

Chapter 25

A trickle of sweat ran down Jay's spine. He'd agreed to help his mum by turning a new veggie patch behind her house. She wanted to grow some exotic flowers and plants he'd never heard of.

Had it been for veggies, he would have said no. There was no point in her growing a few of her own when she could have as many as she liked from him – from a business she was a part owner of, anyway. Not that his mum accepted much in terms of food. She insisted on picking them herself, always choosing the most deformed and wilted looking produce she could find, so that 'nothing would go to waste'. But Mum was Mum, that was fine. Jay's frustration arose from something else.

It had been a month, and he'd gotten nowhere with Nina. Technically, he had had plenty of opportunities. They met regularly. Every week, he delivered the veggie box. And she came over many times to discuss the business plans, drop off print-outs – 'proofs' she called them – and ask his opinion about the next steps. Her work impressed him. His little homemade product suddenly looked like one of the legitimate hot sauces in the supermarket.

Jay trusted Nina to make all the decisions, order the stock and organise the production line. She seemed keen and did so much research online, Jay was sure she was spending more hours than she would admit. Was she doing it for him, or was she just so excited about the business? Surely, bottling and selling some sauce was not that thrilling. Part of him wanted to believe Nina enjoyed his company.

Jay had finally seen the doctor and was waiting for the results of his biopsy. It felt like the longest wait of his life. This wasn't just about his health. He was waiting to find out if he had anything to offer. Was he a healthy, single guy or a sad, sick one? Even if Nina didn't mind the sickness – even if she was happy to be with him – he would always wonder if it was out of pity. Molly had stayed with him out of pity. Only for a few weeks, to avoid breaking up too close to his father's death, he presumed. It had stung Jay to his very core.

Jay sunk his shovel into the dense, packed topsoil, channeling his anger and frustration into the ground. It had always been his favourite way to deal with complicated emotions. He could have brought the tractor and finished the job in twenty minutes, but he needed to wield the shovel. Mum hadn't asked why, which Jay was grateful for, but he also suspected she knew. He'd been like this his whole life. After a sour breakup, Mum always had her firewood chopped for months ahead and every gruelling physical task taken care of.

Mum had casually asked how it was going with Nina, and whether the sauces would be ready for the Christmas markets. She didn't drop even the tiniest hint about their relationship being anything but professional, yet Jay noticed himself acting defensive. He could tell Mum was being extra careful. She hadn't even mentioned his health since their last conversation. It was hard to stay mad at her. She did everything out of love, even the annoying things. So, Jay had told her about the biopsy, emphasising the likelihood of it being just a simple cyst. Mum had given him a hug so tight she may have bruised him.

After an hour of sweating and probably burning his neck in the sun, Jay was ready to cover up the nicely dug up patch with a black tarp – to kill all the weed seeds in the intensifying spring heat. As he rolled out the tarp, Jay heard an engine turning off and a car door slamming. He instantly knew it was Tyron. Even his footsteps sounded arrogant. Jay pretended not to hear and carried on with his job. Stopping within a conversation distance, Tyron cleared his throat.

"Jay, my man! What are you doing with a shovel? Did you sell the tractor?"

He sounded genuinely concerned. One less thing he could turn into collateral for his startup investment?

"Yeah, IRD came knocking. Had to sell the lot." Jay waited to turn around. Once Tyron saw his face, he'd know Jay was bluffing. But he wanted to see a glimpse of his panic. There it was, a brief flicker behind those dark, sharp eyes.

"Dude, you scared me!" Tyron exhaled. "For a moment I thought you'd really..."

"No. Pissing money down the drain, that's your thing."

Tyron assumed a look of tired superiority. "For your information, I've made a decent profit in the last quarter."

Jay blinked. "Funny. Mum didn't mention you paying her any dividends."

"It's not the right time to take money out. She knows that." Tyron shifted.

"Really?" Jay held his gaze, enjoying the hint of guilt behind his brother's eyes.

"It's complicated."

As infuriating as this sounded, it wasn't actually half as bad as their last exchange. Tyron had pointed out that Jay knew nothing about investing and had told him to 'stick to his effing cucumbers'. Jay suspected there was a reason he was holding back. Tyron wanted something.

"I actually came to ask if you wanted in on it. Our stock is going up like crazy, and with the cryptos picking up at the end of the year, you can easily quadruple your money in two months."

Jay stared at his brother, quietly fuming.

Tyron continued. "Look, I know you didn't like me selling my share of the farm. I didn't enjoy doing it either. But it was the only way. And now we're in a great position. This thing is finally taking off."

Tyron dug up graphs and figures from his phone. They all

showed growth – that's as much as Jay could tell. He saw a flash of a new website selling some kind of investment product, promising generous returns.

"With the housing market turning, there are loads of investors looking for new opportunities, better yield, less work, lower running costs. We're right on the verge of a breakthrough."

He seemed genuinely excited. Jay looked at his brother, suddenly remembering a summer when they were in middle school. Tyron had started a lemonade business with him and two other friends. They'd sold fresh lemonade from a simple cart at the side of the village hall. They didn't have proper permits, but Tyron was young and charming and people tolerated their presence. The lemonade sold like hot cakes during the hot summer. Tyron had driven the little business with gusto, making them work so hard that by the end of the summer, they'd each had enough money to buy mountain bikes. Tyron had taken the largest share and gotten a fancier bike, but then again, it had been his idea. He was the self-appointed CEO.

Even if Tyron was now right about the money, the whole thing bothered Jay to no end. Going into business with him felt like endorsing his lifestyle, the heartbroken women he left behind – and Nina. It all came back to Nina. He had got to her first, chatted her up, said all the right things, before Jay had gotten anywhere. Maybe that's why he hadn't made a move, not knowing what had happened between them.

That's right! He didn't lack courage, he just had too much pride to go after his brother's rejects. Jay ground his teeth. It was a lie, but it made him feel marginally better.

Jay could sense Tyron studying his face, trying to read him. Was there a hint of interest or not?

"You don't have to decide right now. I'll email you the proposal with all the numbers. Have someone you trust look over them with you."

Jay scoffed. Bill the surf instructor? Gary the guitarist? Tyron probably relied on Jay having nobody like that within a 10-mile radius.

"So, what's new with you?" Tyron asked. "Mum said you're going into the sauce business?"

"Just making some hot sauce for the Christmas markets." Jay tried to sound non-committal.

"She said you've done branding and everything. It doesn't sound like a small deal."

Jay knew Tyron was just trying to be supportive, but somehow it came out condescending. His little sauce business was small beans compared to his international investment company. So what? He was doing something with what he had. A bunch of chilli, Dad's old bottling machine, and a neighbour who was a graphic designer.

"The girl who bought the lot down the hill, the one who lives in that tiny house ... She's a graphic designer, so she's helping me out with the labels." Jay saw a look of recognition on Tyron's face. He waited.

Tyron's eyebrows flew up. "Yeah, I think I know her. I met her in town once. We had a drink, and I drove her home. She mentioned she was a designer."

"Yeah?"

"Man, that house of hers is small!" Tyron laughed, expecting Jay to join in. He didn't.

"Bed too small for your liking?" Jay's tone was icy, anger bubbling on the surface now.

"Didn't really get to test the bed, to be honest. I got the feeling she was maybe into someone else." Tyron narrowed his eyes. A huge weight lifted off. The Tyron he knew never passed up an opportunity to kiss and tell. Maybe, just maybe, nothing had happened. And if that was true, Nina must have been the first female in the known universe able to resist his brother's charm.

At Jay's request, Tyron rolled up his sleeves and helped him spread the black tarp over the new veggie patch. They secured it with heavy rocks.

"You know," Tyron said, "Mum had me try your hot sauce. It's not like the one Dad used to make, right? It didn't make my eyeballs sweat."

"No. I changed it." Jay tried to control the irritation in his voice. Was Tyron expecting him not to alter Dad's recipe? Was that recipe considered Dad's legacy? In his mind, Jay composed a comeback about Tyron selling their father's actual legacy – the land he'd farmed, but Tyron quickly corrected himself.

"I mean, it's better. Dad was all about burning your taste buds. Yours is more mellow, it has more flavour. It's something I'd actually use, not just swallow because Dad was daring us to."

Jay nodded his thanks. It felt oddly nice to hear Tyron say something real about their dad, something other than the platitudes people repeated about the deceased. Dad had been a tough guy. He'd loved pranks, and that sauce had been his party trick. He wanted to see you cough and sweat as you tasted it. Tyron had acted like he enjoyed the burn. Jay had thought his brother and dad were on the same wavelength – one that Jay couldn't tune in to, even though he swallowed the sauce. He swallowed more than anyone. Damn the burn.

With the veggie patch finished, Jay noticed their mum behind the window, fondly watching them work together. She looked so happy. Jay almost wanted to forgive everything Tyron had done. Almost.

Mum opened the window and poked her head out. "I'm so glad you're both here! I really want to talk to you about Christmas. It's a while away, but I've been planning the menu and I want your input!"

Jay and Tyron exchanged a wary glance and a hint of a smile. Mum must have been desperate for them to bury the hatchet. She rarely started the Christmas planning this early in the year.

CHAPTER 26

Panic tightened Nina's gut. It was time for her second date with Adam. She'd arrived at the local pub, dressed casually for a quiet night of drinks and conversation. The rest of Raglan disagreed. It was the night of the Town Fair, with the night markets spread alongside the main road. The locals had filled every available parking spot and created a buzzing crowd around the pub.

After finding a car park three blocks away, Nina already knew the night would be nothing like what she'd envisioned. It was too late to cancel. Down at the pub, Adam stood at the front door like some kind of out-of-place signpost, dressed in a canary yellow shirt Nina hated at first sight. He looked too tidy for Raglan. She wanted to take him down to the beach and roll him in the sand.

"Is it always so busy here?" Adam gestured at the pub.

"No. Sorry, I completely forgot about the Town Fair. We won't get a seat in here. Do you mind if we go for a walk first? I think there'll be more room when the market ends."

"What time is that?"

Nina shrugged. "No idea. Probably before the pub closes, though."

She could tell her ambiguity made Adam uncomfortable, although he was working hard not to show it.

"Okay," Adam agreed. "Let's have a look around the village first. I haven't been here in a long time. It's changed a lot. I also want to see the beachfront. I hear they've redone that?"

Nina nodded. She would have been perfectly happy to wander around, talking, but Adam seemed to need a solid reason for moving his legs – like a marathon or something.

Once outside, Nina held her breath, hoping no one she knew would spot her. She wasn't ready to introduce Adam. What would she call him? He wasn't a boyfriend. Was he even a friend? She didn't want to say they were on a date. Nina tried to steer them to a quiet side street, but Adam insisted on seeing 'how the town planning had panned out' on the main strip, chattering about differences in council approach to urban development between Hamilton and Raglan. Double yawn. They passed hotdog vendors, grilled chicken, an ice cream cart, and many little stalls selling local art that was more 'Kiwiana' than creative.

And then she saw Jay.

Nina couldn't believe she'd forgotten about the hot sauce stall. They'd talked about the Town Fair and the possibility of testing out the market with their first batch of products.

Jay had shrugged about the idea, and they'd left it at that. The labels were not the final ones. These were a short digital run Nina had done to tie them over – and to avoid using the old handwritten ones Jay still had lying around. Still, they looked good on the new bottles.

Nina stalled, trying to think of a way out, but a steady stream of people pushed them along, nearing Jay's stall. To make matters worse, Adam instantly noticed the sauce.

"Look at this!" he exclaimed. "I haven't seen this in the shops."

Nina glanced at Jay, who smiled back tentatively, probably not knowing what to make of the guy in the yellow shirt.

"It's not in the shops yet," Jay responded politely.

Nina turned to Adam. She had to sort this out. Somehow. "Adam, this is my neighbour, Jay. I've been helping him with these labels," Nina said.

"You've done more than that," Jay said.

Jay looked at Nina, then at Adam. She could feel the question hanging in the air.

"I'm just showing Adam around town," Nina offered, hoping that was enough.

"This is our second date. We met online," Adam chirped, picking up a sauce bottle. "Now, how does this sauce go with fresh pasta? Would you recommend trying it with tagliatelle or maybe ravioli?"

Nina willed the earth to open up and swallow her whole. It didn't. Why would anyone volunteer such embarrassing information? And why did he have to volunteer it to Jay? Nina could feel Jay's eyes on her, but avoided his gaze. Instead, she focused her attention on the hot sauce labels. Jay had placed them a little too high. She would have to talk to him about that.

"Any pasta, really," Jay replied to Adam, turning to Nina. "I didn't know you had a dating profile. Which site?"

"I ... I took it down," Nina stammered.

She hadn't, but she feared Jay would look her up the moment they walked away. She would at least make him look through every site, buying her enough time so she could take it down for real.

Adam beamed happily at Nina. "I didn't know you'd already taken yours down," he said to Nina, delighted. "I'll do the same when I get home."

Nina closed her eyes for a second. She wanted to disappear. She would have rather been back at the dentist, getting drilled without anaesthesia. "You don't have to," she tried to say breezily. It came out croaky, like her voice was deserting her.

Adam beamed at her. "I was thinking about it after our first date. I should have just done it. But I wasn't sure you were in the same place."

His genuine excitement made Nina's insides hurt. Here she was, affirming her brand-new relationship with a guy she barely liked, right in front of a guy she couldn't stop thinking about. Just looking at Jay, with his unruly curls falling on his forehead, made her a little heady. The dark lashes framing those hard-to-read eyes and his hands, ever busy with work, sinewy and strong. Nina had to make a conscious effort not to look at his rolled-up sleeves and tanned forearms, not linger on the way his muscles and tendons tightened as he picked up a cardboard box... *This was ridiculous.*

They chatted for a moment about the hot sauce. Jay had sold about twenty bottles, mostly to locals who promised to test it and give him feedback. It was a good start. As Jay talked, Adam slid his hand at the small of Nina's back, then around her waist.

"Should we go for that walk now, babe? Before it gets dark," he asked.

The word 'babe' didn't fit in Adam's mouth. It was like a foreign object he had accidentally swallowed and coughed up. Nina shifted to lessen the contact of his hand on her body. They left, waving Jay goodbye.

Nina remembered she had a meeting with Jay the next day about the upcoming Christmas market. After this, it would be awkward, but Nina could hardly wait. She wanted to be alone with Jay, away from Adam.

"It's a cute little place," Adam said. "I get why you like it so much."

Nina had to admit Raglan was at its cutest. They followed the palm tree-lined main street to the waterfront and watched a group of kids jump into the water from the little walking bridge. They looked happy, fearless. The sun hung low in the horizon.

"I guess I could imagine living here. If it came to that," Adam announced in his practical tone.

He was already moving here? Nina felt conflicted. Adam was a nice person who genuinely liked her and approached their future with excitement. Nina thought about the future. It was there, approaching her at a terrifying speed. Nina took a breath and tried to relax. The sunset had painted the sky a soft peachy orange. It was beautiful. Peaceful. This was exactly what she'd been looking for. Someone who wasn't afraid to just go for it, start a life together, start a family. She could imagine Adam there, running after the kids, keeping them safe. He seemed so sensible, so organised, so uncomplicated. He would make a brilliant father.

No longer in the presence of Jay, Nina felt more rational, her goals slowly coming into focus again. She was tired. After weeks and weeks of waiting for Jay to make a move, to tell her he liked her – anything, really – she wanted something real. Someone who liked her. Someone who wasn't afraid of having babies.

Adam looked at her. "Are you okay? You seem quiet. But I don't know you well enough to say if this is within a normal range for you."

It was such a weird choice of words, delivered in Adam's earnest style. Yet Nina appreciated his concern. She nodded and gave him a little smile. "I'm fine. I often go quiet when I see something beautiful."

"Okay, that makes sense, like with the cherry blossoms? That's good to know."

He looked like he was making a mental note in his 'Nina' folder and filing it away. Something about that gesture, the way he was orienting himself with their future, warmed Nina's heart. She reached for his hand. "Come on."

Nina pulled Adam onto the walking bridge, and they crossed to the other side where the sandy beach was glowing in the pink evening light. Nina kicked off her shoes. He untied his sneakers, carefully rolled his socks into them, and followed her down to the sand. They walked for a moment and found a grassy bank to sit on. The water on this side was always nice and calm, sheltered from the open sea.

This would be the perfect moment for a kiss, Nina thought.

She wondered if Adam could sense it. She turned to look at him, letting her eyes lower to his lips. Adam didn't miss the universal signal. He leaned in and kissed her, softly, like his lips were asking a question. It didn't make Nina want to tear his shirt off, but his style suited the moment. It tasted like Adam – uncomplicated and earnest. A part of Nina wanted to do something crazy, to take off her shirt and jump into the water, just to see what he'd do. To see if, underneath all the niceness, he was a red-blooded male. But she was getting cold, and the chances were Adam was exactly what he seemed. And there was nothing wrong with that.

They got up and walked back to the village. Adam talked about an upcoming marathon he was training for. He asked

Nina to go for a run with him. As soon as she agreed, she knew she had no desire to run, ever. She got plenty of exercise, shovelling the soil in her garden, and walking up the hill to Jay's house. As the thought hit her, she noticed the market stalls on the main street had all but disappeared. Jay had left. Assuming they were going for a drink at the pub as planned, Adam led them to the door. Nina hesitated.

"Would you mind terribly if we call it a night?" she asked. "I was up early this morning and I'm getting tired. I wouldn't be such good company. Alcohol makes me even sleepier."

"Oh, okay." Adam looked a little thrown. In fact, he looked so disappointed Nina wanted to kick herself.

"I could come in for a cup of tea, maybe?" she suggested, biting her lip.

Adam relaxed and led them inside. They ordered bread and dipping sauce and two cups of tea.

"I wouldn't feel right drinking if you're not," Adam said.

Nina could see his logic. She could see the logic in everything he said and did. It was the first thing you noticed. There must have been more to him. Humans were not that one-dimensional. Adam must have had a messy, dark side, and she hoped to see it – a glimpse of genuine passion, irrationality, something that wasn't so neat and well presented.

Nina let the peppermint tea burn its way down her throat. She hated her own thoughts. She sounded like she was looking for trouble. No wonder she ended up falling for men who weren't so called 'marriage material,' whatever that even meant. The man sitting across the table, expertly using a napkin, was marriage material. He was an advertisement to the male gender – a gleaming example of good upbringing and decency amid testosterone-fueled, commitment-phobic cave men. He deserved a medal, which he would probably display oh-so-proudly in a glass cabinet with his marathon trophies. Nina sighed. She wasn't being fair. The inner conflict had created such a perfect storm in her gut she could hardly digest the Turkish bread. She had to get out of there.

Wolfing down the last piece of bread, which she already felt her tightly wound stomach rejecting, Nina grabbed her handbag and got up. "Sorry, I don't feel too well. I better get back home."

Despite her protests, Adam escorted her to her car. The three-block walk felt endless. Adam wanted to use the time to exchange as many bits of trivia as possible.

"What's your favourite colour?" he pressed her.

Nina blinked. "I... don't have one."

"What do you mean?"

"I think it's because I work with colours. There is an endless amount of different shades. One green can look horrible where another green looks great. It depends on the context, you know? I don't think there is such a thing as a beautiful colour or an ugly colour."

Adam nodded, as if the lack of a clear favourite colour was an unfortunate but acceptable shortcoming on Nina's character.

"My favourite colour is blue," he stated.

Nina wondered if it was his true preference or an exemplary answer. At least, he hadn't said 'canary yellow.' Nina smiled to herself.

"I can give you a Pantone code for this one shade of blue that I'm really into right now," Nina said, feeling cheeky.

Adam turned to her, his interest piqued. He took out his phone, waiting for Nina to continue. "Okay, I'm ready. What is it?"

Dear God, he was going to write it down! Nina searched her brain for the colour code. "540C."

She only remembered the code because she'd just been looking for the perfect shade of deep indigo for Jay's labels. Nina could hardly believe her eyes as she watched Adam type in the numbers. Did he have a file titled 'Nina 101' on his phone? Or did he email stuff to his home computer to populate an Excel sheet? Was this flattering or creepy, or maybe both?

As they reached the car, Nina turned to give Adam a quick kiss. She wanted to pre-empt the goodbye routine, but Adam wasn't so easily rerouted. As soon as their lips touched, Adam grabbed her face with both hands and held on. Had Nina been onboard, it might have felt amazing. Nina wriggled free and slipped into her car. Adam smiled and waved. Either he sensed nothing was wrong, or he hid it well. On the way home, Nina reviewed every moment of the confusing, awkward second date. She tried to skip the most confusing part, the one with Jay, but it kept popping up.

She had to figure out how she felt about Adam.

It wasn't helpful to compare Adam to Jay. She wasn't choosing between the two. She was trying to find someone who wanted the same things she did. So, did she like Adam? Could she imagine a future with him? She couldn't possibly lead him on any longer. He was already getting serious. She had to decide what she wanted, sooner rather than later.

CHAPTER 27

"Why don't you ask Jay out?" said La La, in-between big slurps of green smoothie.

Nina had needed her friend's voice. After a fitful night and a morning pacing around her tiny house – a challenge because of the limited floor space – she'd packed up her laptop and jumped in the car, hoping that La La had time for coffee. They met at the farmers' market. To Nina's shock, La La had answered the phone fully awake, on her way to stock up on organic greens.

They sat down at the outdoor tables, serenaded by an old Māori guy with a beaten-up guitar. The market brimmed with spring produce, spilling out on the sun-soaked yard after being cooped up indoors over the winter months. The strawberries, avocados, seedlings, and baby potatoes were once again available.

"I still don't know how he really feels about me," Nina contemplated. "I can't be sure. If I said something, and it turned out he's not interested... It would be horrible. And it would be so awkward to do business with him. Plus, he doesn't want a baby."

"Yet. We went over this. You said, he said he's not there yet."

"And I don't have time to wait for anyone to get there," Nina sighed.

"You don't really know where he's at. You guys haven't really discussed this. If you like him, ask him out. If he says no, then you at least know where you stand."

It sounded so simple, coming from La La. Although Nina couldn't imagine her friend being rejected that much. She somehow always got what she wanted.

"But I don't want to be the one to ask," Nina protested. "I want a guy who has the balls to ask me out. If he really likes me, that means he's more chickenshit than I am, since he couldn't work up the courage to do it himself. I can't win."

"Jay doesn't strike me as the timid type. But maybe he is out of practice? I suppose he doesn't have that much action where he lives and works."

"Maybe. His brother is a real charmer though."

"Oh yes, the condom guy."

La La laughed and Nina wondered why she'd even shared this story with her friend. She'd also told La La about Adam, and her reaction had been fairly unenthusiastic.

"God, you have a lot of guys in your life!" La La exclaimed.

Nina coughed up a piece of her bliss ball. She never thought anyone would say this about her, especially La La.

Her friend usually had more than enough going on in her own life to rival Nina's hopeless crushes and awkward first dates. However, since La La's interest had shifted from whirl-pool love affairs to having a baby, their roles had changed. Nina felt like she'd first contracted the horrible baby fever and passed it on to her best friend. Or maybe it was just something that happened to every woman on the wrong side of 35. She couldn't ask her mum. She'd had her baby at age 25 – back when the societal pressure exceeded the pressures of any biological clock. This was new territory.

"I don't have a lot of guys! That's ridiculous. I'm not looking for a one-night stand, anyway. I want a baby! Maybe Adam is my best chance at that? I've wasted so much time with guys like Tama who would never in a million years settle down."

La La seemed to flinch at the mention of Tama. "Speaking of Tama ..." she started, and paused to slurp the rest of her smoothie. Nina waited.

"He asked about you."

Goosebumps sprouted on Nina's skin. "What do you mean? Like how I'm doing?"

"No, more like if you're seeing anyone."

Nina felt a familiar heat rise to her face. "I thought he was seeing that new designer?"

La La bit her lip. "He was. Now, he's not. She's gone. They replaced her with a guy. Probably a smart move."

Nina felt guilty for not showing interest in her old colleagues. She was no longer up-to-date on the office gossip. "But why would he... when?"

"It was a few days ago. I told him I'd find out. I wanted to talk to you first."

Nina sighed. Why now? Why, after all the hard work of moving away and moving on with her life? It was not fair.

Seeing Nina relax a little, La La took a deep breath and continued. "It may have been a little my fault he... you know."

Nina froze. She had a feeling she would not like this. "What did you do?"

"I... may have accosted him for leading you on. Sorry, I wasn't having the best day. I missed you and I kind of blamed him for everything. I felt like if he hadn't treated you the way he did, you would have stayed."

Nina felt ashamed. "Tama knew what he was doing. Nobody does that much flirting by accident."

"No, that's the thing. I think he liked you but thought he didn't have a shot with you. So, the flirting was more like... I don't know, like flirting with a married lady. Or someone famous. Or royalty!"

La La grinned from ear to ear. It was the stupidest thing Nina had ever heard, but also sweet. "I'm sure nobody would confuse me with royalty."

"No, but you're exotic. You're from a faraway country. The assumption is that one day you'll go back and marry someone your own kind. I think Tama just instinctively thought it would never work out. Like a holiday fling."

This kind of made sense. Tama had his whakapapa, his extended family. He had the places his ancestors had lived in. There was no way Nina could ever be as connected to any place on earth, but she wasn't a fleeting visitor. She'd held a job and had permanent residency. She'd spent years in New Zealand building friendships and connections. Now she even had property. Her divorced parents lived across the globe. She didn't have a solid home anywhere else.

"I don't think that though," La La said. "I'm okay with you living in Raglan if that makes you happy, but you're not allowed to fly back to Finland."

Nina smiled, blinking away tears. "Thank you."

"So, what should I tell him? Are you available or not?"

Nina paused. A few months ago, the answer would have been a simple yes. But now, she wasn't sure. There was a certain restlessness about Tama. He kept moving, planning the next party, working on the next big thing. Whatever happened, he would make light of it, turn it into a joke and make you laugh. It had been attractive, almost intoxicating, to be around. His buoyancy shielded you from the shitty side of life. Nothing could ever get to him. But, without the stomach-butterflies distracting her mind, Nina knew nobody was like that, deep down. Tama was hiding a lot under that smile. He was one of those people who had to keep moving, lest the shadows catch him. Even if he could get real with her, she wasn't sure she could handle whatever was lurking underneath.

Watching Nina fall into silence, La La picked up a magazine and flipped through pages of vegan party food.

"No," Nina finally said.

La La looked up. "No, what?"

"Tell him I'm not available."

"So, you're officially dating the notebook guy?"

That made Adam sound more attractive than he really was. He was definitely no Ryan Gosling. He was the literal 'notebook guy' – the guy who made notes.

Nina sighed. "No, please don't tell anyone that. I'll deal with it."

"Okay," said La La. "I'll make up something."

That sounded even scarier, but Nina let it go. Did it really matter what anyone at her old office thought about her?

CHAPTER 28

Nina drove home with a little more clarity. Being able to leave her old crush behind felt like an achievement. She wasn't any closer to her goals, but felt freer. Or maybe she had just swapped one pointless crush for another?

As Nina gathered her papers for the meeting with Jay that afternoon, she felt the same butterflies returning. Why was she this weak? Why couldn't she make a sensible, informed decision based on facts and be happy with that? Adam was that choice. The only problem was that deep down Nina knew she couldn't make that choice. She had to let him know.

Nina sat down at her laptop and composed a message. Briefly, she thought about calling him, but then decided she was better with the written word. Seeing him again would have probably been the decent thing to do, but what if she got all confused again and ended up kissing him instead? That would only postpone the inevitable. Nina wrote a long letter, then edited it down. There was too much detail, too much wiggle room. He didn't need to know much, but he needed to know she was serious. The letter got shorter and shorter, then longer again, until Nina noticed she was late for meeting Jay. She saved the email as a draft, grabbed her things, and rushed out the door.

On the way up the hill, Nina suddenly remembered her appearance. She hadn't even looked in the mirror. Was her hair doing the annoying flipping up thing on one side? She couldn't tell by feeling it with her hand. Either way, her face must have been shiny. Jogging uphill didn't really help matters. But maybe this needed to happen. If she properly blew her chances with Jay, she could just focus on growing her own food. Since Jay had begun delivering her vegetables, Nina's gardening had taken a long hiatus. She had let her veggie patch get covered in weeds, every potted herb pushed flowers and her footpath was still unpaved. It was hard to keep yourself motivated when you only answered to yourself. She always got the most cleaning and organising done when she was expecting a visitor. But even La La hadn't visited for a while.

Wading through the long, wet grass, Nina struggled to get a footing with her slippery gumboots. Who tried to run in gumboots, anyway?

Up on the hill, she spotted Jay by his car. She watched him open the door and get inside. Nina took a big breath and sped up for the last spurt, catching him right before the car was moving. Jay lowered the window and gave her a questioning look.

"I'm so sorry I'm late. I got caught up with … something," Nina panted. "Where are you going?"

Jay killed the engine and got out of the car. "I thought you weren't coming, so I was going shopping. But I can do that later."

"Sorry," Nina sighed again. "I should have called. But when I saw I was running late, I just panicked and got on my way and it's really hard to make a phone call when you're running uphill."

"But if you'd called, I would have just waited for you and you wouldn't have had to run at all," Jay said, amused.

Nina felt like an idiot. Her cheeks burned, but she rather enjoyed the feeling. She must have had a masochistic side that enjoyed being wrong – and teased. "You're right. I don't know why I didn't call."

Jay chuckled and led her into the house.

He didn't seem to be into expensive gear and status items. No Bang & Olufsen speakers, leather seats or whatever else guys bought to impress visitors. Instead, Alice's pot plants mingled with well-worn, functional furnishing. Jay's TV was small and pushed to the corner of the lounge as if only need-ed occasionally. Instead, there was a huge sleeping mat for Chloe, and a bookshelf full of random items – books, yes, but also family photos, scotch glasses, pocketknives, and keys. Two unused scented candles had gathered a layer of dust. Maybe Jay didn't host that many candlelit dinners?

Nina loved decorating. She didn't want a territorial man

who'd never let a woman alter his sacred bachelor pad. In her mind, she'd already refurbished Jay's house. The carpet had been replaced, the ceiling painted a lighter colour, and the bare lounge had a few more cushions, a Kilim rug maybe, and a big house plant...

They sat down at the kitchen table, which was half-covered in earlier label mockups, bottle order sheets and other accumulated papers. Having a table so big you could leave papers lying on it felt like a strange luxury to Nina. She had to declutter daily. If she didn't put everything away immediately after use, she had nowhere to eat or sit or lie down.

Jay watched her, his eyes burning with questions. Nina swallowed. She didn't want to discuss Adam, not until she'd sent that email and properly broken up with him. Hoping to quell any questions, she set her laptop on the table and dove straight into work. "Did you get the labels?"

She'd ordered the final labels and had them sent to Jay's address. They should have arrived the day before. The schedule was tight, but Nina trusted her supplier – they went above and beyond to deliver on time.

Jay raised his brow. "No, I don't think so."

Nina drew a deep breath. The market was tomorrow. They didn't have enough of the temporary ones. "Really? Did you get a card to collect? They may not leave it at the door if you're not home."

"But I'm always home."

Nina looked at him pointedly. "Being in the greenhouse or

out in the field doesn't count."

She got up, grabbed the pile of mail Jay had on his kitchen counter, and flipped through it. And there it was. A courier card with yesterday's date on it! Nina waved it triumphantly in the air, but then it hit her. "It's Saturday! Can we still pick it up?"

She read the card. The collection was from a Raglan address, but only until 4 p.m. on Saturdays. It was already past 4:30 p.m. Nina sat down at the table, furious at Jay for not checking his mail, and furious with herself for not checking Jay's mail. She shouldn't have trusted him with that. She'd seen how he let his mail pile up.

Jay grabbed the courier card from her and looked it over. Then he took his car keys and headed to the door.

"Come on," he said.

"Where are we going?"

"To pick up the package," Jay replied, already out the door.

Nina jogged behind him to his car and got in, annoyed at his sparse communication. They were supposed to be a team.

After a moment of driving, she noticed Jay turned away from the town. "Okay, you really need to explain what we're doing here."

Jay grinned, clearly enjoying himself. "We are going to see Old Neil. He's my friend Steve's dad. He works at the courier company. We'll ask him for a favour."

"We'll ask him to drive back to work after closing and spend his Saturday night looking for our package?"

"Exactly."

"He must be a really nice, helpful guy."

"No, he's an old grump. But you are a beautiful young lady, so I'm hoping when he sees you, he'll be inspired to help."

Nina blushed. "I'm not that young," she mumbled.

"You're a hell of a lot younger than old Neil," Jay laughed.

Jay had called her beautiful! This must have been the first time he'd said anything remotely related to her looks. Nina felt flustered. She had to remind herself it wasn't anything romantic. Jay was just focused on getting those labels. Maybe he only meant that no female had visited Old Neil in a long time. Based on the remote hilltop Jay was driving to, this seemed likely.

After ten minutes, Jay stopped the car in front of an ugly seventies brick house with dirty mint-coloured window-panes, surrounded by overgrown hydrangea bushes. An impressive view of rolling hills opened up behind the house.

Jay knocked on the screen door. There was no answer. Of course, he wasn't home. How could any of this work out? Nina racked her brain for a solution. Could she organise another batch of emergency labels from her supplier, begging them to run a batch tonight? It was unlikely.

Not seeming worried, Jay circled the house, heading to a standalone garage. Nina followed. She spotted more hydrangea bushes, an overgrown lawn, and a rusty shovel sticking out of a patch of turned soil. An unfinished veggie patch, maybe? The shovel must have stood there a while since weeds already twined around it. What a shame. It looked like fertile land. You could grow a lot more than hydrangea around here. Jay noticed her looking around.

"He's divorced," he said, as a way of an explanation.

They reached the garage, and Jay opened the side door. Apart from the usual clutter of cardboard boxes, tools, and pesticide, it was empty.

"A-ha! He's fishing."

"How do you know?"

"The boat's gone," Jay said, like it was the most self-explanatory thing in the world.

Nina hopped behind Jay, back to his car. She looked at her watch. It was too late to get anything else printed. They would have to cancel the market or just go without labels.

The drive back felt somber. Nina mulled over their equally poor options and missed Jay driving past their houses. Instead, he turned towards the harbour. When the car stopped, Nina woke up to where they were. "What... are we doing here?"

"I know where he fishes," Jay said.

"Are we planning on swimming to his boat or something?"

Jay looked at her with amusement. "No, we'll take my boat. Unless you prefer swimming?"

"You have a boat?" she asked.

"I have a boat," Jay repeated, amused, like having a boat was akin to having a car or a phone.

They walked down a long dock lined with boats of various sizes. Jay stopped at a white motorboat. It wasn't the largest of them, but it looked fairly new and seaworthy. Jay produced a key and unlocked the chain attaching the boat to the marina. He then untied the two other ropes, helped Nina onboard, and hopped on himself. After a few coughs, the engine started, and he steered them carefully away from the dock, onto open sea.

Nina had been so focused on the chase that she took a while to take in the gorgeous scenery. The sun was low over the horizon, making the water sparkle like an endless diamond carpet. If they hadn't been here for sauce labels, this could have been an amazing date. Nina sighed, watching Jay steer the boat toward a little island ahead of them. The wind caught in his T-shirt, flapping it like a flag. She could see every muscle in his chest.

Looking down at her own shirt, Nina saw she was similarly on display and tried to wrap her cardigan around her midsection. How could she possibly charm the old grump in her worn-out T-shirt, jeans, and gumboots?

This was the first time she'd gone to Jay's house without a session of standing in front of the mirror, seriously considering her wardrobe and fixing her hair and makeup. She looked her absolute frumpiest. The wind would soon complete her look with a bird's nest of greasy, limp hair.

But it was too late now. She could only hope Old Neil was so old he had cataracts.

Closer to the island, Jay slowed down. After a moment,

he pointed at something in the distance. Nina couldn't see anyone. A good twenty seconds later, she finally noticed a small boat anchored in a small bay. An old man, presumably Old Neil, sat at the back, holding a fishing rod. Jay steered slowly within a yelling distance and killed the engine. For a moment, they drifted closer. Neil's boat bobbed in the waves caused by Jay's engine and he craned his neck, trying to see who was coming.

"Damn, Hartley! You're scaring away the fish!" Neil glared at them.

Jay smiled, turned on the engine one more time, and ran it for a couple of seconds to get them closer. Eventually, they ended up within a jumping distance from Old Neil's boat. Jay grinned at the old guy. "Neil! Aren't we happy to find you! Listen, we need your help…"

He explained their predicament. Nina had never heard him sound so humble. Neil barely took his eyes off the fishing rod, his brow still knitted.

"So, I would be most grateful if you could let us in after hours to fetch that one package," Jay finished.

They waited. Neil scoffed and turned to them, now taking in Nina for the first time. "You think you can boss around an old man? Show your girlfriend you're a big shot, huh?"

Nina cringed. This wasn't looking good.

Jay gestured at Nina. "Nina here is the designer. She made those labels I'm talking about. She's helping me out, going above and beyond really."

Neil gave her another look and scoffed. Did he not believe Jay? What could they possibly say to sway this curmudgeon? It was clear he would do nothing out of the goodness of his heart. Did they have any leverage?

Nina raised her hand and flashed another tentative smile. "Jay has a tractor."

Both men stared at her, confused.

"I mean, if you ever need help with turning the soil or anything like that? The summer's coming. A good time to set up a veggie patch."

Neil turned to his fishing, but Nina could tell his ears perked up. Jay didn't miss this either. "Nina's right. I'd be happy to come over and sort you out. You have a good-sized section. You could easily grow enough veg for your own needs."

"Nothing fickle," Neil harrumphed. "I don't have time to weed three times a week."

"We'll cover it up first, kill all the seeds. I'll get you some hardy seedlings and they'll be well on their way before the weeds even make a start. You'll get a decent crop even if you don't weed it once."

Nina turned to Jay, whispering. "Is that true?"

"Yeah. It won't be an amazing yield, but with the right plants, it'll work. He'll want potato and kumara. It'll be fine."

Neil sat quietly, staring at his fishing rod. Then he dug into his pocket, whipped out something and threw it at them. Nina ducked instinctively, but Jay caught the flying item – a set of keys.

"The blue one will get you through the back door. The security code is six-five-five-seven. Turn it back on when you're done, and lock up!"

"No problem," Jay yelled, his voice bursting with thrill. "We'll bring these back tonight."

"Tomorrow's fine. I'm not going back until Monday." Nina wondered if that was the number one reason he wasn't that willing to help; he hated his work and preferred being here, out on the water, as far away from it as possible. Who could blame him?

"Tomorrow then," Jay confirmed. "I'll bring the tractor."

Neil nodded. It seemed he was just waiting for them to leave, to restore the peace and quiet and catch fish.

Jay backed out of the bay and steered them back towards the harbour. When out of earshot, he turned to Nina. "Good call," he said.

It looked like he wanted to say more. Nina waited for a moment, but he must have swallowed the rest.

"Thanks," she replied. "But you realise I just volunteered you to work on someone else's garden?" Jay shrugged. "We do that a lot around here. No biggie."

His statement gave Nina a jolt. Why had she never asked Jay to help her out with her garden? She could have saved hours of back-breaking work, turning the soil with a shovel. Nina wanted to kick herself for being so stupid. Instead of being temporarily delivered fresh produce at her door, she could have asked for gardening help to set herself up for the future. She could get comfortable in gumboots, but deep down, she really was a lazy city girl.

CHAPTER 29

Jay glanced at the woman sitting next to him, her light blonde hair wildly flapping in the wind. Her eyes sparkled and even though she kept wrapping herself in a fluffy white cardigan, Jay could see the shape of her body. The firm, round breast and the lean waist he wanted to wrap his hands around. He looked away and told himself to focus. It was getting late. They had to find the right package and spend the night hand labelling at least a hundred bottles of sauce. He needed Nina's help, and he couldn't risk it by making a move on her.

As far as he knew, she had a boyfriend. Jay hoped the second date with the yellow-shirted man hadn't resulted in a third. He'd been the tidy type, just like Tyron. Someone who probably 'maintained' their nails and cleaned the bottoms of their expensive shoes. Maybe Nina preferred tidiness. She'd invited Tyron to her home and now dated this other city guy.

Taking note, Jay had started showering more frequently and tried to keep his house in order. Well, apart from the mail. But everything he had was worn out and old-fashioned. Neither his wardrobe nor his house would impress any female. He definitely didn't have the 'attention to detail' Tyron always lectured about. Even the sauce label, which contained maybe twenty words altogether, had to be proof-read by Nina and his mum.

"What was the alarm code?" Jay suddenly remembered. Had he already lost this detail as well?

"Six-five-five-seven," Nina replied without missing a beat. "I tried to find a rule to memorise it but haven't come up with one yet. I don't have a pen and my phone is out of battery."

Her phone seemed to be constantly out of battery. Jay memorised this detail for the future. Maybe he could buy her a new phone for Christmas. Or was that too weird? They were just neighbours, working together on a short-lived project of launching one product. Jay had heard Nina talking about other clients and jobs she was pitching for. She would move on to other products and leave Jay selling his sauce. Would Nina still help him get the sauce in the shops? She was already doing way more than he had ever expected from a graphic designer. Jay wasn't sure if she was like this with all her clients or just him.

Ten minutes later, they had already moored the boat and were driving to the courier office in town. Jay circled the building and found the staff car park right outside the back door. It was getting dark, and he regretted not taking a flashlight. He should have had one in the car. But then again, sneaking around with a flashlight might draw more attention than they wanted. They had keys, but he doubted the company headquarters would have approved their visit.

Jay opened the door and Nina stepped in, looking for the alarm keypad. An alarm beeped somewhere, but it was dark inside. Jay reached for the light switch by the door, but Nina stopped him. "Don't. It might draw attention from the road. They have those big windows."

Jay withdrew his finger. "Good call."

"I can't find the alarm," Nina hissed. "What do we do?"

"Just follow the beeping," Jay urged.

He followed Nina inside, but it was dark. Soon enough, he could no longer see her.

"Found it!" Her voice rang from ahead of him.

The beeping stopped. Jay sighed. He heard Nina rummaging around in another room and followed her into a small warehouse full of shelves. She'd found a light, which revealed a room full of undelivered parcels – alongside the walls and on the long, ceiling-high shelves set up in the room's middle. This could take hours.

"Do you think they have a manual logbook or something we could use for a reference?" Nina asked, her voice betraying her doubt.

"No, I think it's all electronic. And we can't turn on the computers, if that's what you're thinking."

"Not what I was thinking, but we have to figure out their system. They must organise these in some logical way."

"You think?"

Jay didn't have that much faith in the courier business. But Nina was probably right. Neil and his colleagues must have had a system for locating a parcel in the storage room. They started going through packages on the two closest shelves.

"These are all town addresses," Jay noted. "Rural must be somewhere else."

He moved on to check the next shelf, then the next. Finally, he spotted an address in their neighbourhood.

"Here, this road is close to us!"

Nina rushed to his aid, starting from the other end of the same shelf. After a while, they met in the middle. Jay's arm brushed against Nina's as he reached for the last parcel. It wasn't the right one either, but he took a moment to study the label, just to be there, right next to her. He could smell her shampoo or something else coconutty, mixed with sea salt. Jay wanted to touch her so badly. But could he, as a friend? Jay snuck his arm behind Nina's back and tapped her on the opposite shoulder.

She jerked around on a frightened gasp, stumbling into his shoulder. "Oh, my God! What was that?"

Jay couldn't help laughing. "Just me. Sorry."

Nina's laugh rang with nerves. "Not cool! It's creepy enough in here."

She tried to shove him. Jay didn't budge, enjoying the feel of her body right next to her. He expected her to step back, but she held right next to him, her eyes glinting in the low light.

Jay fought the urge to lean in and kiss her. She was so close. But before he could make a move, Nina turned her attention to the shelves, eyes browsing the labels on the package. She picked up a small parcel. "Found it!"

The package looked a lot smaller than Jay had expected. "That's it?"

"It's got the printer's logo, and your name on it, so yeah," Nina replied, rushing out the door. "We should go." She punched in the security code on her way out. Jay locked the door behind them. In the car, Nina ripped open the courier bag and pulled out five neat rolls. She held the printing up in the faint evening light, but it was hard to tell what it really looked like.

"I'll have to look at this in daylight tomorrow."

"I'm sure they're fine," Jay said.

"Do you need help with labeling?" Nina asked.

Jay wanted to scream 'Yes!', but could he really ask her to stay up all night? It had been a long day.

"I still haven't even shown you the sales material," Nina said. "You know how we were supposed to have a meeting and then ended up on a boat instead?"

From the corner of his eye, Jay could see she was giving him a teasing smile. "I'm sorry. It's all my fault. I should have checked my mail."

"I kept thinking I should have checked your mail. I thought about it earlier, but forgot."

"Seriously? You expected me to fail?" Jay was both offended and impressed by how well she knew him.

"Kind of," Nina admitted. "I thought you might be busy and not go through your mail. I've seen it piling up on the counter."

Her words hit Jay like a lightning bolt. He had been waiting and waiting for the biopsy results. Was it possible that they had come in the mail? Was there a letter waiting for him at home?

Chapter 30

Nina felt giddy and light-headed. Going after the labels had turned their business meeting into something much more exciting. She didn't want the night to end, which had led her to ask Jay if he needed help with the labels. Of course he'd refused, out of politeness or something equally stupid.

She remembered the moment in the warehouse, how he'd lingered next to her, his breath on her neck, almost like a gentle touch. She'd imagined him suddenly kissing her and them both surrendering to that moment. Then her gaze had magically landed on the right parcel, breaking the spell. In a movie, that would have been the moment the hero and heroine excitedly hugged one another, jumping up and down. But she'd focused on getting out of the building before someone noticed what they were up to.

And Jay... she wasn't sure what Jay was thinking, but here they were, driving back, mission accomplished. Nina felt herself drifting back into her hopeless crush. Any thought of the sensible Adam and starting a family had vanished. She hadn't even sent that email! Technically, she and Adam were still an item. This was not right.

Nina dug up her phone, then remembered it was still out of battery. There was no way she could send that message. She sat back and focused on the scenery. The rolling hills already looked like dark green bumps against the sky. The night was cooling and white fog had gathered at the foot of the hills, reflecting the last of the evening light. It was that magical moment you could see with the naked eye, but could never capture with a camera.

Jay pulled up in his driveway and turned to her. "Sorry. I wasn't thinking. I can drive you home so you don't have to walk."

"It's not that far. And it's downhill." Nina replied. "But I'll come inside for a bit to see the labels first, if that's okay?"

"Of course."

They walked in and Nina placed the labels on the kitchen table. In the proper light, she could see they had turned out great. She grabbed one of the sauce bottles and modeled the label on it.

Jay seemed distracted, grabbing the pile of mail on his kitchen counter and flipping through it. After a moment, he put the pile down and turned to her. "Do you want a cup of tea?"

"Yes, please," Nina replied, even though she felt like something else than tea. She presented him with a newly labeled bottle and smiled victoriously.

"Look! I can't believe we got there. We should celebrate!"

Jay laughed. "We still have at least ninety-nine bottles to label, so I'm not sure we should uncork the champagne just yet." He hesitated. "I mean, I have ninety-nine bottles to label. I don't expect you to do it."

Nina sighed. "I know it's your business, but I feel like I'm invested, you know? I want to see this take off!"

She wanted to say so much more, but this was already a lot. She had to see how Jay would react.

The kettle boiled, filling the room with its loud gurgle. Jay poured two cups of tea and sat down at the table with Nina. "That's great, but I feel like I'm exploiting you. If someone asks if my sauces are fair trade, I'd have to say no, because I'm not paying a fair wage and you've done everything apart from making the sauce."

"That's crazy!" Nina tried to laugh off the notion.

"No, it's not crazy. And I can't pay you. Not yet. But if you want in, you can have a share of the business, whatever it turns out to be." Jay looked her straight in the eye. He was so serious Nina wanted to just blurt out a terrible joke to break the spell.

"Wow."

It was all she could say. Jay was offering her a part of his business. That was huge. But it could also complicate things. She'd only set out to help him, mainly to spend time with him, to be near him. As she'd researched and designed, she'd gotten more and more excited about the project and had spent countless hours on it. Jay's offer was generous, but it somehow tainted the experience – making it almost look like that had been her goal all along. She wanted to say yes, just to have this connection to Jay – even if it was through business. But this wasn't what she wanted. She wanted his arms around her, nothing in between them and yes; she wanted to share everything with him, but not as a business deal. Yep, she'd definitely slipped right back into her crush.

Nina sighed into her teacup. "That's a really generous offer. But I can't do that. It's not right."

Jay leaned in, his tone insistent. "No, it's the only thing that makes sense. I can't do this without you and I can't risk you doing a runner." He tried to laugh, but it sounded hollow.

"But I'm not going anywhere."

"You say that, but you have this guy in town and maybe one day you want to move there, to be closer to him."

"You mean Adam? No, that's not happening." Nina shook her head, grateful for the opportunity to clear things up. The briefest of smiles graced Jay's mouth. "I'm just saying we may not be neighbours forever. But if we're in business together... honestly, I don't think I can run this show by myself. I'll just go back to growing vegetables. That's the only thing I know."

Nina frowned. "But you're so good at making hot sauce!"

"It's not enough. And one product is probably not enough. I'm experimenting with salad dressings but haven't got very far."

"Maybe you should explore other chilli-based things, like marinades and pastes and chutneys?" Nina's mind buzzed with new opportunities. Evidently, she couldn't help getting involved.

"See!" Jay exclaimed. "You already think like it's your business. I want to make it official. Fifty-fifty."

Nina's heartbeat kicked up a notch. "Oh, no! I could never take that much."

"You need to have an equal share so you can vote against anything stupid I might do." Jay winked, but Nina felt too flustered to even smile.

"But I'm not bringing in any investment," she insisted. "It's your ingredients, your recipe, your bottles, your production line... I don't even have anything I could invest in this."

"You're investing your time and expertise. That's valid. Ask Tyron, he does these kinds of deals all the time. He says if you have someone irreplaceable, you need to make them a shareholder. Otherwise, they leave and take your business down with them."

Nina swallowed hard at the mention of Tyron. She really didn't want to involve Jay's brother in this. Maybe it was best to just agree and figure out the details later. "Okay."

"You mean, okay, let's be partners?"

Nina nodded. Oh, how she wished the word partners meant more than owning shares in a small business. It was exciting, sure. With any other client, it would have been a dream come true, but with Jay, it felt like a cold shower. She'd been downgraded from a potential love interest to Marketing Manager – or something else very unromantic. Maybe Jay never even considered the love interest part, and it was all in her head? Either way, they were now officially business partners.

Nina forced a smile. "Did you say you had champagne?"

Jay looked at her, surprised. "I do, actually."

He took a green bottle off the top shelf and untwisted the wire to pop the cork. Nina traced her finger down the length of the bottle, collecting a thick layer of dust.

"How long have you had this?"

"It's alcohol. It won't go off."

Nina rolled her eyes. "Yeah, that's what I'm concerned about."

Jay pulled a face. "Are you commenting on the frequency of champagne-worthy moments in my life?"

Nina laughed. The cork hit the ceiling and a fountain of white froth erupted, covering his hand and dripping on the table.

"Fu... I didn't think this through. Can you grab the glasses? They're up there."

Jay pointed at the cabinet, and Nina fetched two flutes. They raised their glasses, both looking for words to toast with.

"To ... us," said Jay.

"To ... hot sauce," said Nina.

"And success," added Jay.

"And... being good neighbours?"

"And business partners!" Jay confirmed.

"And not moving to town for a boring guy who works at the council," Nina added.

"I'll drink to that," laughed Jay.

They both took a sip. It wasn't Dom Perignon, but tasted decent. They stood for a moment, looking at each other, listening to the gentle fizz rising from their glasses.

"So, it didn't work out with the council guy then?" Jay's voice brimmed with hope.

Nina wanted to agree, laugh it off, laugh so much that Adam faded away with tiny little bubbles rising from her glass. But she couldn't. She knew why Adam had happened. Even if she was about to break it off, she couldn't discount the fact that Adam wanted what she wanted. He wasn't a bad guy. He was a guy who, at that very moment, believed he was in a serious relationship with her. Nina put her drink back on the table.

"I don't know," she said.

Jay set his glass next to hers. "Sorry. It's none of my business."

He fetched a box of unlabeled sauce bottles and set it on the kitchen table. "This is my business. And it's getting late."

Nina nodded. They had to get a move on if they hoped to be ready for tomorrow morning and get some sleep before that. She sat down at the table and quickly showed Jay how to place the label on without wrinkling it. He was a fast learner but worked a lot slower than Nina. She'd finished half the bottles by the time he got through twenty of them and decided he needed a break. Jay made them omelets. While he cooked, Nina explained what she'd planned for the stand. She showed him a poster she'd made advertising their give-away deal. This one, along with other signage and collateral, had arrived from the printers earlier, but Jay hadn't opened the package.

"So, you just don't open your mail?" Nina exclaimed, in-specting the print quality under the brightest ceiling light.

"I wanted to save that for you," Jay replied with a wink.

He served her a beautiful omelet dotted with cherry toma-toes. Nina asked if she could add some hot sauce. She was so used to it now, some foods tasted bland without it.

Jay fetched an opened bottle. "I can't believe I didn't think of that."

Late that night, Nina walked down the hill, head spinning with unsaid things, but a part of her mind was already on the next morning, planning and checking for things they would need to pack and remember. At home, she sat on the laptop and devoted a couple of hours to building their social media presence. It was officially her business now, and she wanted to do things right. She needed to get at least a few more followers before the big market day. After she finished, there were only three hours left for sleep. Thankfully, sleep arrived.

CHAPTER 31

On Sunday morning, Nina woke with a start. She checked the time. 6:30 a.m. She had a lot to do, but if she got organised, she would get there. One of the first things on her list was the letter to Adam. She had to send it.

Fortified with her regular green smoothie, Nina sat at her laptop and read through her draft email. It sounded evasive and cold, but maybe that was for the best. She didn't want to leave room for what ifs. Good enough. Nina hit 'send' and jumped in the shower.

By 8 a.m., she was ready to go. When Nina got to Jay's house, she found him already waiting by the car. The boot was open with everything packed in there - the bottles, printouts, the EFTPOS machine, and even two camping chairs for them to sit on.

"You've thought of everything!"

Jay looked proud. He whistled, and Chloe appeared, giving Nina a happy tail-wagging greeting. Jay tapped on the car and the dog jumped in.

"Do you have a bowl for her to give her water?" she asked.

"It'll be a hot day."

"Good point!"

Jay ran back to the house while Nina packed her bags in the boot.

When they arrived at the market, they found a dozen pickup trucks and trailers; the vendors unloading boxes into their designated spots. Nina and Jay found their slot in the far corner.

They worked side by side, setting up the stand. Nina documented their progress on her phone, composing a couple of social media updates for their newly created Instagram account. She'd got to twenty-five followers, which felt like a major achievement. Thinking of the right hashtags, Nina heard a familiar voice.

Earth, setting up a stall with her mother, three tables away. It made sense she was here, but Nina felt annoyed that she hadn't prepared for the possibility. She'd been happy to leave the entire experience behind her, to forget about ever knowing the pair. But now she had to see what their brand looked like. She craned her neck to see the sign they were hanging up.

Jay appeared next to her. "Ah, the eco-bitches have arrived. Is that the logo you designed?"

To Nina's amazement, it was one of her designs, only in a different colour and printed too big for the board it was on, making the whole thing look tacky.

"I can't believe it," she muttered under her breath.

"What?"

"It's one of my designs, but they've changed the colour. And something else…"

Nina grabbed her phone and found the original email she'd sent to Marlena. Comparing the logo draft and the one now on their board, she could see someone had added two lines to the design, making it cluttered and out of balance. They'd produced it in bright green instead of the original soft mint, but it was the same design. Nina handed her phone to Jay.

"It's the same logo!"

"Well, not exactly, but they've definitely used my file. Earth said they had no use for it and that's why they wouldn't pay."

"It's the same logo," Jay repeated, staring at her phone, then at the sign.

He launched towards Earth and Marlena. Nina grabbed his shirt to stop him. "Please, don't go over there. Not now!"

"Why not?"

"Let's focus on our business, okay? I don't want to start the day with an argument," Nina pleaded.

Jay shrugged. "Fine. But we can't let them get away with this."

"We won't, I promise. We'll deal with it later. But I think it's best if we do our own thing, you know?"

Jay nodded, but looked a little hurt. Nina dug up a couple of raw chocolates from her emergency stash and handed one to Jay. He ate it in silence.

"I appreciate the thought," Nina added. She rarely had

anyone to fight her battles for her.

It was ten o'clock, and the shoppers began arriving, which gave them something else to focus on. The weather stayed sunny, and the morning was busy. By eleven o'clock, they'd sold twenty bottles and gotten twenty-five names and emails on their Christmas giveaway list, all vying to win three sauce bottles with a ribbon around them.

During the first lull, Nina fetched them coffees. Walking past Earth's stand, she noticed a few ladies browsing their clothing racks. She had to admit they'd put together an eclectic, colourful selection that seemed to attract people with a similar fashion sense.

When Nina got back with the coffees, Jay was just finishing with one customer. As the old lady left, they both collapsed in the camping chairs. Nina could feel the previous night's sleep deprivation hitting her. The fertility-friendly decaf would not help, but she sipped it anyway. If she really believed in it, maybe the placebo effect would kick in.

"It's going pretty well," Jay said, turning to Nina just when she was mid-yawn.

"Ye...es."

"Did you get any sleep last night?"

"A little." Nina smiled.

The tired haze didn't bother her at all. She would make it through the rest of the morning and then curl up somewhere, anywhere. Only three hours to go. What she really wanted to do was to rest her head on Jay's shoulder and curl up against him.

It was such a lovely day. If she closed her eyes, she could just listen to the buzz of the marketplace, mixed with distant Christmas carols playing somewhere in the background. A gentle breeze played with her hair. Nina felt her eyelids get heavier and heavier, and before she knew it, she was actually leaning on Jay's shoulder. He didn't move. He didn't even shift. Instead, he wrapped his arm around her and gently stroked her shoulder.

Just a friendly gesture, Nina mused.

But it was too late. Every cell of her being ran away with the sensation. Her spine vibrated. She didn't want to move. This was the only place in the world that felt right.

Eventually, two new customers showed up. Nina straightened up and grabbed her coffee. There was still a mouthful in the cup she could lubricate her throat with.

Jay sold two bottles of sauce, chatting happily like nothing had happened. He seemed so carefree that it made Nina's insides hurt. Could he not feel the nerve wrecking vibration between them? Was it possible he had no part in what was going on in her mind? She may have already been friend zoned. Nina remembered a funny video she'd seen a long time ago, explaining how sideways hugs were a sure sign of being in the 'friend zone'. She may have gotten rid of Adam, but this hopeless crush on Jay would be her undoing.

The next hour was so busy, they barely exchanged two words. Nina kept the table tidy and stacked, explained their

Christmas giveaway raffle at least fifty times, and listened to Jay answer questions about his sauce recipe. The old locals kept bringing up his father, fondly remembering his spirit, his amazing vegetables, and his bowling success. Jay never joined the reminiscing, just smiled politely and nodded along. It was only from the slight tensing of his shoulders that Nina could tell he found it uncomfortable.

Around lunchtime, their side of the market quieted down as most people headed for the food trucks and formed disorderly queues for dumplings, burgers, and churros. Nina sagged down in her chair with a sigh. "We should get lunch too, but I don't want to stand in line. It's too hot out there."

The lovely, mild morning had turned into a sweltering summer's day. Nina knew if she stepped out of the shade, she would burn her shoulders in ten minutes. It was one of those New Zealand quirks every tourist learned the hard way.

"I can order something," Jay offered, taking out his phone.

The phone looked so battered Nina couldn't even tell what brand it was. But it seemed to work.

"Uber Eats?" she asked.

"Uber what?" Jay looked at her blankly.

He'd dialled a number and was waiting for someone to pick up. "Hi! It's Jay here. We're at the market, was hoping to order a couple of meals. I can come and pick up..." Jay turned to Nina. "You want a salad or something? I'm getting a pizza."

Nina wasn't sure who he was talking to, but agreed to a Caesar salad. Anything, really. She was feeling faint and would have eaten anything – even pizza.

Jay finished the phone call. "Twenty minutes," he announced.

"Where did you order from?"

"My mate works weekends at the pub," he said.

The pub was only a little down the road. It seemed Jay's version of Uber Eats was a friend who worked in the nearest commercial kitchen.

"Do you like living here?" Nina asked.

Jay looked at her oddly. "Why?"

"Just wondering."

Jay froze for a moment, staring at something in the distance. "When I was a kid, I used to think I'd go somewhere. I wanted to go to Asia or England. Every place I read about. Anything was better than here. That was the one thing I agreed on with Tyron. He still thinks that."

"And you?"

Jay shrugged. "I made my choice."

He sounded neither happy nor unhappy, but at peace. Nina remembered reading about a study that proved having fewer choices was actually a source of peace and happiness. People who had the freedom to change their minds experienced more anxiety. The study had used shopping-related examples, but maybe the same principle applied here. Jay had his farm, his mum, and his friends. They anchored him.

Nina's life was literally on wheels. She could tow her home somewhere else at the drop of a hat. Maybe that possibility made her more anxious. She could always move back to Hamilton, or somewhere else. Nobody depended on her. Nobody would care.

"Do you ever fantasise about living somewhere else? Doing something else?"

"Not lately," Jay replied, smiling cryptically.

"That's good, I suppose. I wish I could just get stuck somewhere. Make a choice I can't undo and stop thinking about all the options. They are crowding my mind."

"You want to get stuck?" Jay stared at her in confusion. Nina picked up a sauce bottle and rolled it in her hands. Her fuzzy brain fired a weak signal, warning her of sharing too much, but she was too tired to care. "I always wanted to belong somewhere, have this undeniable connection. To be able to tell people with absolute certainty where you're from, it sounds amazing. My family moved around and then my parents split and I never felt that way about any place. I have a cousin, Ingrid. She's never met her father, but she knows he's a Kiwi. She was conceived on this beach in New Zealand. Waihi – "

"Waihi Beach?"

"Yeah, I think so. It's on the East Coast, right? Anyway, she has this connection to New Zealand, and I heard she's saving money to visit ... And it's stupid how jealous I am of someone like her. I don't even know her that well. She's a lot younger, and we never lived very close to each other. But when I first moved here, I felt like a fraud, like I shouldn't have come because I didn't have a good reason. And it's true, I only came because I wanted to leave Finland and go somewhere far, far away. I don't really belong here. I don't belong anywhere."

Jay shifted closer, his voice soft. "I'm glad you ended up here, even if it was by accident." He drew a sharp breath. "Can't you just choose to belong?"

"I thought buying a piece of land would mean I'd finally settle somewhere. But now it feels like it's just another decision I have to make – to sell or not to sell."

Jay looked startled. "Are you thinking of selling?"

His concern warmed Nina's heart. That's what she wanted! Someone who cared whether she went or stayed. "No, not right now. But obviously, if I can't make my life work here, I have to consider it. I love that I have the choice. And I hate that I have the choice."

Jay grinned, and Nina elbowed his ribs. "I know I'm not making any sense."

Jay studied her. He looked like he wanted to say something, but no words emerged. Finally, he looked at his watch. "The food might help. I'll be back in a sec."

He strolled down the road toward the pub that didn't look like it was open at all. Surely, it had to be.

When he returned, Nina was busy opening their last box of sauce bottles. They'd sold far more than she'd expected. It must have been the proximity to Christmas and the affordable pricing. And possibly the crackers and cheese they had been serving so that people could test the sauce.

Nina had also made little holiday cards that people could buy with their bottle. They had messages like 'Because you're hot', 'Have a spicy Christmas!' and 'Be brave – Go beyond ketchup'. Paired up with these and the beautiful packaging, the sauce made the perfect Christmas gift. Nina had sold at least ten bottles to stressed-out people looking for Secret Santa gifts for their colleagues. Nina remembered the frantic, late-night gift-wrapping sessions in her office around Christmas time and empathised with them.

"Is that the last box?" Jay asked, his voice full of admiration.

Nina nodded. "We should have made more."

"What are you talking about? Let's sell out and leave early! That's perfect. I still have to go sort out Old Neil and his veggie patch."

Nina felt a twinge of guilt. She was so tired she wouldn't have even dreamt about running another chore in the afternoon. And she doubted Jay had caught much more sleep. "I was just thinking you could have made more money."

"We could have made more money," Jay corrected. "But now we've tested this out, we can still do another market before Christmas. If you want to?"

Jay delivered his last question with a look of such pure expectation it made Nina's heart ache. She loved the moments when his trademark smirk gave way to something genuine

– childlike enthusiasm or sincerity. If he'd known what Nina was thinking, he would have probably sported a smug grin 24/7.

"I think we should. Christmas is the best time of year for this kind of product. I can get some new cards made and sort out new gift packaging."

"Those were a great idea," Jay said. "Are they all gone?"

"Almost." Nina dug up the last cards from under the table and laid them out nicely on the table. She didn't notice a figure quietly approaching them.

"You guys have had quite a bit of traffic here today."

Nina looked up and saw Earth browsing their table. Before Nina could even say hi, her eyes had landed on Jay.

"What do you want?" Jay barked, unamused.

Taken aback, Earth changed tack. "Just wanted to see what all the fuss is about."

Earth must have heard her customers talking about Jay's sauce. Nina felt a surge of pride.

"How's your stall going?" she asked casually.

Earth looked at Nina, slightly startled, like she'd forgotten about her already. Her face must have been an unpleasant reminder of what had gone down between them. Nina kept smiling, determined not to show her annoyance or hurt. Earth didn't deserve it.

"It's good," Earth said evasively and turned back to Jay. "I just kept hearing about this sauce, and I wanted to try some before it's all gone. Is it vegan?"

Nina knew it was, but suddenly wished Jay's recipe included some animal products. Anything. Maybe he could just throw in a bone or two when cooking it? She turned to Jay and caught his eye and a flash of understanding passed between them.

"Not really," Jay replied. "I use some animal products."

"Huh? Like what?" Earth narrowed her eyes, trying to figure out if he was kidding.

Nina jumped in. "A bit of bone broth. It's very good for you. Full of collagen."

Jay nodded in agreement, and Nina watched Earth's eyes widen. Nina suspected she'd had her mind set on tasting the sauce and complimenting Jay – sharing an intimate moment of him feeding her.

"Well, that's good to know," Earth replied. "I have to warn my vegan friends then. I think some of them mistakenly tasted and bought it."

Nina felt terrible. This little ruse could cost them a lot of business. She was about to come clean, but Jay was faster. "Oh, sorry. We had a batch of vegan sauce too, but we sold out. Quite a few people asked for it, so it's all gone."

"That's a shame," Earth responded. "Maybe next time then."

"Maybe," Jay repeated. "But next time, before you come here asking for free food, maybe you should first pay for the services you've already used."

Earth looked like she'd been slapped. Nina felt her stomach tighten. Where was Jay going with this?

"Excuse me?"

"I think you know what I mean. You hired a designer to do your branding, but you haven't paid her. Nina and I are actually in business together, so if you owe her, you owe me. And I may not be as lenient as her, is all I'm saying."

Nina held her breath. She'd never expected Jay to approach the issue from this angle. It felt like she suddenly had her own debt collection service. She loved it.

Earth looked at them both, now forced to take in Nina as part of the equation. She turned back to Jay, assuming a confidential tone. "Come on Jay, of course I was going to pay. We just need to get the business off the ground first. I explained this to Nina."

Nina wanted to scream that she'd explained nothing of the sort, but the words got stuck in her throat. Jay glanced at her and all she could do was to shake her head.

"Generally, if you can't pay someone as agreed, you need to negotiate a payment plan. I trust that you have done this with Nina then?"

"I was going to email her," Earth retorted. "We've just been so busy with the market. You know how it is."

Jay nodded. "Well, the market is over now, so you'll have time. Perfect."

"I'll email you," Earth told Nina. "We had to do some quick tweaks to your design for this market, but we might need you to look at it again. It's not quite right."

Of course it's not, Nina thought. You butchered it.

She couldn't help rolling her eyes, but tried to disguise it by looking away. No. This was not right. She had to look at Earth and stand her ground.

Nina took a deep breath and focused her attention on the woman. "Sure. As long as you pay for the work that's already done." She held Earth's gaze, her pulse twitching in her throat. It probably looked like a massive muscle spasm.

"Fine," said Earth. "We've sold quite a few garments already, so there should be enough revenue if we hold off on other purchases."

Somehow, she made it sound like it was Nina's fault if her business struggled.

"Sounds like a plan," Jay inserted.

Earth gave him a forced smile. "Toodle-oo then," she said and moseyed on, leaving the familiar scent of incense lingering in her wake.

Chloe sneezed, making both Jay and Nina burst out in laughter.

"That was amazing," Nina whispered. "How did you do that?"

Jay shrugged. "I know her."

Nina couldn't help wondering how well he knew her. Did they use to go out? Had they slept together? She didn't want to ask – mostly because the answer scared her.

"You think she will actually pay?" Nina asked.

"I can't be a hundred percent sure, but I think she will

feel the pressure. My mum knows her mum. You know how it goes."

Of course, Nina thought. When you were part of the fabric of a small town, you had leverage. People couldn't risk angering you. Whereas, until now, she'd just been a random newbie, unconnected and unimportant.

Exhausted by the drama, Nina sat down on the wobbly camping chair and welcomed Chloe's warm, heavy head on her lap. She suddenly noticed she was famished. Jay had brought in the food, but she hadn't had a chance to even look at it. Nina opened the containers and found two perfect, thick chicken wraps with chips and a side salad.

"Sorry, the salad sounded pretty light. I thought you might need more sustenance," Jay explained.

"It's perfect," Nina exhaled, almost in tears.

It was perfect. Sometimes, you didn't get what you ordered but still got exactly what you needed.

That afternoon, Nina drove home with her feet aching and her heart glowing. Hanging out with Jay, even working hard with Jay, was so much nicer than she'd ever expected. Nina replayed their first meeting – that quiet, strange man who had towed her tiny house and driven away, left her there wondering whether he was socially awkward or simple-minded. It seemed like such a long time ago. With most people, you first noticed the charm, the jokes, the entertaining stories, and later the hang-ups, the annoying habits – their dark side. With Jay, she kept noticing wonderful things

like perseverance, honesty, surprising kindness and balls...
well, metaphorical balls. Nina couldn't let her mind wander to his actual balls. It was likely he didn't want to start a
family, or at least start one with her. She could feel herself
getting carried away in her dreams, at the risk of getting
hurt – again. However, she felt like she'd made a friend. At
least that gave them a good foundation for doing business
together.

Chapter 32

Nina teared another piece of paper towel to polish a tiny smudge on her mirror. She'd been cleaning her house all morning and the muscles on her arms were getting sore, but there was no moment to waste. La La had called around ten and informed her she'd volunteered Nina's tiny house as a potential filming location for a marketing video they had in production. The location fee was substantial. Nina needed the money, but worried that La La had oversold the cuteness of her humble abode.

After she finished polishing up and decorating the interior, she moved on to the garden. It needed some serious weeding and tidying up. She still had a good two hours to go, but she couldn't do this alone. She needed help. Nina took a breath and called Jay, hoping he wouldn't be too busy.

Jay picked up on the first ring.

"Hi Jay … I have a business proposition for you," Nina began, attempting a light tone. She explained what was happening and promised to split the location fee fifty-fifty if Jay could help her with the garden.

"Two hours is not a lot of time."

Nina pulled a face. "I know. Sorry."

She didn't want to admit that she'd already cleaned and decorated for three hours. She'd started with the fun things, making some bunting and a wreath on her door. The social media video La La was producing was for Christmas, a 'what we did this year' ensemble of thankyous and well-wishes. Nina understood they needed her house in the mix to provide variety so that the client – an insurance company – could showcase their care and understanding of their clientele. Nina found it slightly amusing, considering she didn't even have house insurance. She'd been advised you couldn't get house insurance for a tiny house on wheels. But La La had told her that this company was the first one to offer such insurance, so featuring a tiny house in their video was a small nod towards New Zealand's growing – but still tiny – tiny house community. Maybe she needed to look into it.

When Jay arrived – as instructed, on his ride-on lawn-mower – Nina was in the middle of weeding her wildly over-grown planter boxes.

"Thank God you're here!" she exhaled.

The grass around her house was nearly knee high. Jay looked around and chuckled. "So, the manual lawn mower is all you'll ever need, right? Because it's such wonderful exercise?"

Nina had once given this lame excuse for why she would

never buy a petrol-guzzling little car to keep her lawn in check. But the spring weather had been unpredictable, with frequent showers mixed with hot days. Two weeks of neglect resulted in growth so high her old push-reel lawn mower choked on it. Nina also needed help in arranging big rocks, but she thought it best to lead with the lawn mowing.

After an hour of working in the overcast but muggy weather, the garden was looking a lot better and Nina a lot worse. She could smell her own sweat, which was now running down her back and being absorbed into her sunhat. Having finished the lawn, Jay moved on to helping her with the big rocks she was inching forward pathetically slowly. After watching him simply pick them up and put them down like they were made of Styrofoam, Nina stepped back and focused on guiding the stones to where they needed to go.

Don't look at him. Focus on the garden, she thought to herself.

Watching Jay's tightening muscles was making her feel hot, and she was already sweaty enough.

Another forty-five minutes saw the footpath transformed from a minefield of rocks and weeds into a nice, even path, lined with various rocks. They used the gravel Nina had ordered when she first moved in to create a nice surface to walk on. It also got rid of the gravel pile on the side of her house – a double win.

Nina couldn't believe her eyes. "We did it! Or rather, you did it. Thank you so much!"

Jay smiled back. Before she could think twice about it, she wrapped her arms around him for a hug. He felt a little stiff and startled for a second, but hugged her back, holding her tightly for a good, long moment. She loved how they fit together, how his arms felt around her body ... and almost simultaneously, she noticed how dirty and sweaty they both were. She could smell her own shirt. Oh God, could he smell it, too?

Nina stepped back and looked at her watch. "Oh my God, what if they come on time?! I don't have time to shower!"

Jay looked at her, possibly assessing her level of hygiene. He didn't seem bothered. "Nobody finds this place on the first try. I'm sure you have at least fifteen minutes."

Nina looked at her driveway. It was still quiet.

She turned to Jay, pleading with her eyes. "Could you stay and keep watch? Just for ten minutes. I'm not high maintenance, I promise!"

Jay looked uncertain. "If they arrive, I'm not sure you want me to introduce... you know... anything."

He looked so uncomfortable Nina wanted to hug him again. "You're much better than you think. I've seen you at the market, you're a natural!"

"That's different. I know most of those people."

"Just tell them to wait a couple of minutes, that's all I'm asking."

"Okay." Jay nodded and sat on his lawnmower. He looked like he needed a shower, too. Thank goodness he wasn't complaining about that.

"Thank you!"

Nina hurried to her house, grabbed a towel and a change of clothes, and locked herself in the bathroom. As soon as she got under the shower, she heard the cars arriving. Oh, crap. Poor Jay would just have to hold the fort. Nina showered in record time, quickly wiped herself and any droplets off the walls. There was no time to dry her hair – she didn't even have a hair dryer – but surely it was better to be wet from the shower than from the sweat.

Dressed up and sort of ready to go, Nina stepped out of the bathroom and looked out her window. She could see La La talking to Jay and at least three other guys. One of them looked familiar. Tama! What was he doing here? He didn't do video!

Nina looked in the mirror and tried to fluff up her towel dried hair, which was definitely not ready for a public appearance. But she had to step out.

Mentally priming herself to show no embarrassment, Nina opened her door and smiled at everyone. "Hi! Welcome to my tiny house! Sorry I made you wait. Trust me; it was the lesser of two evils. We worked so hard on the garden I was sweating out of my eyeballs…"

La La came to give her a hug, probably to shut her up. "Sorry, I should have warned you about Tama," she whispered. "He jumped in last minute and won the pitch."

La La introduced her to the crew: a cameraman, a sound

recordist, and the client's representative – a middle-aged lady in a flowery blouse called Jane. Then she turned to Tama and added: "And I think you know our director?"

"Nina!" Tama stepped in to give her a hug. It was a lovely gesture, but felt almost too familiar. Obviously, they knew each other, but there had definitely not been any hugging at the office.

Over Tama's shoulder, Nina saw Jay looking at them, wearing an inscrutable expression. She tried to give Tama a friendly pat to show the embrace had done its job, but he was going for a full ten-second squeeze. He smelled of after-shave and beer.

"So, the plan is to just take footage today to show our client what we're planning on. We will need to use you guys as stand-ins. We haven't cast the final talent for this just yet." La La looked at Nina, then at Jay, expecting this to be no big deal.

Jay looked confused. "Me? No... no. I just came to help Nina out with the garden."

La La was unperturbed. "Well, now you're here. That's how it works. You turn up, you're discovered, you end up on camera." She laughed, and the crew joined in, chuckling half-heartedly.

Jay shook his head. "I don't ... I'm not..."

"Don't worry, only the client will see the footage. It won't be used anywhere."

"I don't think..."

Jane looked questioningly at La La. Nina knew well that this kind of thing easily put a client off. They were notoriously risk-averse. Everything had to be smooth. Everyone had to cooperate.

Nina pulled Jay aside and spoke under her breath. "Please? I don't want to do it either, but it's clearly important to them... and I don't want to get La La in trouble. Please?"

Jay sighed and nodded. Nina had a feeling he was doing this for her, not for her friend, but did it really matter? Plastering the biggest smile on her face, Nina turned to La La. "He's in!" she announced.

La La looked relieved, and Jane settled down. They planned the shots. As the crew squeezed into her house to scout possible angles, she dipped her head and combed through her hair with her fingers, trying to let the gentle wind do its job. Tama appeared on her side.

"The place looks great," he said.

Nina lifted her head and smiled. "Thank you."

"You know, this was my idea," Tama added, bursting with pride.

"Filming at my house?"

"No, I mean the story. They weren't sure about the direction and we all got to pitch. They liked my idea."

Nina could imagine Tama shining at the pitch. He was always at his best under pressure, charming the client's socks off.

"I didn't know tiny houses looked like... this. But then I

went on Pinterest. There are some pretty epic tiny houses out there," Tama continued.

"True," Nina admitted.

"But I think yours is perfect for this video."

Nina hoped he was right. If this worked out, she would get her money and use it to buy presents and food... and petrol. La La had invited her and two old Hamilton friends whose families were overseas to spend Christmas at an Airbnb, somewhere in Coromandel. Nina hated being the only one with no family around at Christmas time. That invitation was her lifeline.

From the corner of her eyes, Nina could see Jay sitting on his lawnmower, checking on his phone but probably listening to them.

"Couldn't have done it without Jay, though," she added, pointing at her friend.

Tama lifted his brow. "Are you guys...?"

"We're in business together," Nina replied. "Jay makes this amazing hot sauce and I'm helping him launch the product... or a product line, eventually."

"Choice." Tama leaned in. "So... where do you guys go to grab a feed around here? I mean something better than burgers?"

Nina gave him a short list of acceptable restaurants in Raglan, explaining that most of them were in the village but one, her favourite one, was outside of town.

"Totally worth it, though. The food is divine."

"I don't mind the drive when it's worth it," Tama said with a wink.

He was flirting with her. Just like the old times. Nina didn't want to be rude, but she didn't want him to do this. Not in front of Jay. Not ever.

"How's it going with Emma?" she asked.

"She... moved on," Tama said. "Got another job."

"Anyone else since then?"

"Oh, come on, can't I be single for a while?" Tama laughed.

No, you can't be single. Nina smiled back, exasperated. Maybe it would have been better to let Tama flirt to his heart's content. Wasn't that what women did to make a man jealous?

"I was just so sad about you leaving..." Tama's forehead wrinkled.

Nina tried to stop herself from rolling her eyes. He'd been sad all right. So sad that he'd turned to the random person occupying Nina's desk and started dating her immediately. Maybe it was better that Tama didn't finish the sentence.

La La appeared with a crate of soft drinks. "Tama! There's a bag of snacks in the car. Can you go grab it? I think we should take a quick break."

As soon as Tama was out of earshot, La La moved in closer. She looked guilty. "So, a funny thing. I ... kind of ended up telling him you're not seeing anyone. I meant to come up with something, but he sort of cornered me and I think he genuinely likes you ... and I thought, maybe once you see him again and if he's actually honest with you, you might feel different."

Nina stared at her friend. She didn't know how she felt about Tama, but this situation was making her uncomfortable. Jane and the rest of the crew approached La La's crate of drinks, grateful for the breather.

Nina didn't have outdoor furniture, apart from one chair she used when sitting outside, drinking her morning smoothie. She ran to her house to fetch a picnic blanket and they set up camp under the walnut tree, sharing fruit and sausage rolls. After being invited for the third time, Jay sat down with them. He had a slightly sullen look about him, but being wedged between Tama and La La, Nina couldn't talk to him.

As Nina bit into her sausage roll (she hadn't had one in a year) she realised what it was missing: Jay's hot sauce. She ran back to her house to get the bottle Jay had given her earlier.

Tama grabbed it off her. "Is this the sauce?"

Nina nodded. She was happy she'd placed one of the new labels on it. It looked like a legitimate product.

"It looks like your work." Tama inspected the bottle, smiling appreciatively. "You guys are making this sauce together?"

"No," Nina corrected. "Jay makes the sauce. I help with design and marketing."

"I couldn't do it without her," Jay confirmed.

He sounded so matter-of-fact. Why couldn't he say it with a smile and a wink, to show Tama that they were more than business partners, at least a little more? He was so business-like. Nina wanted to go back in time, back to that hug, and just hold on, never mind the sweat.

"So, I was thinking, after we finish here, I could take you out for dinner?" Tama suggested to Nina.

He gave Nina his most charming smile, the kind that, back in the office, would have sent her head spinning. But now, she was sitting right next to Jay, and the question felt like a ticking time bomb she was having to diffuse on the spot.

"I don't know," Nina replied, trying to smile back.

She didn't know how to get out of this without offending him, and she couldn't offend him right now. Not while they were still deciding about filming at her house. Not while the entire crew was listening.

"You guys are getting busy towards Christmas, then?" Nina asked, desperate to change the subject.

"You know how it is," Tama shrugged, "Everyone comes out of the woodwork."

Tama talked about the shift from print campaigns to video, especially social media clips. None of this was news to Nina, but she was grateful for the new topic and nodded along. They finished eating and Nina got up to clean the rubbish.

After an hour of Tama and the crew looking for the perfect angle on the outside of the house (God, filmmaking was slow and boring!), La La took Jane inside the tiny house for one last look and, Nina suspected, a private conversation. The crew waited outside. Nina snuck away to pull the last weeds she'd spotted in her garden.

Tama approached her. "So, how about that dinner?"

Nina tried the non-committal smile again. "It's a lovely offer."

Fortunately, La La and Jane interrupted them, stepping out of the tiny house with happy, excited faces. Jane gestured with her hands, fiercely agreeing with La La on something. Nina hoped it was good news.

As Jane excused herself to get something from the car, La La leaned in to give Nina an update. "Jane loves the house. They want to use both interior and exterior. And they want Jay to star in it!"

"For real?" Nina looked around for Jay to see if he was listening. She located him in the garden, rearranging the stakes supporting her neglected tomatoes.

La La grinned. "They like his look for this. And they're looking for a woman to pose as his partner. We need a couple living in a tiny house. They think a single person makes it look too lonely and sad."

"Thanks." Nina cast her a hurt look.

La La rolled her eyes. "Oh, come on. You know what these people are like!"

Think about the money, Nina reminded herself. If they wanted to use Jay's face, they'd have to pay him, too.

"He might not be that into it," Nina warned her friend. "I

think he only agreed to this one because it's not published anywhere."

"No, he agreed to this because you asked him. I can tell." La La winked at Nina.

The two-person camera crew approached them. "I think we're done here for now," said the cameraman. "Got some candld shots of the farmer too."

"Great!" La La gave them a thumbs-up.

Nina frowned at the way they referred to Jay as the 'farmer'. It was technically true, but their tone, coupled by the way they talked about him as if he wasn't here, made her angry.

"So, are things... progressing with you two?" La La asked Nina when the crew was out of earshot.

"Not really," Nina admitted. "Well, we're in business together, so we see more of each other..."

As La La nodded enthusiastically, Nina noticed her friend was trying to suppress a smile. Her eyes sparkled like she couldn't wait to interrupt and tell her something. "You have something to tell me, don't you?" she hissed at her friend.

La La nodded, but Jane interrupted them with a huge gift basket, which she handed to Nina. "Thank you so much for opening up your home to us. It's been a privilege."

Nina thanked Jane, peering through the cellophane. Her mouth watered at the sight of the treats. Some of them didn't quite go with her diet, but maybe she could relax her standards a little. Or share them with Jay, who'd just joined her side, exchanging a meaningful look with her over the cloud of cellophane.

"We're going out for dinner before driving back," La La said. "You're welcome to join us. Both you and Jay."

"I'm good," Nina said. She wanted to talk to La La in private, but she'd have to do that another time.

Jay didn't seem too excited, either. "I have a lot of work to get through, before it gets dark."

"Ah, evening milking?" asked Tama with a wink, joining their circle.

"I grow vegetables," corrected Jay, unamused.

"Actually," Tama continued. "I was hoping to take Nina out for dinner, if you guys don't mind?"

He looked around, daring anyone to object. La La looked at Nina, her eyebrows raised. Nina turned to Jay, feeling hot and cold, desperate for him to fight for her.

"Have fun." Jay didn't sound friendly, but nothing in his expression betrayed jealousy.

Nina's heart plummeted to her ankles. If he didn't mind, even a little, she might as well go. Just to avoid having to come up with an excuse.

Jay hopped on his lawnmower and waved over his shoulder – his signature goodbye.

"You'll talk to him about the filming, right?" La La asked. Nina nodded.

"Okay," La La confirmed. "We will head out to Orca and you guys ... do your thing?"

Nina stared back, trying to signal La La that she hadn't

actually agreed to this date, but everyone was too busy with their plans to notice her.

La La hugged Nina goodbye and discreetly mouthed 'call me' before she walked to her car with Jane. The camera guys hopped in their car, presumably to follow the ladies to the restaurant, and their two-car convoy drove away. Tama pointed to his car – a brand new Bentley. It reminded Nina of Tyron. She wondered why Tama hadn't carpooled with La La and Jane. Had he been planning this date all along? Oh well, she was starving. And Tama was paying; she knew that. He'd paid for her before, even when it wasn't a date. He enjoyed buying rounds for his friends at the bar and giving lavish gifts.

Nina excused herself for a moment to grab her handbag. Alone in her house, she took a deep breath and looked in the mirror. Her hair had finally dried to nice, soft waves, but her eyes looked startled. She tried to smile, but her face refused to relax. She felt physically sick and couldn't even contemplate eating, especially with Tama. They had no future, not even one that worked on paper like with Adam. She didn't want him anymore, and if she couldn't have Jay, then to hell with it – she wanted no one.

With a strange fire burning in her belly, Nina dropped her handbag on the floor and stepped out. It was time to be honest with everyone and let the pieces fall as they may.

"Look, Tama," Nina said, "I don't want to do this. A few months ago, I would have said yes without even thinking. I admit I was totally... under your spell. But I'm not anymore. And I don't want to waste your time or your money. I hope we can still be friends, but I can't go out with you. Sorry."

Tama cocked his head, a smile spreading across his face. "You were totally under my spell?"

So, that was what he heard? Tama was nothing if not an optimist.

He studied her for a moment, as if to confirm she was serious. "I should have asked you a long time ago," Tama finally said. "My bad."

"Maybe it was for the best." Tama shrugged. "I enjoyed working with you. And I miss you." He looked wistful, but not badly hurt. Nina couldn't imagine it taking him longer than the drive back to town to get over her.

She gave him a meek smile. "We had a lot of fun."

"So, there's someone else then?" Tama winked.

Nina nodded. It wasn't technically true, but stretching the truth was the kinder option. "It's pretty new, but I want to see where it goes."

"Understood. Well, take care!" Tama hugged her briefly, got in his car, and drove away.

Nina let out a deep sigh. One mission accomplished, one more to go.

CHAPTER 33

Jay picked up a crate and made his way to the greenhouse. Thank goodness for the work that kept him busy. He needed the distraction. That guy, Tama, he had been all over Nina. All that hugging and winking and dinner plans... Jay could tell they had a history, even if Nina seemed embarrassed with all the attention.

Tama reminded Jay of Tyron, someone who always got what he wanted. They knew what they wanted and went after it with such charm and tenacity that nothing – and nobody – could withstand it. Guys like Tyron and Tama never got sick or weak. Well, until they got older like his dad, and simply fell down like a tree in its prime, leaving everyone else behind to deal with the messy business of ageing – gradually getting uglier, smellier, and less capable. And full of suspicious lumps, of course.

Jay sighed. He continued picking up ripe capsicums and arranging the supporting stakes of the unripe ones. His hands worked and his mind wandered. Nina was smart and gorgeous. She could take her pick. And when it came down to it, could a guy like him ever get the girl?

***

Before she had time to second-guess herself, Nina headed up the hill to Jay's house. Bracing herself, she knocked on the door. There was no answer. That's when she remembered he'd said something about the work he had to do. He must have meant it.

Nina headed to the greenhouse. She spotted him at the far end, framed by rows of ripening capsicum, picking up produce in a large crate.

Chloe noticed her before Jay did, alerting him to her arrival. Jay turned around with a look of surprise. "What's up?"

Nina took a step closer, not sure where to stand or how she should do this. Only that it needed to be done. "I didn't go out with Tama. I don't want to be with him."

The words spilled out with force, making her feverish. Jay looked at her quizzically. "Okay." He waited for her to continue.

Nina swallowed a lump that rose in her throat, studying his non-committal face. "So, you don't care at all?"

Jay's mouth hung as he stared at her. Nina closed her eyes, the pain of rejection shooting down her arms and legs.

She had to get this off her chest, even if it ruined everything. "I know. We're just business partners and I can date whoever I want and you couldn't care less. You..." Nina's eyes burned, her whole body pulsating with something hot, raw, and uncontrollable.

"Are you okay? What's wrong?" Jay's voice brimmed with genuine concern, which made Nina feel even worse.

"Nothing. I'm just... so stupid!" she cried. "You know, I have these men in my life who want to be with me... and I go after the wrong ones and I end up alone. I'll never have a family!" The sobs rose from somewhere deep inside and she couldn't stop them.

Jay took a step closer and touched her shoulder. "Are you... angry with me or something? What did I do?" he asked.

She shook him away. "No... yes...It's not your fault."

Jay looked at her with such concern she wanted to die. She could take rejection, but she couldn't take his pity. She had to get out of there.

"I'm sorry," Nina gasped and ran out the door.

Jay caught her outside and grabbed her arm. "What happened?" he demanded. "Did that guy do something to you? What did he do? Tell me!"

Nina shook her head. Her tears spilled out on both cheeks and ran down her neck. This was hopeless. "I was in love with him for two years. And I waited and waited for him to ask me out. And now that he did, I don't want him anymore. What's wrong with me?"

Jay's brow wrinkled. "Nothing's wrong with you. He's a douchebag."

If she hadn't been so upset, Nina would have laughed. "I'm sorry I yelled at you," she whispered.

"That's okay."

"From now on, I'll stick to being business partners and will keep my stupid personal life to myself."

"If that's what you want...?" Jay frowned.

Nina could feel a fresh batch of tears behind her eyes again. "No, it's not what I want. But I don't get what I want. I get... this!"

"Are you saying you don't want to do business with me or..."

Was he playing dumb? Nina felt like she couldn't swallow. She could barely speak. "I'm saying I wanted to be more. I wanted you to... I wanted you. And I thought you liked me. I was so stupid!"

Nina turned around and ran downhill, not looking back. Chloe rushed after her, and maybe Jay, but he didn't catch her. She stumbled into her house, locked the door, climbed into her bed, and cried.

CHAPTER 34

Jay cursed his big, clunky gumboots. They were not made for running. He sped up, trying to close the distance. Just when he was about to reach her, he stumbled on a rock and fell on his hands and knees on the wet ground. Shit! The palm of his hand was bleeding and the dewy grass soaked his jeans.

Jay turned back home. He needed a bandage or something. He'd go over later. Maybe it was good if he gave her a moment to calm down.

But when he got back to his house, he saw his mum's car.

Not now! What did she want?

"Hi!" Alice waved as she got out of her car, holding a thick folder.

The damn recipes.

Mum had called him earlier that week, wanting to discuss the Christmas menu. There were only three of them. Why did it have to be such a big deal?

When Jay got closer, Alice noticed his bleeding hand. "What happened?"

Jay gave her an evasive answer, and Alice led him into the house. She raided his first aid kit, cleaned and disinfected the wound, and bandaged it way more thoroughly than necessary.

"So, the Christmas menu..." Alice started.

"Look, anything you want to cook for Christmas is fine. You know we're easy to please." Jay didn't want to throw his mum out of the house, but he needed to sort this out quickly.

"I know," Alice replied. "It's not really why I'm here. I have something in the car."

She looked almost giddy as she ran away and soon returned with a foil-covered oven dish. "I brought a meatloaf."

There was a DVD on top of it. Without even looking, Jay knew what it was. Eating meatloaf and watching It's a Wonderful Life had been their family tradition around Christmas time. It wasn't even a Christmas dish, and Jay couldn't remember how it had started, but he could tell this meant a lot to his mum. She placed the steaming tray on the table and presented him with the DVD, her eyes already glistening. Since their father's death, Mum had shown no interest in family traditions. Jay hadn't pushed for it either. It was easier to do something different rather than create a setup that only reminded them of their loss.

Now Mum was ready. She wanted to watch Clarence the Angel get his wings and cry. He took the DVD and gave his mum a hug. "The meatloaf smells amazing, Mum."

They fetched plates, cups and cutlery and sat down to

watch the film on the living room rug, just like Jay had done as a little boy. Camping in front of the TV was only allowed at Christmas time.

"Do you think Nina would like to join us for Christmas dinner?" Alice asked. "She has no family around, right?"

Nina. Jay felt his chest tighten. He had to talk to her, but he couldn't do it now. This night was a big breakthrough for his mum. Jay was her only remaining family member who was still around. He couldn't abandon her. Talking to Nina would have to wait until the next morning. They also needed to discuss the biggest Christmas market. He'd labeled another two hundred bottles and had everything ready to go. But he needed Nina by his side.

"I don't know," Jay answered honestly.

Would Nina want to spend time with him, his mum, and Tyron? That was a tough one. Even if Tyron was no longer a threat, was Jay able to offer Nina what she was looking for? The biopsy results had not been in the mail and Jay hadn't got hold of his doctor. Was it a bad sign that things seemed to take so long? Jay could have sworn the lump had grown.

Jay felt his mum brush his hair, the same way she had done when they were kids. Straightening curls and letting them bounce free, stroking their temples at bedtime.

"I think she likes you," she said. "But maybe she needs to hear that you like her too?"

She smiled apologetically. Jay hated meddling, but right now, Mum was right on the money.

Chapter 35

Nina woke with swollen eyes to someone banging on the door. Half sleep walking, she stumbled her way down from the loft and opened the door. It was only then that her brain brought back the events of the previous night. Her entire body seized up, ready to slam the door on Jay's face and dive back under covers. But it wasn't Jay, it was La La.

"I tried calling you," La La said, pushing past Nina into the house. "But this isn't on-the-phone news. This is face-to-face news."

Nina remembered La La's sparkling eyes from the day before. The news! She'd been a terrible friend. Instead of texting or calling La La, she'd cried all night, eaten the raw chocolates she had in the freezer (the ones she'd planned to hand out as Christmas gifts) and finally fallen asleep.

"You look like shit," La La observed. "What happened last night?"

"It's a stupid story. It can wait. I want to hear your news!" Nina put the kettle on and sat at her tiny table, opposite her friend. La La drew a breath. Nina could almost hear a drum roll. "I'm pregnant!"

Nina blinked, staring at her beaming face. "Wow. That's amazing. So the sperm donor thing worked straight away?"

"Not exactly," La La said with a mischievous smile. "This kind of happened without the turkey baster."

"Whose is it?" She racked her brain for any guys La La would have talked about in the last few months, but came up with nothing.

La La's cheeks reddened. "It's the sperm donor."

"What?"

"The one I told you about, with gorgeous eyes and..."

"Wasn't he married? Didn't he have a family?"

"He's getting divorced."

This sounded bad.

"Don't look at me like that," demanded La La. "It's not like I chose to fall in love."

"You're in love with him?"

"Yeah, I think I am. Isn't it great that this child is born out of love, not a sperm bank? I thought you'd like that!"

Nina rubbed her forehead, trying not to frown. "But... what about his other children? His wife?"

La La looked uncomfortable. "She was okay with him donating sperm, so maybe it's not such a big deal?"

Nina could tell these other people hardly existed in her little bubble. They were anecdotal, one-dimensional characters, floating about on the fringes of her amazing love story.

"Sleeping with someone else and filing for a divorce is not

the same as donating sperm." Nina hated bringing her friend down, but she couldn't help it. The questions and doubts burst out of her like those stupid words she'd thrown at Jay last night. At this rate, she would lose every friend she had.

"I know. But right now, I'm just trying to get used to being pregnant," La La said in a quiet voice, "And I could really use a friend."

"I'm sorry. It just sounds so..."

"I know." La La repeated, staring at her hands.

"Does the fertility clinic know?"

"Of course not. I haven't even told him yet."

"How do you think he will react?"

"I don't know. First, he was happy to donate sperm. And when we got together, he didn't want to use protection, so he should be okay with it, right?"

"So, you didn't talk about it?" Nina's muscles tensed.

La La fiddled with her nails. "No. Well, I told him about my test results and how difficult it might be for me to conceive. So, I'm sure he'll be happy for me. It's a miracle, when you think about it."

"And any contracts you were preparing through the agency... would they be valid?" Nina sounded like a lawyer and hated it. She wanted to believe in love, but it was getting harder and harder.

"Well, I hadn't finished the paperwork yet. We'd only had the first meeting between me and him... and his wife."

"Wait, his wife was there?"

La La looked up, eyes wide. "Yes, that's how they always do it."

"And he hit on you in front of his wife?"

"No!" La La shook her head. "He called me after and asked me out."

"And you said yes?" Nina asked, feeling queasy.

"Well, not at first, but then I ran into him the next day and we chatted. And he told me about the divorce. And he asked to meet me the next day, at this hotel bar. It wasn't sleazy. It was kind of wild and romantic. And a bit cheeky."

"I bet," Nina said. "How far along are you?"

"Seven weeks." La La dug into her handbag and pulled out a crumpled ultrasound picture of the little bean.

Nina studied the fuzzy image for a long time. No matter how much she wanted to be happy for her friend, she felt a rush of sadness rise into her throat. Her friend had done what she – the over-thinking, self-sabotaging idiot – couldn't. La La had abandoned her better judgement and got pregnant. This was why women like La La ended up having a child and women like Nina ended up old maids – childless, alone, and judgmental of other people's choices.

Nina handed the ultrasound picture back to La La. "She's beautiful. Or he's beautiful. You wouldn't know the gender yet, right?"

"Not until 20 weeks, they said. I don't know how I can wait that long!" La La enthused. "So, I found out you can do this blood test overseas that reveals gender at 12 weeks."

Nina sighed. How drunk out of her mind would she have to be to do the same? And how much danger would she put herself in? Women got murdered by their Tinder dates left and right. Those who still went for it and threw caution to the wind must have been a different species.

She recalled the previous night and how she'd tried to bare her soul to Jay, making a mess of things. It was painful to even think about it. She must have sounded like a stroke victim. But she'd definitely done something impulsive and stupid. Maybe that disaster counted as a step in the right direction? Next time, she would care even less about her dignity and take bigger risks.

"Now, there's something else I need to talk to you about," La La said.

She looked uncomfortable and Nina felt her stomach turn. What now? Was she moving away? Was the tiny house filming deal off?

"I had to cancel the Christmas trip," La La said with a pained expression. "I hate the idea of you alone, here... but Holden's got this summer bach that he's going to over the holidays."

His name was Holden? Audi or Mercedes would have been more La La's style, Nina thought, suppressing an out-of-place smile. "And you want to go there with him?"

"I kind of have to. I'm carrying his baby and I need to break the news..."

"So he's invited you there for Christmas?" Nina asked, relieved that Holden was serious enough about La La to spend Christmas with her.

La La nodded, a dreamy smile lighting up her face. "Will you be okay by yourself?"

"I'll be fine. Will you be okay?" Nina asked back.

Christmas with no one to share a dinner or a drink with. No gifts to exchange, only a few Skype calls with parents. It sounded depressing. She couldn't even go see Alice. How could she show her face there after last night? What if Jay had already told his mum that his new neighbour and business partner had gone nuts and confessed her love for him? She could barely think about it.

Nina could feel herself slipping into the dark side. She had to make a list – a mental list of things she was grateful for. Her house, her freedom, her health, not being broke – especially if she could get paid for the filming.

"About the filming," Nina remembered. "Could you be in touch with Jay directly? I don't want to be in the middle, I can't do it. Not after yesterday."

La La cast her a grave look. "Okay. What happened?"

Nina explained her irrational moves, hoping La La could see the fuzzy logic in it all.

"Wow," La La exclaimed. "You really like Jay, then? It's all about him?"

Nina gave her a pained smile. "I guess it is. But it doesn't matter. He's not onboard. He's a good friend, but he doesn't see me like that."

"How do you know?"

"Did you not hear the story?"

"Well, you said he asked if Tama had hurt you or something?"

Nina waved her hand. "Yeah, he got that wrong. But I told him I liked him, and he said nothing back."

La La narrowed her eyes. "Maybe you didn't give him a chance?"

"I did! I went to see him, told him I didn't want to go out with Tama. He didn't care."

"Did you tell him you wanted to go out with him?"

Nina thought about this. Surely, she'd been explicit enough with her tears and confessions. What had she actually said? It was all blurred in her mind. "Not in so many words, but yeah."

"Men don't read between the lines," La La informed her. "You need to tell him exactly what you want."

Nina bit her lip, nearly hard enough to draw blood. She was sure she'd given Jay ample opportunity to say what he thought of her. Or just kiss her if he didn't want to say anything. If he had any interest, he would have communicated it somehow by now. He knew where she lived, but he hadn't come to see her at all. That was enough to extinguish the tiny flicker of hope Nina had still been holding when running away from him.

"Anyway, you have to talk to him about the filming," Nina pleaded. "I can't."

"Fine," La La said and copied Jay's phone number off Nina's phone. "It's not a big deal, anyway. If he says no, we have a backup the client likes."

"That's good."

A backup would be great. Then she wouldn't have to see Jay at all. But as awkward as the idea of seeing him again was, part of her longed for those eyes, his smile, his scent, his closeness. No longer being friends or business partners... it was too painful to think about.

La La got up to leave. A week before Christmas, even Saturdays were regular workdays. Nina had hated that, but now she missed it. She wanted to escape into the buzzing, air-conditioned office and bury herself in Christmas ad campaigns.

"Make sure you get out of here," La La advised. "Don't be alone on Christmas. Go to the markets. Sing carols. Check out the Christmas lights. Go to church. I don't care, as long as you're not by yourself, okay?"

Nina assured her she'd be okay and they could catch up over New Year. La La got up, holding her non-existent baby bump, and made her way to her car. It wasn't her red Mini Cooper though.

"Tama let me borrow his car," La La said with a smile. "Mine's at the shop."

Tama really was a generous guy, Nina thought.

It felt like a bad joke she no longer felt that way about him.

As La La drove away, Nina went for a walk to pick some oranges. The weather was beautiful, and the air filled with birdsong, but she could hardly enjoy it. There was no Chloe, no Jay. Only oranges. Nina found some early raspberries and walked back home, feeling an acute emptiness, like she'd lost a limb.

Later that night, La La called and confirmed that Jay had said no and that they were going with the backup guy who apparently was gorgeous.

Nina couldn't care less. The filming was happening to-morrow. As soon as it was over, she could get her money and focus on spending it. She had her eye on special Christmas lights she could order online. They were commercial quality, heavy-duty lights she'd always wanted. Ideally, she would have hung them before the filming, but since that was hap-pening day time, the effect wouldn't have been that great. The lights were just for her – a beacon of Christmas spirit for her tiny house, to remind her that… well, to make her feel a little less shitty about spending Christmas alone. If anything could do that, it was money well spent.

Chapter 36

When Jay got to Nina's house, he immediately noticed the other car. It looked like the one that guy had driven. Tama. She had said she didn't want to date him, but maybe she had changed her mind. It was only 9 a.m. Had he spent the night? Jay felt a rising anger, mixed with disappointment at the unfairness of it all. For a moment, he contemplated just knocking on the door. She'd said she wanted him, but Jay had never really understood women. The meaning of their words eluded him. Could he really trust those words, especially if her actions told him something else?

Why hadn't he grabbed her in the greenhouse and never let go? Nina had gone from zero to a hundred in a matter of seconds. It was only afterwards, with her last words ringing in his ears, that he'd understood what she may have expected of him. That had been his opening, his chance to come clean about his own feelings, and he'd blown it. Jay kicked a rock so hard he saw spots and walked back home.

He would wait for the guy to leave and talk to Nina later.

He still needed to know if she could help him at the Christmas market. Once home, Jay's phone rang. It was La La, asking if he was interested in being filmed for the video they were making at Nina's house.

"I'm sorry it's me calling," La La said. "I asked Nina to talk to you but she... well... anyway, we would love to work with you. What do you say?"

So, Nina didn't want to talk to him. Jay felt his heartbeat in his throat. "No, thanks. I'm sure you can find someone else."

"Absolutely, not a problem."

Jay collapsed on his sofa, sighing. If Nina didn't want to talk to him, she most likely didn't want to do the market with him, either. And that probably meant she was involved with that Bentley-driving guy. Was he meant to just swallow his defeat and move on?

The phone rang again. Jay assumed it was the same unknown number from before. What else did the tattooed woman want from him?

"What?!" Jay groaned as he picked up.

"Jay Hartley? This is Elizabeth from Raglan Community Health Centre. I'm so sorry you haven't heard from us. There's been a bit of a miscommunication. I just wanted to let you know your results were negative. The lump is a simple cyst. Totally benign."

Chapter 37

Nina stepped into the courier's office in Raglan. It was Christmas Eve and her Christmas lights had finally arrived. The building looked different in daylight, but the memories of their nightly escapades flooded in regardless. She rang the bell and Old Neil appeared, looking even grumpier than last time.

"Hi! How are you?" Nina smiled with forced ebullience, handing over her 'card to collect'.

Neil grabbed it and disappeared into the storage room. After a long while, he emerged with two packages. Nina wondered if she'd ordered something else. She couldn't remember. Her new pyjama and cute doormat had arrived the day before.

But as Neil shoved the parcels under her nose, she noticed one of them was addressed to Jay.

"Can you take that one as well? Otherwise, he won't get it until after the holidays. And I'm not handing over my keys again."

Nina nodded, grabbed both packages, and hurried away. She really didn't want to argue with Old Neil. She wasn't sure how she would drop off the package at Jay's without having a super awkward encounter with him, but she would think of something. Maybe she could go in the middle of the night. Then it would be like Santa had visited. It was probably a Christmas present, anyway.

Happy with her plan, Nina drove home. She wanted to hang the Christmas lights well before dark. After testing that the lights worked, Nina leaned her stepladder against the wall. Her house was built to the maximum allowed height of 4.25 metres, but with the ladder, she was fairly sure she could reach high enough to attach the lights. Armed with her cordless power drill and a pocket full of screw-in hooks, Nina climbed up the ladder. Securing her foot against the step, she drilled the first hole.

Drilling upwards required more strength than she'd expected. After thirty seconds, her arms shook. But she had to do this. These hooks were the one thing standing between a dark, depressing Christmas and one with a bit of magic. She needed the magic. Something to believe in. Even the story of baby Jesus depressed her. A virgin fell pregnant and had a baby – and her husband raised it with her even though it wasn't his baby. She couldn't find a man who wanted to raise a baby that was his own flesh and blood. And there was no guarantee she could fall pregnant either. As Nina finished drilling the first hole, her arms were already killing her. Maybe she should just cancel Christmas. Why did she have to celebrate other people having babies?

Nina screwed on the first hook. Perfect. Now, the next one. She shifted herself to the other side of the ladder, to reach the next spot without having to move the ladder. Nina hoisted her leg around the ladder and that's when it happened. She slipped. In any other situation, she could have grabbed on to something, but her arms – holding the drill, spasming from the exertion – had turned into noodles. They fumbled, grabbing onto air. Her right leg got wedged in between the steps and she crashed down, bringing the ladder with her.

She ended up on the ground, pinned under the ladder. Thank God it was made of light aluminium. Her body vibrated with the shock, but she was alive. Nina ran her hands over her head and midsection. Nothing was bleeding. She could move her arms. She tried to hoist herself up. That's when she saw her leg was still between the steps, twisted. It didn't look right. She had to get it out.

Nina turned to her side and dragged her leg free. It throbbed, and the shin looked bent. Without thinking, she pushed herself up to sitting and pulled at it to straighten the bone. It was broken, but she couldn't feel the pain, not yet.

Holding on to the fallen ladder, Nina tried to get up on her left leg. At least that one was working. She noticed a bruise on her right shin. It looked swollen. The pain caught up, coming in waves, pulsing through her entire leg like a hot, white light. Her heart pounded in her ears. What if there was nerve damage? She had to get to the hospital, but she couldn't drive herself. How could she even get to her car? Her arms felt like jelly. She would have to wait for a moment before she could pull her body weight anywhere.

Nina let her body fall back on the ground, unable to do anything but feel the pain, pulsating in sync with her heartbeat. This was exactly what La La had worried about, reminding Nina to keep her phone charged and always with her. Nina had failed on both accounts. Her phone lay on the sleeping loft, probably out of battery. How could she even get to it? Her tiny house wasn't designed for the disabled. Her loft stairs didn't even have a handrail.

Contemplating her options, Nina felt faint. The sun was setting, the ground cold under her body. Was she going to die here and be found after the holidays? Who would find her? The initial shock and adrenaline were wearing out, making room for tears. This was rock bottom. The worst Christmas Eve she had ever had. Worse than the throbbing pain or anything else, was that she had nobody. Nobody cared.

Nina lay on the ground and listened to the birds, still chirping away in her walnut tree. She couldn't tell how much time had passed. Time seemed irrelevant. It was getting dark – the light glowing from inside her house seemed stronger as the darkness swallowed the landscape. Thank God she'd left the light on! That would help her navigate once she found a will to move, a plan ... something.

Something touched her face. A raindrop. In a few seconds,

she felt droplets land all over her body, one by one. Her right leg felt nothing but pain. Nina prayed. She had nothing left, so she prayed.

"I'm sorry," she whispered. "I'm sorry."

The raindrops kept falling, one by one, like little parcels of refreshment from heaven. Nina licked her lips. Her chest shook uncontrollably as she breathed in and out. Still alive. Oh, God. Why?

A rumbling thunder made her shiver. Was that God answering? A softer sound followed the thunder, a rustle of light footsteps, then a dog barking. Chloe?

"Chloe!" Nina called the dog. "Please be Chloe!"

Nina had never been happier to see a dog. The floppy-eared pooch ran to her and excitedly licked her face.

"Chloe, go get Jay! Please! I can't move."

Nina didn't know if her canine friend understood what she was saying, but she barked once and disappeared. Nina prayed again and waited.

After several minutes, she heard heavier footsteps. Jay stepped out of the dark, into the light of her tiny house and crouched down next to her. "Are you okay?"

Nina shook her head. The tears tightened her throat, making it impossible to speak. She pointed at her right leg. "I... fell."

Jay examined her leg. "Is it broken?"

Nina nodded. She had to find her voice. But Jay didn't need her to speak. He scooped her up and carried her to her car, like a rag doll. Nina fumbled for the car keys, which were thankfully in her pocket. A handful of screw-in hooks fell out and disappeared somewhere in the long grass. Her Christmas magic. Jay laid Nina on the back seat with her right leg on top of the left. Then he hopped in the driver's seat and started the car. Chloe barked. Jay lowered the window. "Go home, girl! I'll see you later!"

They drove through the night. Nina knew the closest emergency department was in Hamilton. It would take at least an hour. After a few minutes, Nina found her voice again.

"Thank you," she whispered.

"No worries," Jay replied.

"I'm ruining your Christmas Eve." Nina choked up again. Had she damaged some vital part of her brain during the fall and become unable to talk without crying?

"Don't worry about it," Jay assured her. "I'm just glad I found you."

"Me too." Nina sighed.

She felt dizzy, her vision narrowing on the edges. Everything else – Jay, the car, the night – drifted away as she sank deeper. The last thing she noticed were the streetlamps rhythmically flashing past the window, illuminating the car interior – her legs, the front seat, and Jay's powerful arms holding the steering wheel. The arms that saved her.

CHAPTER 38

Nina woke up to bright daylight. What had happened? She took in her surroundings – the hospital room; the line coming out of her arm, the hospital gown against her bare skin. Then she remembered. Nina peered down at her leg. It was in a cast, with only the tips of her toes sticking out. She tried to wiggle them and, to her relief, they responded. She hadn't lost her leg!

"You're up!"

Nina turned to and noticed Jay in a small tub chair, stretching his arms overhead.

"What... happened?" She asked. Her voice sounded unused.

"You had some internal bleeding. They had to do surgery. And fix up your leg," Jay said, "It took a few hours."

Nina swallowed. Her throat felt like sandpaper. "Did you spend the night?"

"Yes."

"Why?"

Jay got up and walked over to her bed. He sat on a stool next to it and leaned over. There was another bed in the room, but it was empty. They were alone. She could feel his breath on her arm.

"Why? Because I love you, Nina. I haven't had a chance to tell you, but I'm doing it now. And I don't know where you're at. If you still like me or not. But I need to tell you before you run away again. Just so that there's no confusion. I am in love with you and have been for a while."

Nina stared into his incredible brown eyes, her bruised and aching body suddenly weightless and filled with warmth. "I love you, too, Jay," she sobbed. "I thought I messed everything up. I thought I was going to die."

"Apparently, you were close." Jay squeezed her hand. Nina reached out to touch him. Jay leaned in and kissed her. It was perfect, both familiar and strange, hot and salty with tears. Her whole body fired up. She never wanted to stop.

They heard an echo of footsteps in the hallway. Someone was at the door.

Jay whispered, "That's the doctor, I think. I told them you're my fiancé. Otherwise they wouldn't have let me stay."

Nina nodded. She loved the idea.

The doctor was younger than either of them, probably straight out of medical school. Who else would be working on Christmas morning? He read from his chart and explained that they'd stopped the bleeding in Nina's stomach and given her one litre of blood.

"Where was the bleed, exactly?" Nina asked.

The doctor peered at the chart. "It says here on the right-hand side."

"Not in my womb... or..."

"I'm... not a hundred percent sure, but I can find out. Are you planning to get pregnant?"

"Um..." Nina blinked. How could she answer that in front of Jay?

"Yes," Jay answered for her. "Could you please find out where the bleeding was and if there was any damage to her reproductive organs?"

The young doctor nodded and rushed away, hopefully to find someone more qualified, or talk to the surgeon who'd operated on her.

"Thank you," Nina whispered. "I didn't mean to spring that on you. It's not like I'm on a mission to... you know..." Nina felt hot. She was lying. "Honestly, I want to have a baby," she confessed, shaking with dread. "I'm getting older, and I don't want to miss my chance. It's better you know that. Even if it means you have to run."

Jay smiled. "Why do you think I'd run?"

"Because you said..."

The door opened again. An older doctor stepped in with an air of authority. He explained kindly that Nina's bleeding had been nowhere near her ovaries or womb. She was as fertile as any 36-year-old could be, which, according to the doctor, wasn't very fertile at all.

"We'll see about that," said Jay after he'd left.

"You're not going to run?" asked Nina again. "Are you sure?"

"No. You're the runner." Jay gave her a pointed look. "It's a good thing you'll be on crutches for a while."

He lowered his lips on her again and Nina closed her eyes, savouring the moment. The room smelt of disinfectant. Someone sang carols in the hallway. Outside the window, a gusty wind rustled the trees. It wasn't the Christmas she'd dreamed of, but it was perfect. She finally belonged somewhere. Not Hamilton or Raglan or even her tiny house. She belonged with Jay.

Chapter 39

After a few days in the hospital, Nina moved about her room, practicing how to use a pair of crutches. Her old Asian roommate watched something Christmas-themed on the TV.

On Christmas Day, Nina had sent Jay home to have lunch with his family. Tyron was visiting with his new girlfriend and Alice had been cooking for days. Nina still had to have a series of tests, but if all went well, she'd be released on New Year's Eve. Jay had visited her twice, bringing delicious Christmas treats, courtesy of Alice. He'd kept his visits short, painfully aware of her roommate who shamelessly listened to their every word. But she'd cherished seeing Jay, holding his hand and eating gingerbread with him.

On New Year's Eve, Nina had told Jay she could Uber her way back, but he insisted on picking her up.

The crutches were hard work. Nina suspected she was strongly right-legged, the same way most people were right-handed. Her left leg, on its own, had no coordination and probably less strength and stamina than the right one.

But Nina persevered, and after a good 90 minutes of hopping around, she felt more confident. As long as she dropped nothing on the floor and always had an available seat within a short distance.

For lunch, the hospital served questionable looking ham with tasteless mashed potato and peas. Nina couldn't wait to get out.

Later in the afternoon, the older doctor stopped by to look at Nina's test results and sign her discharge form. Nina texted Jay, butterflies in her stomach, which felt very out of place in this environment. Ever since Jay had told her he loved her, she'd been suspended in a strange, limbo-like space, waiting to heal and finally get back to her real life – or more accurately – to start a new life with him. The doctors and nurses came and went, and she barely noticed. She hardly even cared about her leg. She only wanted Jay. Finally, a hospital aide wheeled Nina out the front doors to the drop-off zone. Relieved to be in her own clothes, Nina looked around and soon spotted Jay's truck. She couldn't stop smiling. Jay parked right next to her and helped her into the front seat. Jay steered away from the carpark, letting out a sigh. "I'm so glad you're here. I've been waiting to talk to you without that tracksuit guy."

"Me, too!" Nina exhaled. "He was hanging out of his bed, eavesdropping. And I'm pretty sure he recorded us once." She glanced at Jay, her heartbeat kicking up a notch. "Now that we're alone, can I ask you... why didn't you tell me earlier? Why didn't you just… kiss me? I waited and waited."

Jay's voice was gruff. "I thought you just didn't like me that much. Or that maybe you liked someone else."

Nina cast him a cheeky smile. "Nope. You had me at 'zero residue'."

Jay laughed, but then his tone turned serious. "I also had this … health scare, and I just needed to find out I was okay. And I am. Totally healthy."

He made it sound like a prerequisite for dating. Nina frowned. "Do you really think I'm that shallow? That I'd dismiss someone because of a health issue?"

Jay squeezed the steering wheel, eyes on the road. "No. I just didn't want to be pitied. I was stupid."

Nina wrapped her hands around his arm and nuzzled against his shoulder. "We were both stupid," she whispered.

For a moment, they drove in silence. There was so much they didn't know about each other, but they would just have to get there, one question at a time. And there was one more Nina had been meaning to ask.

"How did you find me? How did you know I needed help?"

"I didn't know you needed help," Jay said. "But Chloe did. She was barking like mad. So, I followed her. When I saw she was going to your house, I got worried."

The blessed dog deserved a biggest packet of treats.

They kept driving and more questions emerged, questions of preferences, ideas, values, and habits. At the back of her mind, Nina knew many of those things would later become annoyances, but she wanted to enjoy this part. Who said knowing about how serotonin worked stopped you from enjoying its high? She'd found something, and right there, with the sun setting behind the hills, her leg softly aching, and brain flooded with chemicals, Nina was the happiest she had been in a long, long time.

As they pulled up at her tiny house, Nina gasped. It was already dark, but her Christmas lights were up, filling the night with their magic glow.

"Did you do this?" she gasped, already knowing the answer.

Jay just smiled. Nina opened the car door, ready to go home, but Jay took her hand. "I was thinking we stay at mine tonight? I love your house and I wanted you to see the lights, but don't you think it will be a bit difficult?"

Nina had forgotten she was an invalid. Her house being 'a bit difficult' was a generous understatement. For the next six weeks, her house would be impossible to live in. She needed help, and would have to depend on Jay. The realisation hit her with a jolt. What would have happened if he hadn't found her? Or what if he had just taken her to the hospital and left her there? Before she could really put it in words, even in her head, big tears crisscrossed down her cheeks.

"What is it?" Jay asked.

"I can't stay at my house," she sobbed. "I didn't even think about it. But you're right. I can't live there."

"That's what I'm saying. Stay with me," Jay said, pulling

her closer.

"You mean the whole time? Until the cast comes off?"

"Or longer," he replied, kissing her neck.

"I'll be a burden."

"You're not that heavy," Jay laughed and pulled her in for a proper kiss.

It was so unsettling, so good, so scary, so delicious. She didn't want to come up for air. His hand was in her hair, running down her body, tracing her outline. Every part of Nina wanted to surrender. She was so tired of her independence, tired of making it on her own. Tired of being alone.

"You'll get sick of me," she mumbled into his mouth.

"That's part of the deal," he replied.

He meant it. He would get sick of her. She would get sick of him. But he chose her anyway. She'd worry about the rest tomorrow. Tonight, she would enjoy being carried and kissed and loved. She looked into those amazing brown eyes and nodded. Jay could take her home.

EPILOGUE

On a crisp winter's day, Nina and Jay drove towards the Raglan township. Nina balanced a huge gift basket on her knees. It was full of fresh produce, pies, casseroles, and nappies – all for La La's brand-new baby. Nina could hardly believe her friend now lived only twenty minutes away. She looked at Jay, feasting her eyes on his dark curls and strong jawline. Finally, she could look at him without trying to hide her feelings. She loved him more every day.

Two months ago, they'd gotten married on the farm, right by her tiny house. Her house now stood on Jay's property, enjoying the expansive ocean views from the good side of the hill. At the moment, they both temporarily lived in it while renovating Jay's three-bedroom house. Well, suppose it was their house now. It felt strange that they now shared everything.

The wedding had been perfect, with fairy lights and flowers and Alice's amazing cooking. Nina's parents had made it for a visit, finally, and had stayed for three weeks, individually touring the country, attending the wedding, then touring some more. Nina felt grateful for every single thing, even those that didn't go according to plan, like the sudden shower that interrupted their reception and forced them all to rush into the greenhouse.

They had both agreed that they didn't want to spend money on the wedding. Nina didn't have a big family, and Jay's extended family was mostly on the other side of the country. It wasn't about having a big party; it was so much more than that. After the wedding, Earth and Marlena had finally paid their bill, and Nina had used the money to get years' worth of dog treats for Chloe.

Nina still couldn't believe it. She now had a family, a place where she belonged. Even her tiny house seemed anchored, no longer sitting by itself in a sad little garden overtaken by weeds. In the weeks after the hospital, with her leg in a cast and Jay carrying her around, her garden had definitely transformed for the worse. Nina wasn't a gardener. She was a designer. And now a wife. Nina pulled out her phone to text La La. It was a new phone Jay had given her for Christmas. Well, she had received it in the New Year, when they found the package Nina had picked up from the courier and forgotten about.

After a few minutes, Jay pulled up to a brand-new townhouse right in the town centre. Nina spotted a baby stroller outside her friend's new home. It looked so domestic – except for the red Mini Cooper in the driveway.

Nina knocked softly on the door and waited. La La appeared, smiling, without a hint of makeup, a muslin wrap on her shoulder. She looked tired and dazed, but her smile glowed with something Nina hadn't seen before. Serenity? La La invited them in and they sat down in the lounge. It was beautiful, and cleaner than Nina had expected. But then again, La La had just gotten home from the hospital. The baby was asleep in a little Moses basket, propped up in the corner of the sofa. Nina sat right next to the baby. She couldn't take her eyes off the tiny, perfect human, peacefully unaware of anything going on around her. La La had dressed the baby in all white, but the pile of pink cards on the coffee table advertised what La La had known since week 12 of her pregnancy.

"How are you doing?" Nina asked her friend.

"I'm fine," La La said. "It's like this alien world, where everything's upside down. But it's good." She smiled and stared at her baby, maybe in disbelief, or just spaced out from sheer exhaustion.

Nina got up and unpacked their gift. She placed two meals in the fridge and the rest in the freezer. A lot of the food was made by ever-so-productive Alice, who had got to know La La through Nina and become excited about the baby.

Nina arranged fruit in bowls on the kitchen table, hoping her friend would remember to eat. Nina knew the baby's father would not be around to help, and it worried her.

In January, Nina and La La had caught up at Jay's house.

Nina had glowed with happiness, although hopping on crutches. La La, heartbroken and hormonal, had cried on the couch, hugging Chloe, who could sense the crying lady needed her and had been remarkably willing to stay put. Nina had felt useless. She couldn't change the situation. She couldn't make this sperm-donor-turned-love-interest come back to her friend. He'd chosen his family but had agreed to support La La financially, probably hoping to avoid going to court.

They'd talked and talked, and La La had cried some more. At some point, her friend had decided she would move to Raglan. She'd grown fond of the village during her visits and wanted to be closer to Nina. But La La couldn't stomach the real countryside, so she'd stuck to the village, within a walking distance to the cafes and shops.

Now, La La seemed a lot happier. This was probably the best place for her, under the circumstances. Nina wanted to remind her friend of their earlier conversations, of her plan of having a baby on her own and later falling in love.

"How's the business?" La La asked as Nina joined her and Jay on the couch.

Jay looked at Nina, his face full of excitement. "Nina got us an appointment with the Countdown team. They are interested."

"That's amazing!" La La cheered, trying to keep her voice down, so she didn't wake the baby.

Nina and Jay had continued working on Jay's product range, which now also included two marinades, a salad dressing, and a chutney. They had struggled to get the attention of the larger chain stores, but now it finally looked like a door might open. This was all partly because of Tyron, who had some unexpected connections. Nina still felt uncomfortable around Tyron, but she could tell how happy Alice was to see her sons getting along, so she tried not to dwell on those feelings.

"Also, I found a new client, all by myself!" Nina added.

She was excited that she'd found a little foothold as a freelance designer in the Raglan community. Marlena had recommended her services around town. The word-of-mouth amounted to several calls and email queries, and eventually a couple of new clients. Slowly but surely, she was building a clientele that kept her busy at her computer and out of the garden. She helped Jay on delivery days, but otherwise stayed out of his way, pottering around at home, planning their renovation and finding good deals online.

The baby stirred, and La La picked her up. She lifted her shirt and put her on the breast. Jay watched in amazement. Maybe he couldn't believe it either, this transformation in her friend. Jay had confessed to her he'd found La La scary at first, but now – to Nina's relief – they got along nicely.

Nina looked at her man and smiled. She still wasn't pregnant, and the clock was ticking. But by some magic, it didn't worry her as much. In the past few months, she'd given herself permission to relax and enjoy getting to know Jay. She'd found someone to share her life with and even if she never had a baby, she'd be okay. Now she also had the cutest little goddaughter to dote on.

La La finished feeding the baby and handed her over to Nina. Happy and full of milk, she let out a little gurgle and softly closed her eyes again. Nina lifted the baby on her chest, sniffing the magic scent of rapidly renewing cells, and sighed. Life was rather amazing.